RAY HOGAN was born in Missouri but has spent most of his life in New Mexico. His father was an early Western marshal and lawman, and Hogan himself has spent a lifetime researching the West. He has written over 100 books, including THE DOOMSDAY POSSE, GUN TRAP AT ARABELLA, THE IRON JEHU, THE SEARCHING GUNS, THE HANGMEN OF SAN SABAL, TALL MAN RIDING, and 24 titles in the bestselling Shawn Starbuck series, all available in Signet paperback. His work has been filmed, televised, and translated into six languages.

More Westerns from SIGNET

THREE CROSS

and

Deputy

of

Violence

Shawn Starbuck Westerns

by Ray Hogan

A SIGNET BOOK from
NEW AMERICAN LIBRARY
TIMES MIRROR

Published by
THE NEW AMERICAN LIBRARY
OF CANADA LIMITED

Three Cross Copyright © 1970 by Ray Hogan

Deputy of Violence Copyright © 1971 by Ray Hogan

Originally appeared in paperback as separate volumes
published by The New American Library.

First Printing, Double Western Edition, July, 1978

1 2 3 4 5 6 7 8 9

 SIGNET TRADEMARK REG. U.S. PAT. OFF. AND FOREIGN COUNTRIES
REGISTERED TRADEMARK — MARCA REGISTRADA
HECHO EN WINNIPEG, CANADA

SIGNET, SIGNET CLASSICS, MENTOR, PLUME AND
MERIDIAN BOOKS are published in Canada by The New
American Library of Canada Limited, Scarborough, Ontario

PRINTED IN CANADA

COVER PRINTED IN U.S.A.

THREE CROSS

= 1 =

Near the crest of the butte, Starbuck pulled his horse to a halt, eying a sleek, golden eagle, which sprang gracefully into the shimmering layers of heat hovering over the flat below, and on powerful wings began to climb into the sky.

He continued to watch as the great, russet-colored bird leveled off, slipped into a long glide toward the pinnacled Organ Mountains, rising in somber grandeur on the yonder side of Las Cruces, yet a half day's ride in the distance. Then, lowering his gaze in deference to the glare, he shifted wearily on the saddle, brushed at the sweat accumulated on his face. A few moments later, as if suddenly deciding to indulge himself, he swung down, sighing gratefully as his heels hit the solid assurance of the ground. Leaving the chestnut gelding to tear at the scattered tufts of browned grass, he crossed slowly to a nearby turret of wind-scourged granite and leaned his lank shape against its shaded side.

Again he grunted softly, contentedly. It had been a long ride—ten straight days—since he'd mounted the gelding at Lynchburg where he had gone on what had developed into just another fruitless errand in his search for his brother, Ben. Now, following out still another tip, he was heading for the old settlement of The Crosses in the lower end of New Mexico Territory.

He was acting on strange and somewhat disturbing information. A man, skilled in boxing, was wanted for murder by the sheriff of that town. Their father, Hiram, an expert in the art who could have become a professional champion had he loved the land less and fame more, had tutored his two sons to a level of near perfection. . . . Thus the man sought could be Ben since masters of the science were few along the frontier.

But Ben a murderer—a killer?

Shawn found that part difficult to accept—not that Ben wasn't capable of violent anger; his fiery temper had been one of the principal factors in the break between him and old Hiram that led to his leaving home ten long years ago. It contributed also to the reason why Shawn, now seeking his brother in order to settle the Starbuck estate, was having so hard a time tracking him down; not only was he searching for a man he'd not seen in a decade but also one who undoubtedly lived under an assumed name.

But the need to find Ben was absolute, and while the trails that carried Shawn back and forth across the western frontier seemed to have no ending, merely brief pauses during which frustration and disappointment were his only rewards, he knew he could never stop the quest until he found Ben or knew positively that he was dead. Such was his destiny; he had long since come to recognize that fact.

Las Cruces, however, must necessarily be home for a while. He didn't expect to find Ben there, only hoped to get himself a job, rebuild his depleted cash, and he would garner all information possible from the lawman—a good description perhaps and, hopefully, the name Ben was now living under, if indeed the person in question was his brother.

Pausing to work periodically was no new experience to Shawn Starbuck. Hiram, in setting forth in his will that his younger son must first find and return to the fold the offended Ben, had overlooked the fact that money would be needed to carry on the search; or perhaps the elder Starbuck had figured Ben would be somewhere close-by and easily located, and therefore made no provision for expense. The lawyer in charge of the estate had remedied the situation somewhat by granting Shawn enough cash to get started, but it had only lasted for a few months.

After that it became a matter, a system actually, of alternately searching and working and then searching again until the money he had saved ran out and once more it became necessary to find a job for a time. Shawn had acquired a wealth of experience, both good and bad, pursuing such a program. It had converted him from an affable, somewhat unripe, gray-eyed farm boy a few months past eighteen years of age in the beginning, to a lean, trail-hardened man most thought twice about before challenging. It showed in his overall appearance—one that belied the disarming boyish way he had of smiling when pleased; it showed in the slant of the smooth-handled pistol worn on his left side, the easy, yet coiled slouch to his carriage—in the utterly direct and uncompromising manner he had of looking at a man from below a shelf of dark, full brows.

No less characteristic were the creases in his element-ravaged face—the hard, strong lines cut there by the sun, the sweeping winds, the cold rains—all bespeaking the

6

patience of the man and his unwillingness to admit defeat that, many times when his mood was black, presented itself. . . . He'd never find his brother, a sly voice told him at such moments; Ben could be dead, buried under a false name—and even if alive the land was too vast, too remote for him to find traces of one solitary individual.

He could waste a lifetime—a lifetime during which he might have settled down, built for himself a world of his own, found peace and contentment. "Hunting Ben," someone encountered along the road somewhere, sometime, had said to him, "was like trying to rope a cloud, saddle a moonbeam; it was a hopeless task."

And there were those dreary moments in which Shawn was close to agreement, but there was inside him a quality inherited from Clare, his schoolteacher mother, or perhaps passed on to him by iron-jawed, hard-fisted old Hiram—a stubbornness that would not let him give up, admit failure. He would find Ben, clear up the estate, and claim his rightful share—thirty thousand dollars—and then seek the life he knew awaited him. It might take—

The sound of horses moving along the base of the butte caught his attention. The muted voices of men came to him then, and pulling away from the rock upthrust he made his way toward the lip of the formation and the lightning-struck charred cedar upon which the eagle had been perched when frightened by the approach of the gelding. He moved quietly, carefully. He had successfully avoided parties of renegade Apaches all the way from Lynchburg, and he'd like the record to remain unsullied.

Peering over the rim he saw they were not Apaches; four riders dressed in ordinary range clothing, with the exception that each wore a large, triangularly folded scarf around his neck in addition to the customary bandana cowhands used as protection against dust and the sun.

Shawn watched them pass in single file, cut down into a sandy, brush-lined arroyo, and angle toward the south. Mexico lay in that direction—a long forty miles distant. He frowned, considering that. Riders heading for the border would more than likely stick to the shaded path of the Rio Grande where traveling would be more pleasant, rather than buck the endless, dry flats where the heat was known to go well above a hundred degrees.

Casting his glance ahead of the riders, now moving steadily away, Starbuck's eyes picked up the tan ribbon of highway lying a mile or so farther on. This would be the main road from Las Cruces, Mesilla, and points east, and which led on to Lordsburg, Tucson, and finally to San

Francisco; and incidentally, the route of the Butterfield stagecoaches, he realized.

Turned thoughtful by that, he scanned the upper and lower stretches of the curving, undulating strip through eyes narrowed to cut down the glare. It could be a holdup in the making.

That assumption abruptly crystallized into conviction. Off to his left a yellow cloud began to boil up, take shape. It was the stage—a few hours out of Las Cruces on its westward journey. Starbuck cut his gaze back to the four riders. They were keeping to the arroyo, moving on a direct line of interception.

Shawn murmured an oath. He'd hoped to reach the settlement well before dark, but here was interruption, something luck seemed to enjoy plaguing him with during his search for Ben. It shouldn't be necessary for him to step in, help prevent the crime; the government had troops garrisoned at nearby Fort Cummings for just this purpose —protecting travelers from road-agents and Apaches. . . . Where the hell were they, anyway? Probably doing close-order drill on the parade ground at the whim of some shavetail weighted down by the shiny new bars on his shoulders. No matter, they army wasn't around and that left it squarely up to him.

Turning, he moved back for the gelding. It wasn't that he disliked helping others; actually, he'd more or less grown accustomed to the frequent impromptu demands of the beleagured that he encounered since the search for Ben had begun; but it seemed such occasions always presented themselves at the most inopportune times.

Jaw taut, he reached the chestnut and swung to the saddle. Slicing off the upper end of the formation, and keeping the rocks between the four riders and himself, he rode down into the arroyo. There, ignoring the deeply imprinted tracks left by the outlaws' horses in the loose sand, he set out to follow.

In a short time he caught sight of them. They were now riding abreast and moving more slowly, evidently pointing for another series of buttes just ahead. He could not see the road from where he was but guessed it proably ran along the back side of the squat, brushy formations.

Maintaining a safe distance, Starbuck watched the men veer to the right, dip into a narrow ravine, and disappear. At once he spurred the chestnut, curving to his left in order to keep from being seen. At the lip of the wash he drew up, slipped quietly to the ground, and edged forward to where he could look into the ravine.

The riders were just below. They were sitting their mounts, making ready for the holdup. One, a large man with a sweat-stained black hat, was examining his pistol, twirling the cylinder, slipping the hammer, assuring himself the weapon was loaded and in working order. He paused, glanced sideways to one of companions.

"You got it straight, Kid—he's on this stage for certain."

It was a statement more than a question. The Kid, much younger than the others, had blond, stringy hair that bushed down over his collar. There was a nervousness to him as if he were new to the calling.

"I'm sure, Dallman, I'm sure," he answered in an offended tone. "He's heading for Tucson. Carrying the money with him—five thousand gold."

"You all'd best keep your eyes peeled for that there guard," the rider on a dapple-gray said, fitting his black scarf across the lower half of his face. "Prob'ly be old George Eberhardt—and he's a real stem-winding sonofabitch with that there scatter-gun of his."

"Not if he collects hisself a bullet right between the eyes before he gets the chance," Dallman said drily, and glanced over his shoulder to the fourth outlaw. "Ain't that a fact, Charlie?"

Charlie, a narrow-shouldered man with a rifle cradled in his arms, bobbed, spat a stream of brown juice at a nearby rock.

"Just you leave him to me. . . . Got myself a little score I'm aiming to mark off. He winged me once with that goddammed scatter-gun. Still got sore spots on my ass when I set a saddle. . . . Going to pick him off that seat like he was a crow a setting on a rail fence."

"Well," Dallman said, sliding his pistol back into its leather, "don't get yourself so fired up remembering, that you miss. I ain't honing to get my head blowed off by no half a bucket of buckshot."

"Me—I don't never miss—"

"She's about here," the Kid announced, standing up in his stirrups and looking toward the advancing roll of dust. "Where you wanting me to hide?"

Dallman surveyed the shallow cove before him. "Charlie, you get yourself over there next them rocks at the corner of the bluff, like you figured . . . Kid, expect you'd best keep this side of him. Waldo—you find yourself a place on the right. Means I'll be in the middle so's I can work both sides. Savvy?"

"Si senor," the one called Waldo said in exaggerated Spanish and swung away from the others.

Starbuck turned quickly, retraced his steps to the chestnut. He'd delayed too long to throw down on the quartet while they were together in a group; likely it wouldn't have been smart. Men such as Dallman and his kind ordinarily felt they were living on borrowed time anyway, and took any and all chances to prolong their fragile tenure on life.

Going to the saddle, he cut left and gained a small rise. From there he could see the coach drawing nearer on the road, swaying and rocking on its thorough braces as the six-horse hitch thundered up the slight grade. There were the usual two men on the seat—the driver and a guard, both grizzled oldsters who'd likely made the run many times, knew every bend and turn, and had learned long ago to be ready for anything.

The roll curtains had been lowered in the coach to cut out the sun and discourage the dust that swirled up from the spinning wheels, thus Shawn was unable to see how many passengers were aboard. . . . One at least—the man traveling to Tucson with five thousand dollars in gold.

Spurring the chestnut off the knoll and down the slope, Starbuck cut a straight line for the oncoming vehicle, rapidly drawing in range of the outlaws' ambush.

═ 2 ═

He saw reaction to his appearance immediately. The driver yelled something at the guard—George Eberhardt the outlaws had called him—who laid aside his shotgun and reached down for a rifle lying at his feet.

Shawn, both hands above his head, palms flat and forward, motioned for the driver to pull up. The reply to his request was quick. George opened up with the rifle, and the driver, leaning forward, began to ply the whip to his team. Bullets dug into the sand around the gelding's hooves or droned angrily by. Starbuck swore, began to slow. Evidently this particular stretch of road had witnessed more than its share of holdups and George and the driver were taking no chances.

But they were heading into sure and certain trouble, an encounter that was designed to be fatal for Eberhardt, and would likely prove to be so for the driver and his passenger as well. . . . But somehow the holdup must be prevented, Shawn realized, ignoring the impulse to forget the whole damned affair and let George and his hasty trigger finger cope with the problem.

Again roweling the chestnut, he sent the big horse toward the coach, this time removing his hat and waving it frantically back and forth with one hand while pointing at the buttes with the other. The old guard stubbornly continued to lever his rifle, and as the distance between them narrowed, the slugs began to strike closer.

Disgusted, Starbuck pulled off into a side gully. It was sheer suicide to try and stop the coach. He'd have to accept the alternative—that of riding on ahead and springing the outlaws' trap before the stage could reach that point.

Pivoting the foam-flecked gelding, he used spurs once more, lined out down the draw for the row of squat bluffs. It would have been so much simpler, and evidently far safer, to have moved in on the outlaws from above when he had looked down upon them and heard them make their plans. The four of them could not have posed any greater threat than did old George Eberhardt and the rifle he made such persistent use of. . . . But it was too late to think of that now; the coach was near and there was but one thing left for him to do—ride in ahead of it, hope to catch Dallman and the others by surprise.

He did have one advantage denied the coach and anyone else keeping to the road; he could hug the base of the buttes, taking protection from the rocks and the bulging shoulders of red earth. Such would permit him to work in close to the outlaws before being spotted. Undoubtedly they were now wondering just what all the shooting was about.

Eberhardt had ceased his use of the rifle and that was a relief. Either the guard was assuming he had turned back a would-be road agent, or doubt had seeped into his mind as to the actual intent of the rider who had sought to flag down the stage. In either event he was now simply watching and waiting.

Shawn looked beyond the chestnut's cocked ears. Charlie would be posted at an outermost wedge of rocks jutting from the front of the first butte. The others would be strung out in a more or less curved line across the cove. Dallman and the two with him would simply hold back until Charlie got in his promised deadly shot, and then all would converge on the coach as the driver, no longer with protection, would be forced to brake his horses to a stop.

Charlie, therefore, was the key to the situation; he must be downed before he could use his weapon. Shawn probed the rocky outcropping with squinted eyes. The outlaw should be at the forward edge where he would have an unobstructed view of the stagecoach's approach. . . . His nerves tightened. He must get to that point as quickly as possible; he would be running a long chance—that of unexpectedly coming face to face with the outlaw and braving a split-second shoot out with him. If he were lucky he'd get off the first bullet; if not—well, he'd played the cards he'd been dealt.

Drawing his pistol he thumbed back the hammer, pulled the chestnut down to a fast walk. There was no sign yet of Charlie, nor of the other outlaws, but they could not be far off; the hollowed out area in the bluffs was just ahead.

He glanced to the road. The coach was dipping into a swale, the plunging horses running at top speed, manes flying, mouths gaped to the sawing of the bits. Eberhardt was hunched forward, rifle or shotgun, whichever, across his bony knees. The driver, whip curling out over the backs of his team, was a ramrod-straight figure beside him.

Charlie. . . .

12

The outlaw was before Starbuck abruptly. It was as if he'd turned the corner of a building and walked directly into the man. Shawn saw the startled look on the man's bearded face, saw the blur and glint as he pivoted to use the rifle held in his hands. Instinctively he threw his weight to the right side of the saddle and triggered his pistol. The explosions of the two weapons came together as an identical blast.

Starbuck felt the bullet whip at the slack in his sleeve, heard it slam against the rocks now behind him and scream eerily off into space. Charlie, on his feet and twisting slowly, was frowning darkly. He stared at Shawn for a long moment and then took a faltering step backwards. An instant later he was gone, dropping from sight as he went over the ledge on which he had crouched, down into the gully below.

Starbuck wheeled. Already the remaining outlaws, recovered from their surprise, were sweeping toward him from the depths of the cove. Guns began to hammer. Bullets thudded into the rocks beyond him, spurting sand over the chestnut's hooves. He cut sharp again. A rider loomed up immediately to his right, coming in from the ravine into which Charlie had fallen. Shawn snapped a shot at the man, missed, pressed off a second. The outlaw—Waldo, Starbuck recognized him in that next fleeting instant—buckled forward as his horse slowed, and then fell from his saddle.

Eberhardt opened up from his position on the road, the heavier crack of the rifle distinct above the sharp, quick reports of pistols. Shawn again changed course, realizing the two remaining outlaws, Dallman and the Kid, were somewhere on the far side of the cove—that the stage-coach guard apparently had them pinned down.

He spurred the gelding, broke into the open, praying that Eberhardt would not mistake him for one of the outlaws and start pumping lead in his direction. Strangely, at that precise instant, all shooting ceased. From the tail of his eye he saw the coach slowing to a halt, and then far to his right he caught a glimpse of Dallman and the blond Kid, topping out a ridge as they raced off to safety.

Sighing, Starbuck mopped at the sweat covering his face. It had worked out better than he'd had reason to hope. Pulling the chestnut about, he walked the gelding through the drifting dust and smoke toward the vehicle, now at a stand-still in the road. The driver, a wiry, elderly man with a bristly moustache and leather gauntlets that reached almost to his elbows, greeted him with a smile.

13

"Sure obliged to you, mister! Appears we was running smack dab into a ambush!"

Shawn nodded, again brushing at the moisture clouding his eyes. He glanced at Eberhardt. "Tried to warn you but your guard—"

Instantly George Eberhardt was on his feet. "Now, how in blazes was I supposed to know what you was up to?" he demanded testily. Like the driver he was lean, sharp-faced, and well up in years; unlike his partner, there was an irritability to him, an impatient sort of petulance. "You figure me for a mind reader?"

Starbuck shrugged indifferently. "Doubt if any road-agent would be fool enough to ride straight into you the way I was doing."

"Just what I told him, dammit!" the driver said vehemently. "But ain't nobody never told George Eberhardt nothing—no, sir! Never!"

"My job is to keep this here coach from getting held up," the guard countered. "I ain't about to take no chances when I ain't sure of nothing."

"Maybe, but a man ought to use some horse sense—"

Shawn smiled, wondering if the two oldsters fiddled away the miles between stage stops with continuous bickering. He shifted his attention to the coach. The curtains had been rolled up. The door opened and a well-dressed man stepped out. Starbuck could see two other figures inside but they made no move to dismount. Women, he thought. . . . The passenger came toward him.

"Name's Winston. Regardless of what the guard and driver have to say, I'm obliged to you," he said in a deep toned voice. "A holdup would have been a disastrous experience for me."

From the man's appearance and manner of speaking, he was an easterner; going to California to invest, build himself a fortune, Shawn guessed. He'd heard things were really booming up San Francisco way.

"Expect it would," he said. "Next time you plan to carry a lot of gold with you, best you take pains to keep it quiet.

Winston frowned, glanced to the driver, to the guard, and then came back to Starbuck. "I—I don't understand how—"

"One word's all it takes. Somebody overhears it, adds up a couple of things—and you've got a holdup waiting down the road."

"Must have been it—that saloon last night. Town where

we stayed—Mesilla. Just happened to mention where I was going—plans I had—"

"That was it," Starbuck said, and rode in closer to the coach. Looking up at the two men on the seat, he jerked a thumb in the direction of the dead outlaws. "Can't leave them there for the buzzards. Mind helping me boost them onto their horses so's I—"

"Got a better idea," the driver broke in. "Boot's empty, or nigh onto it. We'll load them aboard, haul them to the next way station. Can bury them there. . . . Might save you a passel of trouble."

"Suits me fine," Starbuck said, happy to be relieved of taking the bodies to Las Cruces and making the necessary explanations to the sheriff. Occasionally, in such instances, complications arose that caused a man, doing only what he considered his public duty, considerable grief. "Might as well tie on their horses, too."

"Why not?" the old driver said, gathering up the lines and kicking off his brake. "Something a stage line can always use is horses," he added as he cut the coach about and headed it toward the cove.

Pulling up halfway between the two outlaws, he again locked the wheels, and then climbed down. Starbuck, ground reining the chestnut, moved toward the ravine where Charlie lay. The older man followed, paused suddenly, and flung a speculative look at Eberhardt.

"You hamstrung, or something? We can use a mite of help."

George wagged his head. "I ain't stirring off this here vehicle. I'm not forgetting two of them owlhoots got plumb away."

The driver shrugged. "Ain't likely they'll come back—not with two of their partners dead. But suit yourself," he said and hurried to overtake Shawn.

Together they loaded the bodies into the baggage compartment in the rear of the coach, and then, catching up the loose horses, tied them to the axle.

Dusting himself off with his hat, the driver nodding to Starbuck said, "Again sure want to thank you, friend. Was a good turn you done us. Old George there thanks you too, only it just ain't his way to be beholden."

Shawn smiled and extended his hand. "Lucky I came along at the right time."

"For us it sure was, maybe not for them two in the back. They had us cold, then you showed up. . . . Where you heading—say, reckon I forgot my manners in all this here hullabaloo. I'm Henry Mason."

15

"Starbuck—Shawn Starbuck. I'm riding to Las Cruces. Got to find myself a job."

Mason pursed his lips, clucked softly. "I ain't in 'Cruces much so I don't know whether jobs around there are scarce or not. Most places, seems they are. . . . Wish't I could steer you on to something, but, like I said—"

"Looking for my brother, too. Name's Ben, but it's likely he's not going by that." Shawn had made it a hard and fast rule to always ask, make inquiry. There was always a slim chance—the hope—

He was aware of Mason's curious expression. "Then how can you find—"

"Think he might look something like me. Maybe a bit shorter and heavier. Got reason to think he was around this neck of the woods a year or so ago—in Las Cruces, probably. Could have put on a boxing exhibition. Maybe you'll remember him from that."

"That what you are—one of them boxer fellows?" Mason asked, leathery features lighting with interest as he pointed to the engraved silver belt buckle that Shawn was wearing, with the superimposed ivory figure of a trained fighter centered on it.

"My pa taught us both. The buckle was his. Friends gave it to him. You remember seeing a man in town that put on a boxing show who might've looked a little like me?"

Mason's shoulders stirred. "Sure don't, but like I said, I ain't in 'Cruces much. Sometimes I ain't around for a week or more. Could've happened and me being away, I wouldn't knowed a thing about it. . . . When you get there, look up Abel Morrison. He's the sheriff. He'll recollect."

Shawn nodded, turned to the chestnut. Morrison might remember—and only too well. It appeared, however, that the lawman was going to be his best bet. Swinging to the saddle, he raised his hand in salute to Eberhardt, to Winston, peering out of the coach window, to Henry Mason, climbing back onto his seat and taking up the leathers.

"Luck—" he called.

"Same to you," the driver shouted back, and sent his team lunging against their harness with a sharp command.

Eberhardt twisted about, lifting his gloved hand almost reluctantly. "Sure was a nice fellow," he admitted. "Seems I've seen him before, somewheres."

"More'n just nice!" Mason snorted. "Know what he told me? That there road-agent that was holed up at the point was laying for you special. Said he had a score to settle.

16

Something about you filling his backside with buckshot once."

George scrubbed at his ear. "Done that to plenty of yahoos in my time of being a shotgun rider. Never got no look at him. We get to the station, I'll have me a gander."

"And about him looking familiar—he's here hunting his brother—name of Ben Starbuck."

Eberhardt continued to claw at his ear while he repeated the name slowly. Finally he shook his head. "Nope, don't ring no bells. What was this boy called?"

"Shawn—Shawn Starbuck."

"Well, I ever see him again I'll ask him about this brother of his'n—and where maybe I could've seen him."

"Might've done that back there, polite like, and sort of paid back the favor he done us," Mason snapped.

"Just didn't have no chance—"

"Sure you did! Them outlaws wasn't about to come back—and you know it!"

"Don't know nothing of the kind! They could've just been holding off, waiting to catch us not looking. . . . I got to think of things like that—my job."

"Could've watched from the ground—"

"Not good's I could've from up here—"

Mason, with the coach back on the road, his team running smoothly, settled himself on the seat and glanced sideways at the guard.

"Oh, the hell with you," he said affectionately. "Got any more of that chawin' handy?"

3

It was past mid afternoon, with the sun burning in hot for September, when Shawn rode into Las Cruces. Something like a year had elapsed since he was in the settlement clustered along the east bank of the river—the Rio Grande—and he saw little change. But recalling that he had paused there only briefly as he made his way northward from Laredo where he had hoped to find Ben, he reckoned he was not in a position to judge well.

Now, as he halted in the shade of a giant cottonwood at the edge of town, he wondered if this visit would prove any more productive than the first—or all the other places he had journeyed to. He had so little to go on; no name, only a vague idea of personal appearance, and one distinguishing mark—a small scar above the left eye that was all but invisible except at close range.

No one, it seemed, ever took note of the defacement, and likely such was to be expected. Ben had acquired it when they were small boys playing on the rocks their father had dragged in from a field he was clearing. In the years that followed, the mark became covered over by Ben's dark brow, and a man needed to make close examination if he was to find it. Several times Shawn had followed out what appeared to be certain and definite leads based on a scar, only to find when he looked upon the mark that he had failed again. . . . But someday, somewhere, it would end differently.

Wiping sweat from his face and neck, he touched the chestnut lightly with the rowels and moved on down the street, idly glancing at the names of the business houses as he passed. It was habit with him, a subconscious hope, perhaps, that one day he would see somewhere on a window or printed across a signboard, BEN STARBUCK, and the name of his trade or calling.

It was a foolish dream, and he was aware of it. It would never be that easy, for when Ben had left home that day when Hiram Starbuck had thrashed him unmercifully for his failure to perform a given chore, the boy had declared he was through, not only with the parent but with the family name as well. Thus Shawn knew he'd

18

never see a sign or window so lettered. Ben was the stubborn kind and he'd stick to his vow. . . . Still, there was always the chance, the hope. . . .

Amberson's Gun & Saddle Shop . . . Dr. Edwin Christie, Hours at All Times . . . Hunick's General Store . . . Rodriguez Feed & Seed Co. . . . The Golden Horseshoe Saloon, Gambling-Dancing, Gents Welcome . . . Segura's Restaurant . . . The Border City Bank . . . The Amador Hotel— Stable In Rear . . .

That was the only name to awaken memory in Shawn Starbuck's mind. Likely the other merchants had been there too, when he rode through before, but he had taken no notice. He'd spent the night in the Amador—a hostelry erected by a red-headed, blue-eyed Spaniard who gave the place his name, and then, as if reposing small faith in the profit possibilities of an inn, had continued his regular vocation as a freighter, hauling merchandise in and out of Mexico.

It had been a comfortable place to stay the night— cool, friendly, and to young Shawn, just well embarked on the quest for his brother, a welcome relief from the clap-trap hostelries that he'd had occasion to tarry in.

Now, as he swung into the yard at the rear of the building and dismounted, he sighed in anticipation at the prospects of being off the trail, of a good bed, fine meals in a restaurant, and a bit of relaxation in the Spanish Dagger, the saloon which adjoined.

Pulling his rifle from its boot and taking his saddlebags, Starbuck turned the gelding over to the young Mexican who trotted forward from the stable to meet him.

"Take good care of him, *amigo*," he said, fishing into his pocket for a coin. "Tell the hostler I want him rubbed down, grained, and watered slow. Understand?"

The boy nodded, seized the chestnut's reins, and with a shy smile, hurried off toward the adobe brick barn.

Moving on into the Amador's shadowy lobby, Shawn halted at the desk. The clerk, barely noticing his arrival, pushed a pencil and register at him. He wrote *Shawn Starbuck, Lynchburg, Arizona,* in a firm, legible hand, thanks to the schooling his mother had insisted on his getting, and rested himself against the counter.

The clerk handed him a key to which was attached a wooden tag bearing a neatly carved eight, and glanced at the registration. "How long'll you be staying?"

Shawn was looking into the Spanish Dagger, separated from the hotel by a wall in which an arched doorway had been cut for mutual convenience. . . . A beer would taste good, he decided.

"Hard to say," he murmured.

The clerk crossed his arms and settled back patiently. A man in the far corner of the lobby turned the pages of the newspaper he was reading, the sheets making a noisy crackling as he folded them.

"I mean, it depends on how soon I can find myself a job," Starbuck continued, facing the man behind the desk. He wasn't sure if it was the same clerk who had been there before or not. He didn't think so. He had a good memory for such things.

"Know of some rancher around here needing a hand?"

A pained expression crossed the features of the clerk. *Another saddle-bum passing through;* the thought was written in his eyes.

"Nope, sure don't," he replied. "Like to say, it's customary to pay in advance for the room."

None of it was lost on Shawn. Temper lifted slightly within him. "The hell it is," he snapped. "Wasn't when I stopped here before—doubt if it's been changed."

Tossing his saddlebags into a nearby chair and standing his rifle behind it, Starbuck broke the stiffness of his manner with a smile. "I ever take the notion to beat you out of something it'll be for more than a night's lodging."

Turning lazily, he passed through the archway into the darker area of the saloon and crossed to the bar gleaming softly under the lamps. Three or four men were at the tables, and a tall, well-built individual with intense eyes and the rigid carriage of the military was talking to the bartender.

As Starbuck halted, the aproned man said: "Just a minute, Mr. Gentry—got myself a customer," and moved along the back-bar to where he confronted Shawn, question in his manner.

"Make it beer," Shawn said, and laid a coin on the polished surface before him.

The bartender nodded genially, filled the order quickly from the keg partially hidden under the counter.

"You need a refill, sing out," he said and picking up the money, turned away.

Starbuck lifted the mug, had a swallow of the yeasty liquid. It was far from cold but it was refreshing and it relieved the dust-dry coating that lined his throat. He sighed, took a second swing at the glass. . . . Those past ten days or so during which he'd crossed a big chunk of Arizona and a fair sized piece of New Mexico had seemed more lengthy than usual. He supposed it was because he'd had to use such caution in skirting the Antelope Hills and the Cerro Magdalena. Apaches had been reported active in both areas.

"You seen anything of Vern?"

Idly listening, Shawn heard the man called Gentry ask the question of the bartender. . . . One of the men at the table swore loudly, slammed his cards down. The others laughed.

"Sure ain't—leastwise, I've not seen Mr. Ruch since this morning."

Everybody was *mister* to the bartender, it appeared. Shawn guessed for a man in business it was probably a good idea. He helped himself to more beer, considered whether to first pay a call on the sheriff, make inquiries as to work in the valley—and maybe get the conversation swung around to the boxer who was being sought as a killer, or go to his room and clean up.

As he gave it some thought, a slightly built man with dark, close-set eyes and a thin, bloodless line for a mouth entered by the rear door. He wore a smooth-handled, well-oiled pistol low on his hip. The holster was thonged to his thigh with rawhide string which caused it to tip forward, holding the butt of the weapon it pocketed at the favored, quickly-grasped angle preferred by professional gunmen. Starbuck wondered who he might be.

The bartender answered the question for him. "The usual, Mr. Ruch—rye?"

This was the party Gentry had asked about, Shawn realized as he watched the gunman take up the shot-glass the bartender had set before him and follow Gentry to one of the tables. At once the aproned man behind the counter swung to Starbuck.

"Ready for that refill?"

Shawn shook his head, draining the glass. "One'll hold me for a spell. Sheriff's office here close?"

The bartender lifted the mug, rubbed at the circle of moisture it had left on the counter. "Sure is, Mister— Mister—"

"Starbuck. Don't bother with the mister."

"Habit of mine," the barkeep grinned. "Sheriff's office is down the street, and across. Ain't in town, however. Gone east for a visit with his folks. You got yourself some trouble?"

"Looking for a job—"

"Job? Well, Dave Englund's the deputy. See him, but I

don't know's he can do you much good—him already holding down the job."

"Not looking for a deputy job. I'm a ranch hand."

"I see," the bartender said and cast a thoughtful look at Gentry and Ruch. Whatever it was he had in mind passed, and he added: "Talk to Dave . . . expect he'll be able to help."

"Looking for somebody here, too—or information on him. My brother. You been in town long?"

"About three months. Just bought the place. . . . When was your brother here?"

"Not real sure he ever was, but it'd be a year or better."

"Let's me out, I reckon."

"Seems. Well, obliged to you. I'll go have a talk with the deputy right away."

"Sure thing, Mr. Starbuck. . . . Appreciate your trade."

Shawn grinned. When he returned to the lobby he took up his gear, and under the watchful eyes of the clerk, mounted the stairs to the balcony, off which turned a hallway leading to the rooms, some with numbers, others bearing the names of women.

He located number eight, unloaded his tack, and delaying only long enough to wash his face and hands, since he planned to treat himself to a tin-tub bath at the barber-shop later. Returning to the street, he scanned the store-fronts, located the lawman's quarters, and made his way to them.

An elderly man glanced up from the desk where he sat thumbing through the yellowed pages of a magazine as Shawn entered. He appeared to be the sole occupant in the heat-stuffed building.

"Yeh?"

"You Dave Englund?"

The older man snorted. "Ain't likely to be. I'm Kitch, the jailer. Deputy's out. Something I can do for you?"

Shawn noted a sudden, fixed interest on the jailer's part in his belt buckle. Kitch seemed to be taking in each minute detail of the scrolled, silver oblong.

"Could be. Looking for work. Thought maybe you'd know of some rancher needing a hand. Wrong time of the year, but I still need a job."

Kitch seemed to recover himself. He straightened, then frowned. "Well, man can probably hire on at Three Cross. Jim Kelso owns the outfit. Hear he needs hands."

Starbuck said, "Fine. . . . How do I get to his place?" He was thinking of the older man's interest in the buckle, wondering if it had deeper meaning—something more than simple curiosity. It would pay to question him.

"Not far from here, ten mile more or less, . . . Where you staying?"

"The Amador."

"Well, just come out the front door, turn right 'til you cross the river, then head south. Misdoubt, however, there's any powerful hurry. Jobs at Three Cross are mighty plentiful."

"Meaning what?"

"Well, things've been happening out there, and the way it's going for him—say, that's him coming now. . . . Can save yourself a ride and do your asking right here."

Starbuck stepped to the doorway, smiling at his good fortune. He wasn't too enthusiastic about taking on an additional twenty miles in the saddle for the day unless it was absolutely necessary. Moving out onto the landing, he prepared to hail the rancher. Kelso was pulling in to the hitchrack that fronted the sheriff's office.

= 4 =

Kelso, a harried, bleak man with shadowed eyes and graying hair, swung down stiffly from the tall bay he was riding. Spinning the tag ends of the reins about the cross bar of the rack, he strode into the sheriff's office. Glancing about, he halted in the center of the stuffy room.

"Where's the deputy?"

Kitch said, "Out—ain't sure where. Something I can do for you?"

"There's a plenty the law can do," the rancher said wearily. "When'll Morrison be back?"

"Week, maybe ten days. Unless he changes his mind and stays longer. . . . More trouble at your place?"

"Never quits. Another line shack was burned down two nights ago. . . . Now, about two dozen of my steers've been slaughtered."

"Slaughtered?"

"What I said. Bastards run them down into an arroyo, shot them through the head, left them piled up there."

Kitch wagged his head dolefully. "A hell of a thing. I'll tell Dave about it. All I can do."

"Not all he can do, by God! I want the law moving in on this! Something's got to be done about all this hell-raising. Nobody else's having any trouble but me—and that must mean something. Totes up now to where I've had three line shacks burned to the ground—and have lost close to a hundred head of beef, one way or another. It's got to be stopped—hear?"

"Sure, Mr. Kelso, but—"

"You tell the deputy everything I've said—and you make sure he's listening." Abruptly the rancher pivoted on his heel, started for the door.

Shawn, ignored throughout the conversation, took a step forward. "Kelso—"

The cattleman paused, looked impatiently over his shoulder. "Yeh?"

"Name's Starbuck. Just rode in from Arizona. I'm looking for a job—cowhand. Was told you might be wanting a man."

"Wanting!" the rancher echoed bitterly. "That's the

24

wrong word—needing's more like it." He cocked his head to one side, squinted at Shawn. "You know what's going on at my place?"

"Only what I heard you telling the jailer. Just came in, like I mentioned."

Kelso's eyes narrowed, filled with suspicion. "That the truth—that you just got here?"

Shawn's temper lifted. "The truth," he said stiffly. "Why the hell would I lie about it?"

He could have added that he'd been west of the settlement earlier, involved in preventing a stagecoach holdup—a fact the driver, Henry Mason, and the guard, George Eberhardt, could verify, but the stubbornness in him would not permit it; either Kelso took his word, or he didn't.

"No offense," the rancher said, no apology in his tone. "Hired help's one of my problems—and I'm mighty sick of the way I'm being treated. Can't get a man to stay with me more'n a few days. Some come to me and tell me they've got a job somewheres else. Others just pull out and I never see them again. I get the feeling they hired on just long enough to do some damage—or they're scared off."

"Scared off—by who?" Kitch asked in a voice that made it plain it was an old question often asked. "You've never give us nothing to work on. You tell us who to go after and we'll do it—like the sheriff's always saying."

"How the hell can I tell you who it is when I don't know myself? Ought to be the law's job, stepping in, finding out who and what's at the bottom of the burnings and poisonings and killing off of my stock—"

"Ain't nothing we can do unless we've got something to go on. The sheriff—"

"Sounds like you've got more than your share of problems," Starbuck cut in, realizing that he was once again about to get involved in another man's trouble. . . . But he needed the work—and jobs were scarce.

"My share and then some," Kelso said. He studied Shawn for a long moment. "Reckon that means you ain't asking for the job now."

Starbuck's shoulders moved slightly. "You're looking to hire a hand, I'm needing work. It's that simple. Got to admit, however, my belly's about full of taking on somebody else's grief."

The rancher nodded. "Something I can easy savvy, and I don't blame you. No sense hunting trouble. Comes to a man without him half looking for it. . . . Reckon any man

with a lick of sense would never sign on at Three Cross—
not the way things are going."

"Didn't say I was turning down the offer, just said I was
tired of being in the middle."

Kelso brushed his hat to the back of his head. "That
mean you're hiring on?"

"Up to you."

The rancher stared at Shawn, grinned, bobbed in
pleased agreement. "All right, you're working for me—
and I've got me a hunch you ain't the kind I've been
having to put up with. . . . You're on as a regular hand."

"Suits me. Got my gear and horse at the Amador. Give
me a few minutes to go pick them up, then I'm ready."

"Nothing wrong with me going with you," Kelso said
briskly. "Could stand a drink. Then we can ride out
together."

The rancher moved toward the door. Starbuck, nodding
to the jailer, followed. Together they crossed to the rack
where Kelso freed his horse. Shoulder to shoulder in the
afternoon's bright heat, they walked to the hotel.

Shawn, summoning the same boy who had met him on
arrival, ordered the chestnut saddled and brought up. As
both men entered the Spanish Dagger by its rear entrance
and stepped up to the bar, the man behind the polished
counter greeted them cheerfully.

"Mr. Kelso—good to see you again! And Mr. Starbuck!
Let's see—it'll be whiskey and a beer, as I recollect."

"Right, Arnie," the rancher replied with no particular
show of friendliness. He lifted his brows to Shawn. "Beer
all you drink?"

"Make it a whiskey this time," Starbuck said, and added
to Kelso: "While it's coming I'll run upstairs and get my
stuff."

On his return he halted at the desk. "Got myself a job
so I won't be needing the room. What do I owe you for
washing up?"

The clerk frowned painfully. "Four bits'll cover it," he
said tiredly, and hung the key back on its proper hook.

Starbuck paid off, retraced his steps to the bar, noting
as he crossed from the archway that the gunman, Vern
Ruch, and the military-like Gentry were still at the same
table. His drink was waiting for him on the counter, and
stepping up beside Kelso, saddlebags draped over one
shoulder, he propped his rifle against his legs and wrapped
his fingers around the glass.

"*Salud!*" the rancher said in a hopeful voice as he lifted
his whiskey. "Here's to better days."

26

Shawn nodded, said, "Luck," and downed the fiery liquor.

Kelso drew a coin from his vest pocket, looked expectantly at Shawn. "Another?"

"One does me good—two's too many," Starbuck said. "Go ahead if it suits you. I'm sure in no hurry."

The cattleman shrugged. "Enough," he said and came about. His glance touched Gentry and the gunman. "Howdy," he murmured, and moved on toward the door.

Outside they found the young Mexican waiting with the chestnut. Shawn dropped a dollar—one of his last—in his hand to pay for the gelding's care, slid the rifle into its boot, and slinging the saddlebags across the skirt of the hull, stepped up. Kelso was settled and waiting.

"Place's not far from here—ten miles, about. Got to ford the river, head south. . . . Ride'll work up an appetite."

Jim Kelso seemed in better spirits. The drink probably, Starbuck thought as they pulled away from the rack. Abruptly his head came up as his eyes caught the figures of two men entering the Golden Horseshoe at the upper end of the street. He had only a fleeting glimpse of the pair but there was no doubt in his mind as to their identity—the two outlaws who had escaped during the attempted holdup of the west-bound stage—Dallman and the Kid.

Deputy Dave Englund, his red hair plastered to his skull with sweat, alkali dust loading his stubble of beard, thrust his face into the pan of water he'd poured from the prisoner's bucket and scrubbed vigorously. Then, snorting and blowing appreciatively, he straightened up. Grabbing the towel that hung above the basin at the rear of the jail, he swiped at his dripping features, slanting a look at Bud Kitch. "It's hotter'n hell caved in out there," he said, and then added: "Now, tell me again."

The old jailer swore irritably, moved to the doorway, and spat into the powdery dust beyond the stoop. "Goddangit, pay attention this time!"

"Was paying attention—just trying to get it straight."

Kitch looked up and down the street, near deserted at that supper hour, spat again. "Which you needing to get straight—what Kelso said or what I said about this here Starbuck?"

"Hell with Kelso. He knows there ain't nothing I can do for him. It's Starbuck I'm interested in."

"Like I said, it come to me first off when he come

27

walking in here that he was the killer Morrison's been looking for."

Englund paused, digging the towel into his ears as he studied the floor. "Don't make sense. . . . Was it him, why would he show up here? Be natural for him to stay as far away from this town as he could, not come sashaying right into the sheriff's office."

"Not 'specially. Got to remember that jasper he tangled with didn't die right off. Was several days—and he'd already pulled out by then. . . . Dave, I'm telling you for sure, he's the one!"

Englund hung the towel on its peg, swore. "Too goddam bad there ain't at least one picture of him a man could go by—"

"I don't need one. Know you never seen this Friend, but I have, and Morrison has. Starbuck's a mite taller and skinnier looking, but he could've lost some weight. That'd make him seem taller."

"Guess it would at that."

"And he's one of them boxers. Wears a real fancy belt buckle with some kind of a carving on it—a man standing there in them long drawers and a sash around his middle with his fists held up like they do—"

"Could've bought the buckle, or maybe stole it, or won it in a poker game—"

"Sure," Kitch said in disgust. "Moon's made of green cheese, too."

The deputy grinned at the older man, checked his chin in the cracked mirror above the basin. . . . The hell with it, he'd wait until morning to shave.

"Now, don't get all het up," he said. "Just trying to find all the holes in what you're saying—and thinking. You know how Morrison is."

Kitch turned back into the sweltering room. "Then you're agreeing?"

"Only saying you're maybe right. A lot of it sure fits. Biggest thing that don't is why he'd come back here. Had trouble once in this town, what'd bring him back?"

The old jailer was silent for a time. Finally he raised his head, nodded thoughtfully. "Yeh, why? Now, that's got me to wondering, too. Him coming here to 'Cruces, saying he needed a job—and just happening to be handy when Jim Kelso rode in."

"Exactly. He could maybe be mixed up in this trouble that keeps popping up at Three Cross."

"Does sort of look like a hired gun."

"And him jumping at the chance to go to work for Kelso . . . seems kind of funny."

Kitch shrugged. "Well, I ain't sure there's any hookup there, but I'll swear he's this jaybird Morrison's hunting. Be smart to haul him in, lock him up until the sheriff gets back and can have a look at him."

"Ought to have a reason first. He's probably a pretty smart one when it comes to the law—and all we've got to hold him on is a hunch. I can ask around town, see if anybody else recognized him."

"Wasn't hardly here long enough for that."

"Can ask, anyway. Besides, him hiring out to Kelso means he'll be around for a few days at least—unless he gets run off like the others."

"Misdoubt that. I don't figure him for the kind somebody's going to scare off."

"Maybe. . . . Could be he ain't supposed to get drove off," the deputy said, reaching for his hat. "Let me do some feeling around. . . . Things shape up right, I'll run down to El Paso, send a telegram to Morrison, ask him what we ought to do."

Kitch grunted in satisfaction, drew out his plug of black tobacco. "If you do, you can tell the sheriff for me that I'm willing to bet he's our man."

"Way it looks," Englund admitted, moving to the door, "I'd be a fool to take that bet. . . . Going to get myself a bite to eat. Be back in a hour or so. . . ."

5

Ignoring the bridge, Starbuck and Kelso forded the Rio Grande a half mile or so below town, and in the hard, whiskey-colored light of late afternoon, rode up onto a well-rutted wagon trail paralleling the river's west bank.

A hint of fall was in the air, and the light wind drifting in from the north carried a tang of woodsmoke and burning brush. The cottonwoods—great, spreading umbrellas with trunks six feet and more in diameter, that had furnished relief from the searing sun for the Spanish *conquistadores,* centuries earlier, as they marched up the valley in search of the fabled Seven Cities of Gold—were already tipping their leaves with flaming yellow.

As if to further the fashion in color, rabbit brush, the sunflowers, crownbeard along the marshy sinks, oddly round snakeweed, and even the tangled clumps of wicked, prickly pear cactus—all showed blossoms in varying shades of yellow. Only the asters were at contrariety, proclaiming their individuality with rich, purple faces.

Starbuck drank it all in as a man thirsting, never tiring of nature's flamboyant offerings, his wandering gaze missing nothing—a covey of blue quail scampering along a sandy arroyo, hurrying for the hills to their right; he saw the doves, noted they were gathering, preparing to wing their way south into Mexico for the winter months; he watched a lone jack rabbit spring from beneath the horse's hooves, bound off, his foot-tall, black-tipped ears starchily erect.

All seemed lost to Jim Kelso, however. Shawn slid a glance to the man from the corner of his eye, noticed the preoccupied grimness, the near-desperate manner of the rancher.

"Your brand—Three Cross—you take that from the name of the town?" he asked, hoping to break the rancher's silence.

Kelso shifted on his saddle. "No—from the land, or from a hill that's behind the house, actually. Found three crosses standing there, all sort of bunched together. Graves, I figured. Nobody seemed to know."

"Probably some of the folks heading for California and the gold rush—but didn't make it."

"Doubt it. Crosses had been there a long time. Not much left now—they were just wood. Daughter of mine, Julie, piled rocks where they were so's they wouldn't be lost. She said somebody meant for whoever it was to be remembered and she'd do her part by marking the spot."

"How long've you been ranching in this valley?"

Kelso brushed at the sweat on his face. "Most of ten years. Came west after the war. Found this place, liked it. Done right well—up until this trouble hit."

Starbuck nodded. "Was listening to you talk to the jailer. Sounds plenty bad. Usually a reason why a thing like this happens."

The rancher turned to Shawn. His eyes were dull, tired looking. "Reason—you think maybe I've done something to—"

"Not specially—just that whoever it is, is doing it for a purpose. . . . You have any trouble getting your land?"

"Trouble?"

"Yeh, like having to drive off squatters—something along that line."

Kelso shook his head. "Land was vacant—clear. Got near a hundred thousand acres, not all mine, of course; a lot of it is open range that I'm using. But I've never had to run off one solitary soul—not one. Was never anybody living on any part of it, the free or the deeded."

Starbuck mulled that about in silence as they rode steadily on, following now the crest of a long, running ridge that was beginning to slant toward the west. . . . There had to be some reason for the trouble plaguing Kelso's Three Cross ranch; things like wantonly slaughtered cattle, poisoned water holes, and burned down line shacks didn't just happen for no cause.

"There been anybody around wanting to buy you out?"

Kelso made an indifferent gesture with his hand. "Been a few over the years, as I recollect. Only one lately. That was several months back."

"Who?"

"Don't actually know. Banker drove up from El Paso one day and made me an offer. Was good enough but I didn't see no point in selling. Wife and daughter don't want to move—and what the hell would I do with myself if I wasn't raising cattle? So I turned him down."

"He get riled up over that?"

The rancher rubbed at the side of his neck where the sun was making itself felt. "Not so's I could notice. Blais-

31

dell was making the offer for another man, not himself. All in a day's work to him, I expect . . . Why? You think maybe there's a connection?"

"Somebody who wanted your place real bad could be trying to force your hand."

Kelso shrugged. "Hell, that was months ago, and I've heard of Blaisdell. Big man in that part of Texas—well thought of. He'd not be mixed up in something like you're talking about."

"Might not know anything about what's going on. But if that was several months ago we can probably rule him and whoever he was working for out. . . . Your range run up close to the Mexican border?"

"No, stops quite a ways this side, in fact. Sort of had that idea myself once, that it could be *bandidos* coming across the line. Makes no sense, though. They'd maybe run off a few head of beef, steal everything in the shacks, but it wouldn't be like them to kill off a bunch of steers and let them lay."

"Expect you're right," Starbuck agreed. But the fact, lodged firmly in his mind, remained; there had to be a reason for all the trouble besetting Kelso.

"That belt you're sporting," the rancher said, pointing. "Buckle's mighty fancy. It mean something special?"

"Belonged to my pa. He was a boxer," Shawn replied. He'd gone through the explanation countless times, had often considered not wearing it just to avoid the need for the telling of its history, but he knew that would be a mistake. It was a magic key that opened many conversational doors and prepared the way for inquiries concerning Ben.

"Must've been a champion. . . . That's silver and real ivory, ain't it?"

Shawn nodded, went into the explanation, and then concluded: "Pa's dead now, and I'm trying to clear up the estate. Reason I'm in this country. I'm looking for my brother, Ben. Left home about ten years ago."

The cattleman's brows lifted. "You figure he's around here?"

"Could be—and he's just as apt to be working cattle in Canada or growing wheat in Nebraska. Could be dead. There's nothing for sure and all I can do is what I've been doing now for quite a spell—hunt for him."

"Oughtn't be too hard. Name like Starbuck's not the commonest."

"Probably goes by something else. Swore he'd never use the family name again when he ran off. . . . Sort of got the idea he was around Las Cruces for a time. Would probably have put on a boxing show. You remember anything like that? Would've been a year or so ago."

Kelso thought for a long minute, finally said: "Seems I recollect something about a fancy boxer being in town, but I ain't for certain. Never saw him myself, do know that. Fact is, I don't go into town much. Leave it to my womenfolk and the hired help to do the trotting back and forth. . . . Sorry I ain't much help."

Starbuck sighed heavily. "Just a hunch, anyway. Something comes to your mind later I'll be obliged if you'll mention it."

"Can bet I will. Ten years is a long time, however. You couldn't've been much more'n a button when this—this—"

"Ben—"

"This Ben run off. How do you expect to recognize him if you ever do come face to face?"

"Has a scar over his left eye. Only certain thing I can depend on."

They fell silent after that as the road swung down into a fairly deep arroyo. Large rocks and thick stands of Apache plume, with occasional clumps of mesquite hemmed the twin ruts on either side, and here and there a tall, grotesque agave thrust itself high above the shorter growth as if anxious to feel the first sun's rays in the morning and their last, lingering touch at night.

"Saw you speak to a couple of men in the saloon. Gentry and Ruch, the bartender called them. One called Ruch looked familiar."

Kelso shrugged. "He's a fancy gun-hawk from over Texas way. Don't know what Gentry's got him hanging around for. Man like Vern Ruch just naturally draws trouble."

Shawn agreed. There was always someone, usually with just enough liquor in his belly to fortify his courage, who would call out such a man as Ruch and promptly get himself shot to death for his pains. . . . The Ruchs of the world were bloodless machines, geared to one thing— ruthless, cold murder.

"What's Gentry do? Carries himself like he might've been in the war."

"Seems I heard somewheres he was an officer of some kind. Don't know much else. Been around 'Cruces for a time. Lives at the hotel. Seems to have money. Somebody said he was a buyer."

"Cattle?"

"Could be. Never once talked to me about my herd, though. Always figured——"

Jim Kelso's words were lost in a sudden hammering of pistols coming from the higher ridge to their right. The rancher cursed wildly as a bullet cut into his arm. He swore again as another slammed into the horse he was riding with a meaty sound, and sent the animal plunging headlong to the ground.

"The rocks!" Starbuck yelled, throwing himself off the chestnut. "They've got us cold here in the open!"

6

Starbuck hit the ground flat-footed, the impact jarring him solidly. A bullet whipped at him. He spun instantly, lunged for the shelter of a massive boulder a wagon bed length away. He saw Kelso as he whirled, realized for the first time that the rancher was wounded. He'd thought the horse was the only casualty.

Doubling back, and crouched low, he hurried to where the dazed Kelso was struggling to rise. Throwing an arm around the cattleman, Shawn lifted him bodily off the ground, and turning, dashed for the protection of the rock as lead spanged angrily from its weathered surface.

Heaving for breath, he propped the man against the thick segment of granite and said, "You hurt bad?"

He put the question to the rancher more as a matter of course than in the sense of needed information, since he was already pulling aside the bloodied sleeve to get at the wound.

"Not sure," Kelso murmured, frowning into Starbuck's sweating face. It was as if he were uncertain as to what had occurred.

"Was close—plenty close," Shawn said.

The rancher jerked involuntarily. "Goddammit to hell! What's happening to me?" he cried suddenly in a desperate, baffled voice.

Starbuck shook his head, paying little thought to the frantic words. He had cleared away the fabric of the rancher's shirt, and by pressing with his thumb, had checked the steady flow of blood in the furrow the bullet had gouged from the flesh. It wasn't a serious wound if treated properly, and soon. He looked closely into the man's eyes; the dazed wonderment had vanished and now there was only a dull, hopeless sort of defeat. By that he knew Kelso's senses had returned to normal.

"Press down here," he directed, and taking the rancher's fingers into his own, placed the thumb at the essential point. "Got to keep the bleeding stopped while I find something for a bandage."

Kelso bobbed his head, pointed to his downed horse by jutting his chin. "In my saddlebags—some clean rags."

Starbuck, on all fours, made his way along the side of the boulder to its front and paused. The shooting from above had ceased when they ducked out of sight, but he knew the bushwhackers had not gone; they were simply waiting—patiently.

He glanced about seeking a route to the dead horse that would afford better cover. The animal lay near center of the road, fully in the open and thus exposed to the marksmen above. He doubted he'd have much luck reaching it, but keeping low, he edged away from the boulder. Instantly the arroyo echoed with gunshots. The sandy earth ahead of Shawn leaped and boiled as bullets drilled into it.

"Forget it," Kelso called tiredly. "I'll make out."

Starbuck wormed his way back to where the rancher was slumped. He again examined the wound. The continual pressure on the vein involved had all but stopped the blood flow, but the instant application was released, it surged forth anew. A bandage was the only answer; Kelso, already showing signs of extreme fatigue, would not stand the strain much longer.

Resorting to the bandanna about his neck, Shawn drew it free, snapped it sharply to dislodge as much dust as possible. Then taking up a small pebble he substituted it for Kelso's thumb and secured it in place with the folded cloth. The wound began to bleed the instant the rancher removed his hand, but as Starbuck cinched down with the bandanna, and the small stone pushed deep into the flesh, the flow once again ceased.

"Need to ease up on that now and then," Starbuck said, pulling back. "But it'll work until we can get you to the doc." Drawing his pistol, he checked the loads in the cylinder and glanced to the ridge above the arroyo. "Next thing is to get out of here."

Kelso stirred, reached for his own weapon. "Not alone, you ain't. Up to me to help—you're hardly working for me yet."

"Minute you put me on the payroll back in town, I started. Makes me a Three Cross man, and I take what comes with the job. ... Now, sit quiet. I'll circle around and try coming in behind those bushwhackers."

"My fight," the rancher protested weakly. "I ought to go along. ... Maybe if we can nail one of them, I'll find out what this is all about."

"Do my best to get one for you," Starbuck promised grimly. "But you stay put. Easier for me to go it alone."

Immediately he pivoted on a heel, and keeping low and

close to the base of the butte lifting above them, hurried along through the brush until he came to a narow ravine that broke the smooth face of the formation.

Halting there he studied the road, the place where Kelso was lying was easily marked by its position to the dead horse and the general look of the land. The ambushers would be almost directly above the horse. The bullets, he recalled, had come pouring down from straight overhead. . . . Therefore, he should be well below the marksmen at that point where the wash broke onto the flat.

Removing his spurs and hanging them on a stump, he began to climb the declivity, doing it as quietly as possible, steadying himself by clinging to the tough scrub oak growing from the sides of the storm-slashed gully, bracing himself whenever possible against jutting rocks. By the time he gained the top and could look onto the level, he was sucking deep for wind, and sweat clothed him from head to foot.

Sagging against the edge of the wash, he mopped the mist from his eyes and squinted into the pale glare. Two horses, tied well back from the rim of the bluff, were a quarter mile or so distant. The bushwhackers would be holed up about opposite, he reasoned.

Reaching down, he laid his hand on the butt of his pistol, assuring himself that it had not dislodged during the climb, and then heaved himself out of the ravine. He could have used a few more minutes' rest to ease the trembling muscles of his legs, unaccustomed to such strain, as well as to allow his breathing to subside to normal; but he felt he had little time to spare.

Kelso, while not wounded dangerously, should get medical attention as soon as possible. He was not a young man, and the injury, if neglected for an appreciable extent, could mean trouble. Dropping back a short distance from the lip of the butte, Starbuck, again bent low, moved hurriedly forward.

Motion off to his far left, just over the lip of the bluff dropped him flat on his belly. The stained, peaked crown of a hat bobbed into view along the rim, disappeared, showed once more. Starbuck clucked softly. Now he knew where the outlaws were hiding.

The hat vanished. Shawn raised himself, probed the near-flat surface of the butte. It offered no arroyos or depressions along which he could make an approach. He'd simply have to go straight in, depending a great deal on luck.

Pistol in hand he edged forward, doubly careful now to

37

stay below the lip of the butte and not allow himself to become silhouetted against the sky.

He halted abruptly. A man was standing upright just below the rim, staring at him in surprise. The rider reacted. His arm streaked down for the pistol at his side, came up in a blur of glinting metal. Starbuck dipped to one side, triggered the weapon in his hand. The explosions came together, slapping loudly, setting up a rolling chain of echoes.

The bushwhacker staggered back. His knees buckled as the pistol fell from his nerveless fingers. He took several stumbling steps and disappeared over the edge of the butte.

Shawn, muscles taut, nerves keyed to smoothness, hunched low, waiting for the second man to make his move. Jim Kelso was going to get his wish. He had a dead man to see, and from him perhaps he would learn who it was that was trying to ruin him and Three Cross. . . . Whoever, they were playing for keeps—there was no doubt of that.

The minutes dragged by as the sun began to spread its last, steaming rays across the hills and flats before relinquishing dominion to night. . . . What the hell was holding back the other bushwhacker?

Starbuck squirmed in the uncomfortable heat, brushed at his eyes again. Suddenly out of patience, he moved on, working his way cautiously, attention riveted to the lip of the butte and the narrow slope just below it that extended, like a shelf, for a few feet before it broke off into a sheer drop.

Another storm wash appeared immediately ahead offering him an avenue by which he could get off the flat and down onto the bench. It would be a good move; there was ample rock and brush there to cover his movements. Sliding into the cut, he lowered himself to the bench. He should be able to locate the second outlaw now with no trouble.

Continuing, he made his way quietly along the shelf, placing each booted foot carefully, avoiding the loose shale, the swish of disturbed bushes, and crackle of dead brush as much as possible. He halted, swore deeply as the quick pound of a horse leaving fast reached him.

Lunging upright, he threw his glance to where the bushwhackers had picketed their horses. Only one remained. The other, ridden by a man in dark clothing and hunched low over the saddle, was racing off into the trees.

Shaking his head he stared after the man until he had

disappeared. He had hoped to be of real help to Kelso; a live prisoner could have been made to talk, answer a few questions. Turning, he climbed up onto the little mesa capping the butte and crossed to where the horse waited; a dead man couldn't speak but perhaps his identity would mean something.

The outlaw was a stranger to Jim Kelso—a man he'd never laid eyes on during all his years in the valley, he declared, when later, astride the dead man's horse, Shawn took him to view the body. Nor was there any identification in his pockets or among his gear that was of help. The buckskin he forked wore an unfamiliar brand.

"Just some drifter what hired out to whoever's doing this to me," Kelso said, and then as Starbuck started to hoist the body to the back of his saddle on the chestnut, he added: "Leave him be. I'll send one of the hands back with a wagon, have him toted into town. . . . Maybe the deputy or somebody around there'll know him."

Shawn nodded, swung onto the gelding. The rancher appeared weak and evidently was experiencing considerable pain. He needed to be in the hands of a doctor.

"We far from your place?"

"Less'n an hour," Kelso replied, and then wagged his head. "Ain't no sense going back to town, if that's what you're thinking. Myra—my wife—can do a better job of patching up a man than any doc—seven days a week! Living out like we've done all our lives, we learned to make do and get by. . . . Anyways, been hurt worse than this many a time."

Starbuck nodded. If Three Cross was that near it would be wiser to continue. Wheeling the chestnut about, he aimed for the road, Kelso following silently while a deep frown pulled at his lean features.

"Obliged to you for stepping in the way you did," he said.

"Why not? Was part of the job, far as I'm concerned."

"Not the way most of them I've been hiring would look at it. . . . Can see how you're built. . . ." Kelso's words faded as the horses began to pull up out of the arroyo for the flat above. He was clinging to the saddle horn with one hand, and clamped the other over his wound. There was a translucent look to his features.

"Would like to think," he continued, when the pain from the sharp jolting had ended, and they were on the level, "that you'd stick with me a spell—as my *caporal*—foreman, I expect they call it where you come from."

Starbuck glanced at the rancher in surprise. "I appreciate the offer, but I doubt if it would set well with your other men. Probably some of them've been with you a long time and have earned the job."

"All too old for it. They know it, same as I do. Be no grumbling on that score. Fact is, I've hired on three *caporals* in about as many months—and all quit me. Pay'll be good. Ninety a month and found—and I'll sure not butt into your way of ramrodding things."

"Not meaning to argue, but you hardly know me—"

"Learned all I need to know about you back there in the canyon. Ain't hard to gauge a man once you've seen him standing up to trouble."

"Something else—I'm not the kind to stay long in one place. Got to keep moving on, looking for Ben."

"Well, that's your business but, far as your brother's concerned, my advice is to forget him, settle down before you waste your life away."

"Probably good advice," Starbuck said slowly, "only I can't take it. Ben's got to be found."

"It's that important to you, eh?"

"It is. . . . But if it'll help some I'll take over, work for you until the first of the year. Came here figuring to find a job for that long. Then I'll be moving on."

Kelso sighed wearily. "All right—reckon a while's better'n nothing. I'll nod you off to the crew, such as I've got, tell them you're the new boss. . . . Anything special you want them told—or don't?"

"Can't think of anything. Something comes up, I'll do my own talking."

Shawn looked ahead into a shallow, green basin in which stood, in quiet serenity, a collection of neat buildings, spreading trees, and splashes of brightly colored flowers. A strip of silver marked the course of a small stream making its way across the swale, and near dead center a windmill wheeled lazily in the slow breeze. . . . This was Three Cross.

7

With the last of the sun turning the sky into a golden dome, Starbuck and Jim Kelso rode into the yard. Immediately two women burst from the back door of the long adobe and wood ranch house, and came hurrying up anxiously. Kelso's wife and daughter, he assumed, allowing his eyes to run over the orderly place with its well-kept corrals and structures.

A fine place, he thought, and wondered as he had so many times, if the day would ever come when he could stop, have a home such as this; and as before the answer was the same—first find Ben.

"Now, don't fuss over me!" Kelso's complaining voice broke into his consciousness. "Ain't hurt bad, only nicked deep."

An elderly Mexican wearing a cook's apron had appeared at the door of a smaller building near the main house. A second man, also well in years, was trotting up stiffly from what evidently was the crew's quarters, his seamy face grim. . . . It was a fine place, Starbuck decided again, but tension lay across it, a breathless sort of restraint that was almost tangible. It was as if the trees, the corrals, the buildings—Three Cross itself were waiting, wondering what would befall it next.

Shawn left the saddle, listening to the cattleman make his explanations to all within range, unconsciously giving the girl closer study. Julie, Kelso had called her. She was probably about his own age, maybe a year younger. She had dark-brown hair with reddish lights that the sun brought out, and against the creamy tan of her face her wide set eyes were very blue. She had an attractive figure that even her man's style shirt and corduroy riding skirt failed to conceal.

Mrs. Kelso—Myra, he recalled her name, too—was an older edition of her daughter except there was a gentleness to her as she went calmly about examining the wound in her husband's arm, despite his objections.

"Want you all to meet Shawn Starbuck," the rancher said, finally pulling away. "Wasn't for him I'd not be here now."

Shawn was aware of the instantaneous hostility that sprang to life in Julie Kelso's attitude. She wasn't one to trust any man far, he reckoned, and supposed she had good reason.

"My missus, my daughter, Julie. ... And this here is Aaron Lambert, one of my best men—and best friends," Kelso said, pointing each out individually. "Cook over there by the shack is Candido Aragon—we call him Candy. ... Been with me a lot of years, too." He paused, glanced about and added, "Seems there ain't nobody else around right now. You'll have to meet the rest of the crew later."

Starbuck had shaken hands with each. Mrs. Kelso appeared grateful, Lambert cordial, Aragon polite. But there was a distinct suspicion and mistrust in Julie's manner.

"That's the *caporal's* quarters there next to the bunkhouse," Kelso said as he turned away with the two women at his sides. "Aaron, be obliged if you'll see Starbuck settled, get him what he needs. ... And tell Felipe to hitch up the wagon. There's a dead man lying out in Coyote Canyon. Have him hauled in to town and turned over to Dave Englund. Want to find out who he is. ... Maybe the law can do that much for me."

The old puncher bobbed his head, said, "Sure, Jim. Tend to it right away," and gathering up the reins of the two horses, beckoned to Shawn and moved off toward the barn.

Features sober, Lambert turning his watery eyes on Starbuck said, "mind telling me what happened out there? Didn't like pressing it in front of Jim's womenfolks."

"Ambush," Shawn replied. "Two men hiding on the bluff. Cut down on us when we rode through. One of them got away."

"That's it, then," Lambert muttered. "First blood's been drawed. Wonder what'll come next."

"Something make you think this is the start of bigger trouble?"

"Well, sure ain't never been nobody shot before, only cows. ... You get a look at that bird who got away?"

"Too far off."

The older man swore. "Way it's been. Like a bunch of ghosts. Something always happening but nobody ever sees anything."

He'd be expected to change that, put a stop to all such problems, Starbuck realized, halting in front of the small cabin designated as his living quarters.

Stepping up to the chestnut, he pulled off his saddlebags

and drew his rifle, laying them on the small, square stoop that fronted the door. Then untying the strings, he removed his blanket roll.

"From what Kelso said you're one of the long-time hands."

Lambert hawked, spat. "Longest. Been here longer'n anybody 'cepting maybe old Candy."

Shawn picked up his belongings, pushed the door open. "Later I'd like talking to you. Few things I'd appreciate knowing."

"Sure enough. Can be back soon's I get these horses in the barn and start Felipe out with that wagon."

"I'll be inside," Shawn said, and stepped into the single room.

Its most recent occupant apparently had not been gone for long, he guessed, tossing the blanket roll onto a bench. Propping the rifle against a wall, he hung the saddlebags over the foot of the bed, sat down, tried out the mattress. It was hard, crackled noisly, and the springs protested his every move, but it would do. The way things were shaping up he'd likely spend damned few hours on it, anyway.

Rising, he unbuckled the straps of the leather pouches and began to distribute his belongings. He'd learned to travel light, accumulate nothing other than the actual necessities such as razor, soap, towel, a change of clothing, and extra ammunition for his weapons. A man on the move was foolish to load himself down with—

The rap of quick, firm footsteps on the landing brought him around to the doorway. The screen jerked back and Julie Kelso, features taut, stood in the rectangle of half light.

Shawn swept her with a calculating glance, assessed her manner. Here was trouble—a problem. He nodded coolly. "Something gone wrong with your pa?" he asked, getting in the first word.

She shook her head irritably. He could see the anger in her and it at once stirred temper within him. What the hell was eating her? He wasn't responsible for what was happening on Three Cross—or for her pa getting shot. He was just one of the hired hands.

Pulling off the new hat he'd bought in Lynchburg, just before beginning the journey, he tossed it onto the dusty table, folded his arms and waited. ... It was Julie Kelso who had something sticking in her craw—therefore it was up to her to open the ball.

She looked him up and down, inventoried his scant

43

possessions with a sweeping glance, and said, "You don't seem much like the others."

The words meant nothing to Shawn. He shrugged. "So?"

"You don't fool me any. Maybe you can the rest, but I see you for what you are—another of the bunch that's out to ruin us. Expect you had that ambush all arranged so's you could put yourself in good with my father."

"Sure did," Starbuck drawled. "Was so anxious that I plugged one of my own pals—the one that wagon's going out after right now," he added, pointing into the yard.

"That could have been a slip-up—your shooting him," Julie said, flatly dismissing the point. "I notice you didn't get hurt."

"Was born lucky, I reckon. ... Anything else on your mind?"

"Plenty, Mister Starbuck! Like I said you may have fooled my father but not me. I figure you're just another of the bunch that's causing us trouble, and as soon as you do what you've been sent to do, you'll pull out like all the others who've hired on for a few days—"

"Pull out?"

"You know what I mean! Every rider we've put to work in the last three or four months just up and left."

"Not what I'm figuring to do."

"Expected you to say that—but I want you to know one thing sure," the girl rushed on ignoring his words, "maybe you're the *caporal,* but I'm keeping my eye on you—on just you every minute I can. ... I see you make one wrong move and I'm going to put a rifle bullet in you! That clear?"

"Clear," Shawn echoed mildly. "Anything else?"

Julie stared at him. She was furious, beside herself, and her eyes were snapping. "Don't you laugh at me—I mean every word I say! I'm not easily fooled like my father—and I don't have a soft heart like him either!"

Shawn was tempted to say: *you're a hell of a lot prettier, too,* but he checked the words. Julie Kelso was in deadly earnest, worried to the peak of distraction. It would be cruel to show he did not take her seriously. ... But his own nerves were a little on the raw side and he was laboring to keep his temper under control.

"Make you a deal," he said slowly. "You go right ahead keeping an eye on me. I won't mind that a bit—just as long as you don't get in the way of me doing a job for your pa."

"For my pa—father!" she scoffed. "For your boss, whoever he is, you mean!"

"For your pa," Starbuck repeated coldly. He was tired, sweaty, hungry, and his patience was rapidly running out. "Now, we've both had our say. You don't like me and I've got you figured for a nuisance. That's settled. I'll be obliged if you'll get out of here, let me clean up—that is unless you want to stick around and watch me strip off naked."

Reaching up he freed the buttons of his shield shirt, pulled it over his head, baring a bronzed, muscular torso. At once the girl spun, hastened for the door.

"If I—"

"If you've got anything more to say," Starbuck supplied, "best you tell it to your pa. He's the man who hired me. He'll have to be the one who fires me."

Abruptly Julie bolted through the doorway and into the yard. Shawn stood motionless, listening to the quick beat of her heels as she crossed the hardpack, and then turned again to the bed, resuming the interrupted chore of laying out his gear. He paused again, wearily, as a noise drew his attention. Harsh words rose to his lips. If it was Julie coming back—

It wasn't the girl but Aaron Lambert. "It all right if I come in?" the old puncher asked, and entered without waiting for Starbuck's answer.

Shawn grinned. "Sure. Find yourself a chair and get comfortable. Need to hear a few things about this place."

"Fire away," Lambert said, sitting down. "First off, howsomever, want to put in a word for the little gal. Just seen her go flying across the yard, tail feathers stiff, and head up like the heel flies was after her. Don't you feel too mean towards her. She's fretting plenty about her pa and about what's happening around here."

"Not hard to see that."

"Now, I don't exactly know how I ought to say this, but Jim's sort of easy going and nice like. He just don't quite seem to savvy how to buck up against things and straighten them out—if you get what I'm saying. ... Was she running the place, you can bet thing's would be different."

"She's given me a sample of what she'd do—or like to. Got the idea she not only doesn't trust me half as far as she could throw Durham bull, but unless I comb my hair the way she likes, I'm liable to wake up with a 44-40 bullet in my head."

"That's her all right," Lambert chuckled, and then sobered. "But don't poke no fun at her, son. She ain't deserving of it. Shouldering a powerful big load, that girl, and soon's she finds out you're on the square, she'll be all for you." The old rider paused, looked directly into Starbuck's eyes. "You are, ain't you?"

The bluntness of the question, the direct and simple honesty of it hit Starbuck hard. He nodded soberly, took a step nearer the oldster and extended his hand.

"I am," he said, enclosing Lambert's gnarled fingers in his own. "That's my guarantee. I aim to give Jim Kelso the best that's in me. Goes for everybody and everything on Three Cross. Now, what I want to know is, who's out to kill him?"

$=8=$

The old rider stared thoughtfully at the warped toes of his scuffed, worn boots. After a time he reached into his pocket and drew forth a charred briar pipe. Knocking the dottle into the palm of his hand, he leaned forward, tossed the crumbs into a wood box beside the small White Oak heating stove, and settled back.

"I purely don't know—and that's a fact," he said, digging out a muslin sack of twist tobacco. Pinching off a quantity, he deliberately crushed the shards into fine bits, and stuffed them into the blackened bowl. "Same as I just can't figure why anybody'd be so all fired sot on ruining him."

"What about people who don't like him—other ranchers, maybe, or somebody in town."

"Jim's always been a good friend to folks. I can't think of nobody that'd be hating him."

Starbuck shrugged. "He's got an enemy somewhere, which is about normal, I suspect. Never met a man who didn't have."

"Sort of goes with being alive—like breathing and eating and such," Lambert agreed.

Shawn had asked the question of Kelso himself, now he asked it of the man's best and oldest friend. "There somebody wanting to buy Three Cross?"

The old puncher considered the thin stream of smoke snaking upwards from his pipe. "Recollect there was this lawyer from El Paso. He come up here, made an offer for some friend of his'n. Jim told him he wasn't interested and that was the end of it, far as I know."

"How long ago was that?"

Lambert sucked at his lower lip. "Let's see, this here's September. Was two, three months back—July, that's when it was. We'd just sold off a big chunk of the herd."

The offer to buy had been made more recently than Kelso had led him to believe—at least that was the impression he'd gotten. The rancher, however, had taken the offer lightly; it could be that the time had not registered definitely in his mind.

"How big a herd you running?" Shawn asked, moving

47

to the sink in the corner of the room and levering a pan of water from the pump.

"Somewheres close to two thousand head. Sold off better'n twenty-five hundred this summer. Market was plenty high and Jim grabbed the chance to clean up."

Starbuck washed himself thoroughly and toweled off; that complete bath he'd been looking forward to would still have to wait, however. There were a few things that needed doing first.

"From what I gathered from talking to Kelso and listening to his daughter, you're having no luck keeping hired help."

"Ain't no big mystery to it. They get scared off. All these goings on—fires and shootings and the like, it sure brings the yellow out in some, but maybe you can't fault them. Ain't no man in his right mind going to like bucking for the graveyard. . . . Been a few who didn't even wait to collect their wages."

"Any of them ever actually get hurt?"

"Was some who claim they was shot at, but there weren't none that ever got hit. Jim's the first, like I told you. Had one fellow who got hisself caught in a little stampede."

"Stampede?"

"Yeh. Herd had been split into a couple a dozen bunches. Somebody or something set a jag to running. Puncher name of Gillespie got sort of trapped in front of them when his horse stepped in a gopher hole and throwed him. He got out of the way by jumping behind a mesquite. Wasn't hurt none, but it put the frost into him good. Quit that same day. Said he knew for certain somebody'd started them critters to running, done it just to get him tromped on."

Shawn, pulling on a clean if badly wrinkled shirt, walked to the doorway, looked out into the yard. The hill beyond the structures, mentioned by Kelso, was a round-topped bubble of lava rock covered with a thin grass. It appeared deceptively smooth in the faint light.

The ground at the foot of the formation was in shadow, but complete darkness was creeping up swiftly, swallowing all in its path as it swept skyward. He could not see the mounds where the crosses had stood, and had a quick wonder as to who might lie buried beneath them: simple peasants? adventuresome soldiers? Spanish noblemen in crested armor?

Shawn's interest sharpened. A horse and rider had appeared, and were now outlined on the crest of the hill.

"Somebody up on the *malpais*," he said, beckoning to Lambert.

The older man got to his feet, shuffled to the door. He squinted at the solitary figure for a long minute, shook his head.

"Ain't sure but it looks like that there *vaquero* we've seen hanging around now and then."

"Who is he?"

"Ain't nobody seems to know."

"Little strange, somebody like that just hanging around."

"Maybe not. We're close to the border and these *vaqueros* are funny birds. Work when they want, loaf when they take the notion. Independent as a hoot owl in a hollow log." Lambert looked up, glanced toward the corrals. "You want to meet the rest of the boys? They're coming in—leastways them that's been out with the herd. . . . Night crew's done rode off."

Shawn pulled on his hat. "Like to meet whoever's here now. Figure to ride out and say howdy to the others after I eat."

Stepping into the open, he glanced to the *malpais*. The rider had vanished. Tomorrow he'd do some scouting, see if he could encounter the man, and find out just why he was on Three Cross range. No drifter would stall around the same locality for any length of time without reason.

"Happened again—"

He swung to Lambert. The old puncher's gaze was on two men dismounting at the rack fronting the barn.

"What's that?"

"Them last hands Jim put to work—about a week ago. Two jaspers that blew in from over Texas way. They ain't with the others. Means they've pulled out."

"Maybe got busy—hung up—"

"Doubt it. They wasn't that anxious to work. Would've come in with Pierce and Dodd. The four of them's been working day shift with Jim and me pitching in to help out now and then. . . . Dan, where's them other boys?"

Pierce, a small, wiry man with a limp, jerked at his cinch strap. "Skedaddled," he said disgustedly. "Took off around sundown. Said to tell the boss they was quitting."

Shawn crossed to where the pair were removing their gear. "Name's Starbuck. Kelso's put me on as foreman," he said, offering his hand. "Those two give you any special reason why they were leaving?"

Dodd, a lanky oldster with glittering, dark eyes and a

saddle-leather face, spat into the dust. "Same reason they all give—it ain't healthy around here."

"They been shot at or threatened by somebody?"

Pierce wagged his head, looked questioningly at Dodd who also gave a negative response. "Didn't say nothing about it if they did."

Shawn turned away, hesitated. "One thing more, either of you notice a *vaquero* on the range lately?"

Again the riders exchanged glances. Dodd said: "Sure. Reckon we've all spotted him, just sort of ambling along. Don't do nothing or even get close enough to talk to. Just hangs around, lonesome like."

Starbuck nodded, continued on with Lambert at his side. "Who's doing the nighthawking?"

"Rafe Tuttle, Pete Helm, and Isidro Ortiz—with me spelling them off once in a while. Was three others on the night crew, but they took off a couple of days ago."

"Not many riders to be looking after two thousand head of beef," Shawn commented. It appeared to him that matters might be drawing to a head on Three Cross—the attempt to ambush Jim Kelso, the abrupt departure of half the hired help, which stripped the crew down to only a few elderly, ineffectual if loyal members. Something must be done, and done quickly.

"Like to get myself a bite to eat," he said then, coming to a decision.

"Sure. . . . Candy'll have supper waiting. . . . Come on."

Shawn ate a hasty meal, returned to the yard, and made his way to the barn with Aaron Lambert tagging at his heels.

"Need something to ride," he said, halting at the doorway. "Chestnut of mine's had a long day and needs some rest."

"Fermin!" Lambert bellowed. "You in here?"

From the black depths of the building a young Mexican appeared.

"You want something, *senor?*"

"This here's the new boss—the *caporal*. Get him a horse—that big black'll do."

"My gear, there on the rail," Starbuck said, smiling at the boy and pointing to his saddle straddling the adzed log placed in the first stall for such purpose.

He turned back into the yard to wait. Lamps had been lit in the main house and he could see Myra Kelso moving about inside her kitchen preparing the evening meal. Once Julie passed across the window, but he saw no sign of Kelso himself; most likely his wife had him resting in bed.

"You got something special in mind to do?" Lambert asked.

Shawn nodded. "One thing—see if I can find out what's going on around here. Got a feeling the next time they set an ambush for Kelso, he might not be so lucky."

"Thinking that, too. You got yourself an idea?"

"Not yet. It's what I'll be hunting for." Hearing a sound at the barn's entrance, he stepped aside as Fermin led a tall, black gelding into the open.

"You want some company?"

Starbuck smiled at the old puncher and mounted. "Obliged to you, but I'll go alone. Work better that way. Expect you're needing rest, anyway."

Lambert bobbed his head. "Ain't going to deny that. Now, you have a care. The range ain't exactly safe around here no more—'specially at night."

"I'm figuring on that."

The oldster stared, murmured, "Reckon I savvy," and then added, "Like to say it's mighty good to have somebody calling the turn here on the ranch again. . . . Good night."

"Good night," Starbuck answered, and rode off.

= 9 =

Moving into the pale night, Shawn let his mind dwell upon the words Aaron Lambert had spoken. The old puncher made it sound as if Jim Kelso was doing little to keep Three Cross alive, that the ranch was more or less floundering along on its own strength. Perhaps that was true: it could be Kelso was a man not accustomed to fighting, and found himself at a loss as to what should be done.

His thoughts drifted to other things—to the cattle and the fact that with trouble apparently lurking behind every bush, only three men were riding herd on two thousand head. That was a situation that needed correcting as fast as possible, otherwise Three Cross would find itself out of business in short order. More cowhands, of course, was the solution—and likely some were available in Las Cruces, or certainly in the larger settlements of Albuquerque to the north and El Paso, only forty miles or less to the south.

But the catch wasn't finding men—it was keeping them once hired. Evidently the word was out and spread wide that Three Cross wasn't a good place for a man to hang his hat—not if he wanted to remain among the living. ... And the only way that reputation could be erased was to remove the threat—the source of the trouble.

Shawn sighed, realizing how fully he had become enmeshed in another man's problems. All he had intended doing was come down into the lower Rio Grande Valley, or the Mesilla—as some people called it, and find himself an ordinary job by which he could rebuild his depleted finances while he made discreet inquiries concerning a man who might be his brother.

Now, within hours after he'd arrived, where did he stand? He was the foreman of a ranch that was hock-deep in adversity; somebody was taking pot shots at the owner, and he, himself, was suspected of being a double-crosser by the rancher's own daughter. Added to those items was the fact that he had a couple of thousand steers to look after, and not half enough hired hands to assist in the doing.

Someday—someday he was going to find it possible to start out from one point, ride to another without any interruption, do what he had planned to do, free from detours and side issues, and then if the lead on Ben that had taken him to that particular destination proved false, just ride on. . . . Someday—maybe.

The black was enjoying the steady run in the evening's coolness, apparently having been stabled for some time, and Shawn drew him in, wanting to have as good a look at Three Cross range as possible. He was some distance from the ranch house, he noted, and crossing a broad, undulating plain of silver that was bordered on the west by rugged hills, and on the east by a band of trees. The river would lie there—the Rio Grande.

Other small groves marked the land with shadowy patchwork, and just below him he caught the circular shine of a water hole. Likely there were several of those scattered about, spring fed or possibly filled by seeps from underground streams.

A rider loomed up suddenly to his left, and came out from behind a clump of brush. Starlight glinted off the pistol held ready in his hand.

"Friend," Shawn said, and pulled to a halt.

The puncher came forward cautiously. A scar tracing down the side of his face looked white and slick in the half dark.

"Friend—who? Don't recollect ever seeing you before, cowboy."

"Name's Starbuck. Kelso put me on as foreman today. Which one are you, Tuttle or Helms?"

The rider, his eyes running over the black in recognition, relaxed gently, slid his pistol back into its holster.

"I'm Rafe Tuttle. Heard Jim'd brung in a new ramrod. Cook told us. Looking for something?"

"For anything and everything. Figure the biggest job I've got is to find out who's causing all the hell around here, and put a stop to it. Got any suggestions?"

Tuttle drew up one leg, hooked it around his saddle horn, and methodically began to build himself a cigarette.

"That's the devil of it," he said in a tired voice. "Can't nobody figure what it's all about. Things're just a happening, crazy like."

Shawn studied the old puncher. "We both know there's a reason for it. I've dug into the easy ones, got no answers. Could use some help."

Tuttle lit his quirley, the flame of the cupped match

placing a yellow shine on his taut, lean features and accentuating the high cheek bones.

"Was I knowing something I'd a done spoke up," he said quietly. "Three Cross is home to me, and the Kelsos are the only family I got. Same goes for Lambert and Pete and a couple others. We'd be fools to mess in our own nest, specially at our age."

Shawn nodded. What Rafe said made sense. All the riders who had stuck by Kelso were elderly men, past their yen for drifting, thinking now of the quiet years, and the need for a warm place to sleep, and a table at which they could sit down regularly. He could figure all of them—Aaron Lambert, Tuttle, Helms, Dodd, and the one with the limp, Dan Pierce, would do nothing to wrong Kelso.

That left the cook, Candy, the stable boy, Fermin, and a couple more: the one Kelso had sent after the outlaw's body, Felipe, and a regular range hand, Isidro. The first two he could count out; they'd have neither reason nor opportunity to be involved. Felipe he'd have to see later. Isidro was with the herd.

Tuttle leaned forward, eyes on Starbuck. "You aiming to stay, or you like them others—just passing through?"

"I'll be here. I don't aim to pull out tomorrow or the next day—or the next. But I've got to straighten things out fast. The herd on ahead?"

Rafe bobbed his head. "In the east valley. Going to start them drifting towards the river in the morning."

Starbuck swept the land before him with a hard glance. "Who's orders?"

"Kelso's."

"Won't that put the stock pretty far from the ranch?"

Again the puncher nodded. "Just about as far as it can get, 'cepting the far-south line. Way we've been doing for years. Jim wants to give the grass along the high range a chance to grow back, get set for the winter."

"Makes sense on one hand," Shawn said, "but considering we're short of help, and everything that's going on, it don't on the other."

Tuttle flipped his cold cigarette into the night, settled himself on his saddle. "Come to think on it, it sure don't. Be mighty hard to keep tab on things—and if a man was to run into trouble, it's sure a far piece to the house."

"I'm changing it," Starbuck said. "Pass the word to the others. Morning comes, head the stock north for the hills."

Tuttle shrugged. "You're the boss. . . . What about Jim?"

"I'll tell him. Way I see it we're better off with everything—cattle, horses, and men, all bunched up as close to the ranch as we can get. We'll worry about grass later."

"Just what I'm thinking," Tuttle said, permitting himself to smile for the first time, and then touching the brim of his hat with a forefinger, he wheeled off into the darkness.

Shawn watched him fade into the night, and then sent the black on ahead, slanting now in the general direction of the river. A short time later he caught sight of the herd, or a fair portion of it, bedded down in a broad swale, in the lower center of which water stood in shallow depth. A campfire flared like an angry red eye in the blackness of the slope beyond the sleeping cattle, and he could see the vague shape of a man hunched nearby.

The remainder of the stock would likely be on to the south, he supposed, judging from what Rafe Tuttle had said. Either Jim Kelso was too stubborn for his own good in not moving the herd to a point where it could be more easily watched over, or else he was so worried and preoccupied with the problems besetting him that he was not thinking clearly.

That probably was it, and having no foreman to shoulder the responsibilities of the cattle, make the necessary decisions as to how the beef should be cared for, probably accounted for what appeared to be sheer carelessness—so obvious to an experienced man coming in from the outside.

He rode on, circling the swale, and came in to the fire. The squatting man drew himself erect and stepped back into the shadows of a doveweed clump.

"I'm Starbuck, the foreman," Shawn called.

At once the puncher reappeared, a squat, round-faced Mexican who cradled a rifle in his arms, and stared at Starbuck impassively.

"You Ortiz?"

"Si, mi caporal—Isidro Ortiz. I have wonder if you would come."

"Everything quiet tonight?"

"All is quiet. The cattle sleep."

"Going to start moving them in the morning," Shawn said, and repeated the instructions he had given Rafe Tuttle.

Ortiz made no comment. He simply nodded and waited in silence.

"How long've you worked for Three Cross, amigo?"

55

Starbuck asked then, staring out over the dark mass that was the herd.

"Three years, *senor*."

"Then you know Jim Kelso and the ranch well. Can you tell me who is causing him trouble?"

Isidro shrugged. "This I do not know. Someone with a big hate for the *patron*."

"A hate for sure—but why?"

Again the Mexican's shoulders stirred. "Who is to say? All are friends of the *patron*, yet there is one who is not a true friend, but a *lobo* who strikes when the back is turned. Who this is I do not know."

"You see any strangers around lately—a *vaquero* maybe?"

Isidro Ortiz once more moved his shoulders in the time honored way of his people, a gesture that meant little, meant much—and nothing.

"No, *senor*, no one."

Shawn smiled, said "*adios*," and rode on. He was wasting time talking with Ortiz, doubted if he could supply any information of value, anyway. He was probably a good and loyal employee of Jim Kelso's but it would not go beyond that; he was one who would tend strictly to his own job, and close his eyes to all else.

Pete Helm was at the extreme southwest edge of the herd and came forward to meet him, gun raised. Tuttle had already given him word of Shawn's presence in the area, but he was one who took nothing for granted. When he recognized Starbuck, either by the horse he rode or from a description Rafe had given him, he holstered his weapon and sat back in silence.

Tuttle had advised him of the change in plan for the herd. If he approved or disapproved, he made no observation. He was content with giving monosyllabic answers to the few questions Starbuck put to him, and furnished no more helpful information than his two night shift companions.

Shawn turned then for the ranch and his quarters. He was discouraged in that he had failed to turn up one single thing of value that would enable him to get to the bottom of Kelso's troubles, but he felt the ride and time had not been entirely wasted.

He had looked over the herd, obtained a general view of the ranch, if at night, and met the remainder of the Three Cross crew; and he had made what he believed was a much needed change in the handling of the cattle.

What he wanted now was to sit down, mull it all about

in his mind, and see if anything emerged that would fit into some niche, perhaps make a little sense, and lead to a pattern. Once he could tie onto something meaningful, however small, he believed he could get on the right track. It simply made no sense that someone was striving to kill Jim Kelso, and destroy his ranch without cause.

But first he needed rest—sleep. He'd been a long time in the saddle. . . . Bed was going to feel plenty good.

═ 10 ═

Worn as he was, Shawn was up early, fully rested and feeling at his best. His pure, animal vitality had, in a few short hours of sleep, washed away the weariness that had finally overcome him.

He should first of all speak with Jim Kelso, he decided, and explain the change he had ordered and outline his reasons. The rancher had assured him he would not interfere with his way of doing things, but he still felt Kelso was entitled to know. Now, as he stepped out into the gray light of pre-dawn, he looked toward the main house. Lamplight glowed in the kitchen window and he could see Myra Kelso moving about.

Lambert, with Pierce and Dodd, appeared at that moment, coming from their quarters at a shambling gait, yawning, stretching, hawking in the way of men on their feet but not fully awake, and angled toward the cook shack.

Shawn joined them, greeting each with a short nod, and took his place at the oblong table where Candy had set platters of fried eggs, bacon, browned potatoes, and hot biscuits, backed with a pot of strong, black coffee. The meal was consumed in silence, and only when it was over did Starbuck give them his orders for the day on the moving of the herd.

"Tuttle and the others will stay out for a bit, help you get the stock turned and drifting. Be obliged if you'll carry some grub to them when you go. I'll be along as soon as I have a talk with Kelso."

Lambert wiped at his mouth with the back of a hand, pushed back his chair. "Reckon we'd best get at it. Ain't going to be no Sunday sociable—not with no more help'n we got."

The two other punchers got to their feet. Carl Dodd dug into his pocket for his pipe and said: "Not wanting to complain, but there a chance you can scare up some extra hands? These here long hours are about to lay me by the heels."

"Same here," Pierce said.

"Aim to try," Shawn answered. "Thing is I've got to

58

guarantee a man he'll live long enough to draw wages. Way it stacks up now I couldn't do that."

"I've got the feeling it's going to get worse," Lambert added morosely. "Them two trying to bushwhack Jim don't auger good. Been a lot of cussedness going on before but nothing like that."

"I got the same feeling," Pierce said. "Like maybe hell was about to cave in."

Starbuck watched the men stamp through the doorway, out into the yard, and veer toward the corral where Fermin had their horses waiting. In the attempt on Kelso's life they, too, were seeing the possibility of a showdown, and the resulting disclosure of whoever was behind it.

He would almost welcome it. As it stood now he was fighting a ghost, someone he could neither see nor anticipate. If he could get Kelso's enemy out into the open, force him to tip his hand, matters would then be a lot easier since he would know who and what he was up against.

Nodding his appreciation for the good meal to Candy, who was busy at the moment assembling lunches for the crew, he rose, left the kitchen, and bent his steps for the main house. The side door was closed, and halting there, he knocked. It was opened immediately by Julie who greeted him with cool questioning in her eyes.

"Your pa—I'd like to see him."

Her brows arched. "Quitting—that it?"

Starbuck gave her a tight smile. "Not yet."

She unhooked the screen, pushed it open, and fell back a step to admit him into the large combination kitchen and dining room. Kelso and his wife were sitting at a table in the corner. A third chair, partly pushed away, indicated the girl had been seated with them. Myra Kelso smiled over her shoulder to him and the rancher beckoned.

"Come in—come in. Just in time for coffee."

Kelso seemed well recovered from his wound, and betrayed no ill effects other than a carefullness in the way he moved his arm.

"Obliged, but I've got to get out on the range," Shawn said, and then told the rancher of the change he had ordered.

"Sounds smart to me," Kelso said when he had finished. "Figure you can handle all that stock with the men we've got?"

"Have to. Be hard work, but I think we can do it if nothing happens."

Julie, hands resting on the back of her chair, considered him quietly. "Just what could happen?"

Her hostility had not lessened, he noted. "Maybe nothing and most anything, ma'am."

The reply brought a tinge of bright color to her cheeks. "Don't you—"

"Now, Julie," Kelso broke in, "mind your tongue." He swung his attention back to Starbuck. "Could be I'll ride out a bit later, lend a hand."

"No, James," Myra Kelso said promptly and firmly, "you'll do no such thing. I'll not have you aggravating that wound."

"Well, there's nothing to keep me from helping," Julie declared.

Shawn stirred. Another rider would be most welcome, but he'd as soon it wouldn't be the girl. If trouble developed he did not want her on hand and in possible danger. He'd have more than enough to do without being forced to look after her.

"Not a very good idea," he said bluntly.

She folded her arms across her breasts, and gave him a steady, penetrating look. "Why not?"

"No reason I can say now, but—"

"Is it that you think I might see something that I shouldn't?"

"Now, Julie," Kelso began again in the same, placating way. "You know—"

"I mean it!" she broke in. "I don't think our new *caporal* wants me around because he's afraid I'll find out what he's up to!"

"Not that at all," Shawn said, hanging tight to his temper. "Just that if we do have trouble I won't have the time, or the men, to look out for you."

"I can take care of myself!" Julie shot back defiantly.

Jim Kelso pushed away from the table, chair scraping noisily against the floor, and got to his feet. "Starbuck's right. No place out there for you today. Something could bust loose, and I won't chance your getting yourself hurt."

"I'll be all right," Julie snapped, and spinning on a heel, marched from the room.

The rancher watched for a moment, then shrugged. "Bullheaded as she can be, that girl. . . . You go on, I'll try to keep her out of your way."

"For her good," Starbuck said. "That bushwhacker probably won't care which member of your family he draws a bead on next time."

"Know that, and like I say, I'll do my best to keep her

60

close, but if she shows up—well, look out for her. To hell with the cattle and everything else if it comes down to a choice. She's what counts with me."

Myra Kelso, suddenly worried, rose and went into the hallway down which the girl had disappeared. What Julie needed, Shawn thought grimly, was to be turned over somebody's knee and given what for; that would have been his parents' solution to what the rancher termed bullheadedness, and if she continued to act as she did toward him, by God, he just might undertake the chore himself!

To Kelso he said: "Don't want to have that come up, but that's the way it'll be, of course, if it does."

"Figured you'd understand. You think I ought to run into town again—if I use the buggy it'll probably satisfy my wife—see if I can hire on some hands?"

"Probably have no better luck than before. Nobody's going to sign on until they're plenty sure it's safe to work on Three Cross. . . . Doubt if it'd be smart anyway, your being out on the road."

Kelso shifted helplessly. "Dammit, feel like I'm caught in a box—"

"We get the herd moved to where it won't be so hard to look after, I aim to start digging into what's going on around here, see if I can put an end to it. Meantime, thing for you—your whole family—is to stick close to the house, not give anybody a chance to finish what those two started yesterday."

"Seems so—"

Shawn turned for the door, hesitated. "Whole crew'll be working for a while, so don't get to wondering why the night men haven't come in. By the way," he added as the thought came to him, "what about that outlaw? Anybody know him?"

"Nope," Kelso said, shaking his head. "Stranger to everybody. Deputy couldn't find a single solitary man who'd ever laid eyes on him before."

"Hard to believe. . . . Somebody had to hire him."

"What I thought—but that's the way things've been all along! Never able to tie down nothing!"

"Maybe it won't be that way much longer," Starbuck said, and went back into the yard. Crossing to his quarters, he dug into his saddlebags for the extra cartridges he carried. Taking a handful for his six-gun, he wrapped them in a handkerchief, thrust them into a pocket, and turned to go for his horse. He hauled up short.

A man—a *vaquero* by his gear, was standing in the

doorway. He was not old, probably in his thirties, was clean-shaven and wore cross-belted pistols. There was no way of knowing for sure but he looked to be the rider silhouetted on the *malpais* hill that evening before.

"*Senor caporal?*"

The Mexican's voice was soft edged, pleasant, yet there was a firmness to it.

"That's me."

"I am Pablo Mendoza. I have been told you are in need of riders. Such is true?"

Shawn considered the man narrowly. "The word's pretty well spread but there's no takers. You know the reason why?"

"There is trouble. This I was told."

"By who?"

Mendoza shrugged. "*Senor*, there are few who do not know."

Starbuck moved on into the yard. He could use a good hand, but he had doubts concerning the man. ... And if he were the one on the hill? ... He put the question to the *vaquero* bluntly.

"I see you up on the *malpais* last night?"

Mendoza's eyes flared slightly, and then a half smile cracked his lips. "Yes, I look at this place. A very beautiful *rancho*, owned by a fine gentleman, it is said. . . . I think it would be good to work here."

"Kelso's needed hands for some time, and you've been seen hanging around. If you wanted work, why didn't you come ask about a job sooner?"

Mendoza shifted, and the sun, breaking over the hills to the east at last, caught the silver trim on his broad hat and made it glitter softly.

"A man must think well on such matters. It is not good to hurry."

"You ever work cattle in this valley?"

"In Mexico."

"How about friends—cattlemen—people who know you and will stand for you?"

"I have none here. I can give only my word, which is sacred."

Starbuck considered. He should probably leave the decision of hiring the *vaquero* up to Jim Kelso. But, when he gave it further thought, he realized that it was a part of his responsibilities, and what he was being paid for. He was supposed to use his own best judgment.

It could be a mistake. Mendoza was a stranger to everyone. He admitted being the one seen hanging about the place, had been in the valley for some time and never before sought work. Now he was asking to hire on at Three Cross. His explanation of the sudden change in attitude made little sense—at least to Shawn; but he had come up against the Mexican people enough to know their reasoning was not always logical to the mind of a Yankee.

And if Mendoza was a plant of Kelso's enemy, one sent there to become a part of the ranch someone hoped to destroy, would it not be better to have him close by, where he could be watched, rather than hiding in the shadows? The words of an old cowpuncher with whom he'd once worked came to Starbuck in that moment; "*long as I know where a rattlesnake is laying, I ain't ascared of it. It's the not knowing that rags my nerves.*"

"You a good hand with cattle?"

Mendoza inclined his head slightly, once more setting up a shimmer of silver. His smile revealed even, white teeth.

"I am a *vaquero*," he murmured.

Shawn nodded. It was as good an answer and recommendation as he could get. "All right, you're hired. I'll get my horse and take you out to the herd."

"*Muchas gracias,*" the Mexican said, turning toward his own mount. "I shall prove to you my worth."

= 11 =

Again on his own horse, the big, blaze-faced chestnut with white-stockinged legs, Shawn rode from the yard with Pablo Mendoza at his side.

"Moving the stock, or starting to," he said as their horses climbed out of the swale and broke onto the grass flatland lying to the south. "Want to push them up nearer to the ranch—along those hills in the west."

"The trouble the *hacendado* has—it grows worse?"

"Worse," Starbuck admitted. "Somebody tried to ambush him. He was shot in the arm."

A stillness came over Mendoza. After a few moments he said, "It is a sad thing that is happening to a fine gentleman. These assassins, did they escape?"

"One did. The other is dead."

"He is known?"

Starbuck shook his head. "Kelso had him taken into town. Nobody there ever saw him before."

Again the *vaquero* was silent. Finally, "It is the way of such men, strangers hired with money to do a job of killing—one who is sometimes known by my people as a *foraneo*—an outsider. . . . It is best that way for the one who wishes the death of another."

Shawn agreed. "You talk to somebody about Jim Kelso? Think you mentioned somebody telling you he was a fine man."

Mendoza said, "To the *muchacho* who works with the horses. He speaks highly of him, almost as if he was the father. Also it was he who told me where you might be found."

Starbuck looked away. He was getting no help from the *vaquero*. He had hoped the man had overheard someone speaking about Kelso, but that had not been the case. He glanced beyond the chestnut's head into the southeast. A dust cloud was lifting, beginning to hang over that section of the range. The crew had the cattle on the move.

An hour later he and Mendoza ·topped out a rock-studded hogback and looked down upon the herd. The brown haze stirred up by the churning hooves was so dense that he could see only the puncher riding point, and the line of lead steers strung out across the front.

He had intended for the men to bear more directly toward the hills, get away from the bluffs that overlooked the river as quickly as possible—just in the event something went wrong. But he had not remembered to tell them, he guessed. It could be remedied quickly. He glanced to Mendoza.

"Ride down to the left, get between the cattle and the river. Want them turned more to the west. I'll carry word to the others."

The *vaquero* touched his hat brim, wheeled away, handling the close-coupled black horse he rode with ease and grace.

Starbuck struck off in a direct course for the rider at the head of the herd. As he drew near he saw it was Pete Helms. The weight of long hours on the job showed in the man's haggard features and in the heaviness of his eyes. He looked up at Shawn's approach, listened to his words, merely shrugging when told of the hiring of Mendoza. Then, swinging off, Helms spurred in alongside the old brindle steer that had taken over leadership of the cattle, and began hazing him in the direction of the low-lying peaks.

Shawn pulled away, curving around the mass of slowly moving animals. He found Lambert at swing position, and gave the word to him. Continuing on, he circled the entire herd until he met up again with Mendoza, trailing along at drag just outside the boiling dust.

"It goes well," the *vaquero* said, pulling his bandana down from his mouth and nose. "There is never trouble with the cattle when they have full bellies. They are like sheep."

"Hope they stay that way," Starbuck commented.

It would require most of the day to make the transfer, he had figured, after looking over the range that previous night, and at the herd's present pace it would appear that he had estimated correctly. Later on in the day they could expect the steers to move faster, even if the grade increased. They would be hot and thirsty and the smell of the upper sinks and water holes in their nostrils would act as a goad.

Suddenly there was a shifting in the herd. It was as if some powerful force had collided with the opposite left flank, causing the right to bulge. Shawn whipped away, cut toward the rear of the heaving mass. Gunshots sounded then, lifting above the dull thudding of hooves. In the next moment he saw a bright flash of fire through the yellow haze.

Fire—but how?

He didn't wait to ponder the question, just roweled the gelding hard, sending him plunging into the wall of spinning, swirling dust that blanketed the cattle. A rider loomed up, saw him, swerved in close. It was Carl Dodd.

"Stampede!" the old puncher shouted. "Whole tail end of the herd!"

Starbuck cursed. "Stampede!" he echoed. "How the hell could—"

"Somebody filled a wagon full of hay—set it afire and turned it loose at the cattle!"

That was the flash of flame he'd seen through the pall. "How bad?"

"Don't know for sure," Dodd answered, fighting his panic-stricken horse. "Got the wagon stopped—had to shoot the horses. . . . There's maybe four, five hundred steers legging it straight for the bluffs."

"Who's over there?"

"Ortiz and Pierce—and me. What I come for—help. Need it bad."

Shawn made no answer to that, simply rode in beside the older man, and with him wheeled toward the river and the rim of the buttes rising above its west bank. It would be up to the four of them to stem the onrushing tide of frantic steers; the others would be needed to keep the remainder of the herd under control.

Shortly, Starbuck caught sight of the running cattle. They weren't moving fast but at a more set, determined pace. Ahead of them he could see the two riders whipping back and forth, firing their pistols. The steers seemed neither to hear nor see them.

Shawn reached back for his blanket roll, swore as he remembered removing it along with his saddlebags at the ranch. He threw a glance to Dodd, began stripping off his shirt.

"They're crazy blind! Got to catch their eye somehow—flag them down!" he yelled. "Use anything you're packing. Only way we can turn them!"

Waving his shirt madly, Starbuck cut directly in front of the pounding cattle. Pierce, face caked with sweat and dust, gave Shawn an understanding look and twisted about. Digging into his leather pouches, he produced a dirt-streaked white towel. Swinging it over his head, he spurred toward the leaders of the stampede.

Dodd was also moving in for that point, an old shirt

wigwagging in his hand. Uncertainty began to show in the front-running steers. Several attempted to veer, were caught up by those pressing in close behind, carried on. But the break was there. Seeing it, Shawn wheeled the chestnut about to right angles, driving straight into the teeth of the cattle.

Again the leaders faltered, swerved, were crowded on by the mass behind. Several managed to turn, and the forward momentum of the mass slowed. Suddenly an entire segment began to curve away. Dodd was upon them at once, waving his flag, and firing his pistol.

Shawn hauled the blowing chestnut about, stiffening as alarm rocked through him. The lower part of the splinter herd—a hundred steers or so—were still racing in a direct line for the bluffs. Pierce and Ortiz were slicing back and forth, doing their utmost to turn the bunch into the others, force them to follow the main body. But it was a losing battle; the lip of the bluffs was too near.

"Get out of there!" he yelled, standing up in his stirrups. He knew he'd not be heard above the hundreds of pounding hooves, but the warning came out anyway.

Pierce and Isidro Ortiz recognized the danger. In another few moments they would be trapped, caught between the edge of the cliffs and the oncoming herd. Both spun, jammed spurs to their horses, and bent low over the saddle, rushing to get out of the cattle's path.

They made it with only a stride to spare—and then the bawling, struggling mass of hooves and horns was pouring over the bluff to the ground fifty feet below.

Grim, Starbuck rode slowly to where the two men sat in stunned silence staring at the empty flat. The sounds of the dying cattle seemed distant, almost muted. Pierce turned to him as he came up, and shook his head.

"Done all we could—reckon it weren't enough."

"No fault of yours," Shawn said, brushing at the sweat and dust clouding his eyes. "We got the biggest part of them turned in time."

"Was maybe a hundred head there—all prime beef. You be telling Jim about it?"

"I will," Starbuck said in a clipped voice. "You two go on, help with the others. I'm going to do some looking around."

"For what? There ain't nothing—"

"That wagon had to come across here somewhere. Couldn't have driven it in from the north—we'd have seen it. And they never brought it through the hills. Too damned rough. Leaves only the river—and there ought to be tracks."

Dodd pursed his lips, nodded. "About right. Expect I'd best tag along, however. Isidro can give the boys a hand."

"No!" Starbuck's reply was unduly sharp, but the loss of the steers and the possibility that at last he might be in a position to uncover the identity of whoever it was dealing all the trouble to Kelso, was pushing at him hard. "Better if I go alone. If things get tight I can move about easier."

"Just what they'll do! We ain't dealing with no greenhorns—made up my mind to that when Jim got hisself shot up. Man doing what you aim to do sure ought to be sided."

"Maybe, but I'll make out. Be more of a favor if you see to it the herd gets to that valley close to the hills."

Dodd shrugged, spat. "Whatever you want."

"That's it," Shawn said, and pulled away.

The bawling at the foot of the bluff had all but ceased, and he guessed most of the animals were dead. He swore deeply, angrily, thinking of the waste. . . . A hundred good steers—food now for the buzzards and the coyotes.

Riding on he came to what he sought, a break in the bluff. At once he saw the neat, flat grooves of a wagon's iron-tired wheels, together with a welter of hoof prints. All led up from the river.

Descending the wash, he reached the flat lying between the ragged-faced formation and the stream easily following the wheel's imprints to where the vehicle had emerged from the silted water. Dismounting, he squatted, studied the marks of the horses carefully, striving to determine the number of riders there had been in the party. It was impossible to tell. Prints were everywhere—and there were none with distinguishing characteristics that would aid in locating the owner.

But one thing was certain—wagon, riders and all, had come from Las Cruces. The wheel grooves made that a foregone conclusion. Accordingly, it was simple logic to assume the men who had been involved had by then or were at that moment returning to the same point. . . . But he should be sure of the latter.

The hoof prints where the wagon entered the river all pointed in the direction the vehicle had taken. The riders had apparently forded the broad stream at a different place on their return. Mounting, he continued along the soft bank, eyes searching the moist soil. Within a short distance he pulled the gelding to a halt.

The tracks of three horses, walking abreast, came out

of the shallow water, crossed the narrow beach, and disappeared into the brush. Starbuck swung onto them, following them with no difficulty to where they reached, and turned into the road. A hard grin pulled at his lips. The riders were heading for Las Cruces, as he had anticipated. Roweling the chestnut, he set out in pursuit at a fast gallop.

12

He slowed the gelding to a walk at the south end of the settlement, and came to a full stop when he turned into the main street. There were no horses moving along the curving roadway that separated the double row of business houses, and he had not overtaken any riders on the way in. Evidently they were much farther ahead of him than he had thought.

Regardless, they were somewhere in the town, and there was nothing to do but search about until he found them. It shouldn't be too difficult; simply locate three horses that showed signs of having recently forded the Rio Grande—caked mud on their legs, still wet cinches, stirrup leather dark from water.

Easing forward on the saddle, he hitched his pistol to where it rode a bit higher and was more accessible, then clucked the chestnut into motion. Keeping to the right-hand side of the street, he moved on, eyes cutting back and forth, probing the animals pulled up to the various racks.

There were several saddled mounts, along with two or three wagons and buckboards, in the yard behind Hunick's store. He veered into that enclosure, made his careful inspection of the horses, and returned to the street. None of them appeared to have been in the river.

His roving glance came to a stop on the mounts in front of the Spanish Dagger. One had a definite caking of mud along its fetlocks. Shawn looked closer. The belly of the bay alongside it had a coating of tan, as if the hair had been wet and then sprinkled with dust. He could get no good look at the remaining animals.

Swinging past the saloon and the adjoining Amador Hotel, he rode in behind the structures. Tension was beginning to build within him, and he found himself touching the nearby area with a sharp glance, searching for men who might be the riders of the horses.

He still wasn't completely sure; he'd have a closer look at the animals standing at the rack, and if he discovered one more showing signs of having been in the river, he felt he could then be fairly certain he had found the men responsible for the stampede, and, logically, for the attempt on Jim Kelso's life and all the other woes that had befallen Three Cross.

The hostler appeared in the doorway of the Amador's stable, an expectant expression on his swarthy features. Shawn waved him off, guiding the gelding into the rack provided by the hotel for riders just dropping by for a brief visit with its tenants.

Dismounting, he made fast the chestnut's reins. Nerves taut, he moved to the corner of the building where he could get a better look at the horses in the street. There was a third one, standing slack-hipped among the others, that definitely had been in the river.

Starbuck needed no more. Anger now lengthening into a cool, steady pulse within him, he drew back, prepared to circle around and enter the saloon by its rear door. He hesitated, an ingrained respect for the law, and all it stood for, surfacing within his mind.

He should bring Dave Englund into the matter. After all, the deputy ought to handle it—an opportunity he likely would welcome, since the law had maintained it needed only something of a definite nature to bring it into the situation. But the need to locate Englund quickly was urgent; the three riders could slip away, and with them would go the one opportunity he had for clearing up Kelso's troubles.

Brushing at the sweat collected on his face, he pivoted, walked back in behind the Amador once more, and moved by the chestnut into an inset of other structures littered with discarded packing boxes, whiskey kegs, and wind-blown trash, pointing for an adjoining passageway that led to the street.

He slowed as the rear entrance to one of the smaller saloons standing farther down swung open, and two men swaggered into the enclosed area—two men both vaguely familiar at first glance, and then as they drew nearer, fully recognizable. Dallman and the Kid. Shawn swore softly. He had given the pair no more thought after getting what he believed was a glimpse of them in the street that day before; it would seem, however, they had devoted considerable attention to him.

The older man brushed his hat to the back of his head, hooked his thumbs in his gun belt and grinned broadly.

"Seen you prancing around here. . . . Proved what I told the Kid yesterday—that we'd be meeting up again. . . . Told you that, didn't I, Kid?"

The blond, taking no chances, had already drawn his

71

pistol and leveled it at Starbuck. He nodded, an eager glint in his eyes.

Shawn glanced around. He had no time to waste on this pair. It was imperative that he find Englund, take him to the Spanish Dagger, and make his accusations against the men he'd trailed into town before it was too late.

"Move on," he said impatiently. "I'm in a hurry. Forget this until the next time we meet."

Dallman laughed, winking broadly at the Kid. "You hear that? He's in a powerful big hurry right now. Was in a rush yesterday, too, when he stuck his nose in my business, and got poor old Charlie and Waldo killed."

The Amador's hostler appeared again, coming out onto the hardpan fronting the double door. He glanced curiously toward them. Shawn raised a hand to signal but the man turned away in the same instant, and ambled off in the direction of the hotel.

Grim, angered at the interference, Starbuck brought his attention back to the outlaws. "You want trouble with me—all right. But not now—later. Got a chore to do that can't wait."

"The hell it can't!" Dallman snarled, dropping his bantering manner. "Hold that iron on him, Kid, while I draw his fangs. Then we'll take us a little ride into the hills. Ain't nobody pulling what you did on me, mister, and getting away with it!"

There was no avoiding the encounter. He could only hope the three riders in the Spanish Dagger did not leave. Settling himself squarely, Shawn watched the outlaw move toward him. A few steps beyond, the Kid waited nervously, the tall hammer of the pistol in his hand pulled to full cock.

Dallman, a crooked grin on his face, halted in front of Starbuck. "I'll just take that there hogleg you're wearing," he said, and reaching for the weapon hanging at Shawn's hip, plucked it from its holster.

Starbuck's hand was like a striking rattlesnake. It flashed out, caught Dallman's wrist, and clamped down with the force of an iron-jawed vise. In that same instant he threw his weight to one side, spinning the outlaw about.

"Goddammit—shoot!" the outlaw yelled, dropping the pistol.

The Kid rushed forward. Shawn, still holding to the older man's arm, released his grip, heaved Dallman straight into the oncoming blond. The pair coming together with solid impact, rebounded.

"Shoot!" Dallman shouted again, floundering on hands and knees.

The Kid recovered his balance, and triggered his weapon. The explosion set up a deafening echo in the pocket between the buildings, and the bullet made a hollow, slapping sound as it buried itself in the wall behind Starbuck.

Instantly he lunged forward, caught Dallman just as the man was regaining his feet, and sent him stumbling once more into the younger outlaw. As both went down, he wheeled, scooped up his own weapon, and then closed in on the pair scrambling to disentangle themselves.

Snatching Dallman's pistol from its leather, he threw it into the piles of trash. Wrenching the one held by the Kid from his fingers, he tossed it into a close-by rain barrel. And then, breathing hard, he looked down at the two outlaws.

"I'll say it again—I've got no time now for you. Later—if you think you've got a call coming—"

"Now!" Dallman yelled furiously. "We're settling it right now!"

Before Shawn could move, the man flung out his arms, caught him around the legs. Heaving to one side, he dragged Starbuck down. Striking out at the distorted face pressed close to him, Shawn tried to break the grip locked tight to him, tried to pull away. In the next moment he felt the Kid slam into him, and then all three were prone in the dust.

Lashing out with a knotted fist, Starbuck broke clear. He rolled to one side, jerked away as Dallman kicked out with a booted foot, winced as he felt a blow to the head. Twisting, he saw that the Kid, with that same wild, eager light in his eyes, had bounded upright, and was boring in, both fists flailing.

Throwing himself backward, he spun to his feet, came erect, and meeting the Kid with a stiff left arm, stalled him abruptly. In the next instant he became aware that Dallman was also up and surging in. Spinning, Starbuck unconsciously dropped into the cocked stance of a trained boxer—arms in front of him, elbows crooked, knotted fists poised.

He surprised Dallman with a hard left, crossed with a right to the ear that dropped the outlaw to his knees. The Kid, recovered, was rushing in from the side. Starbuck, neatly sidestepped the blond's awkward approach, caught him by the collar and belt, and taking a few accompanying steps to increase momentum, sent him reeling headfirst into the nearest wall.

Rock-hard knuckles smashed into Shawn as he whirled. He felt his knees buckle and his senses drift, but only briefly, and as he sank he allowed himself to fall away from Dallman, now standing over him and hammering blindly with both fists.

Suddenly he ducked forward, came up under the outlaw's arms, crowding him close. Dallman, hindered, sought to back off, to free his movements. Starbuck seized the slack in his shirtfront, rocked back and pivoted. As the outlaw, badly off balance, fought to retain his footing, Shawn drove a savage right into his jaw.

Dallman seemed to pause, a dark, wondering frown on his sweat-streaked features as he hung there. Starbuck, pressed by his urgency, lashing out with a vicious left, nailed the man with a hard right. Dallman wilted, took two or three backward steps and collapsed into the trash piles.

Shawn turned quickly, once more retrieved his dropped weapon, aware for the first time of the dozen or more men gathered about. Ignoring the hurried rash of congratulations and aside comments, he started for the Spanish Dagger. There was no time left now to find Dave Englund; he would have to act on his own.

"Hold on there, Starbuck—or whatever you call yourself!"

At the command Shawn stopped, turning slowly. It was the deputy. Englund had his pistol out and was moving up cautiously. Apparently he had been standing in the crowd watching the encounter.

"Was aiming to get you," Starbuck said, eyeing the lawman narrowly as he endeavored to assess his intentions. "Trailed three horses in from Kelso's. Men riding them are some of the bunch who've been—"

"Sure," Englund cut in drily. "Suppose you just raise your hands. No tricks now; I'd as soon shoot a killer as jug him."

Shawn stared. "Killer—me?"

"Nobody else but," the deputy said, glancing around at the crowd of surprised, silent men. He was enjoying his moment of eminence, there was no doubt of that. Stepping up to Starbuck he lifted the tall rider's pistol from its holster and thrust it under his own belt.

Anger brushed aside the astonishment in Shawn. "You're way out in the woods, Deputy. If you're aching to do some arresting, take in these two," he said, ducking his head at Dallman and the Kid. "They tried holding up the west-bound stage yesterday. The driver and guard'll tell you that when they come in again."

Englund nodded genially. "That so? Well, I'm obliged for the information. . . . Seems I'm going to have me a whole jail full of desperate outlaws waiting for the sheriff when he gets back. . . . Two road-agents and a killer, my—my!"

Starbuck swore angrily. "Climb down off that high horse, Deputy!" he snapped. "There's three men inside that saloon that've got to be arrested. They stampeded Kelso's herd this morning. Caused a hundred or so to go over the bluffs. You've been yapping about needing something to go on before you could give Kelso some help—I'm offering it to you now."

"Could be," Englund said with aggravating disinterest. "Point is, I've got you three—and like they say, a bird in the hand is worthy a plenty in the bushes." He looked around at the crowd again, making the most of his moment. "What I'm doing now is take you over to the lock-up, and put you in a cell where you can cool your heels until the sheriff gets back."

"You fool around acting biggety," Starbuck cut in, "and those three I told you about will get away. First chance we've had to nail whoever is giving Kelso trouble, and you sure as hell had better not muff it!"

"I get your under a lock, then maybe I'll look into it," the deputy said grudgingly.

"You're a fool—a damned fool!" Starbuck raged, anger boiling over. "Forget that pair of two-bit owlhoots, and the two of us can go in there, grab those—"

"One thing at a time—that's my motto," Englund prattled. He made a gesture with his pistol at Dallman and the Kid. "Come on you jaspers, I'm marching you and this here killer over to my jail."

The accusing word slashed through the yellow haze that was fogging Starbuck's mind. It was the second time the lawman had called him that.

"Killer—who am I supposed to have killed?"

"Who? You trying to say you don't know?"

"Be a favor if you were to tell me," Starbuck replied sarcastically.

Dave Englund cocked his head slyly. "Maybe it'd be better was I to call you by your real name."

"Starbuck's the only one I've got."

"The hell it is! Your right name happens to be Friend—

Damon Friend, and you're wanted for killing a man right here in town."

Shawn stared at the deputy. A rumble of conversation swept through the crowd.

"Either you're loco or—"

"Just telling you the facts," Englund said with a wave of his hand. "Sheriff's been looking for you ever since. Bud Kitch, the jailer, recognized you yesterday when you come in. Then I watched you fight these two—all that fancy dan way of using your fists and dancing around. One of them professional boxers, ain't you?"

"I've been taught—"

"Ties right in with what Kitch told me. Said you looked like the killer—and the killer was one of them boxers. All adds up—and there ain't no doubt in my mind. You're Damon Friend."

The crowd had grown considerably, and comments were becoming louder, assuming a threatening note. Several men now suddenly remembered Damon Friend and the exhibition he had staged, the fact that he had later killed someone. . . . Dave Englund was sure a good man, right on his toes. . . . Bud Kitch, too. . . . Morrison ought to be mighty proud of his deputies. . . .

Shawn, jaw clamped tight, studied the lawman while the irony of the moment spread through him. He was being mistaken for the very person he had come to inquire about—a skilled boxer he hoped might be Ben.

In that next instant, realization flooded through him. This man they were talking about—this Damon Friend—*was* Ben! That name, Damon, from the old legends of the Syracusans—Pythias and his friend Damon—it had been one of his brother's favorite stories when they were small boys at their mother's knee, listening to her read from the books she so treasured.

That remembered fact, plus the apparent resemblance, and the statement that the man sought was a trained fighter, could be added up to but one conclusion; he was at last definitely on Ben's trail!

13

Kitch, sweating freely, shouldered his way through the crowd. Brandishing a sawed-off shotgun, he stepped in beside Englund, bobbed his head approvingly.

"Got him, eh? Mighty fine. . . . Who's these others?"

"Tried holding up the Tucson stage, according to Friend. Aim to lock them up until George Eberhardt gets back to town, see if there's anything to it."

"And him?"

"Locking him up, too, of course. Claims he ain't the bird we're looking for—but they all say that. We'll keep him in the cooler for Morrison. I'll take a run down to El Paso this afternoon, soon's it cools a bit, and send him a telegram, tell him what we got."

The jailer nodded again, made a sweeping motion with the old double-barrel. "All right, you jaspers, start walking—"

Starbuck turned toward the passageway that led to the street, fell in behind the Kid and Dallman, who was cursing steadily in a low monotone. He glanced in the direction of the Spanish Dagger, to the men gathered there. He recognized the bartender, Gentry, and the gunman, Vern Ruch. The others he did not know and could only wonder which among them were the three he had trailed from Three Cross range.

Sudden frustration rushed through him. He whirled on Englund. "Dammit—those men will be getting away unless you move in—"

Kitch pulled up short, weapon leveled, stiffly alert. The deputy laid his hand on the barrel, pushed it down, and shook his head at the jailer.

"They'll keep," he said then to Shawn. "Keep moving. I got you, and that's what's counting with me. Like I said, a bird in—"

"Oh, go to hell," he muttered in total disgust, and continued on. A moment later he added: "That thick skull of yours is going to get you in a bale of trouble. Those three I keep harping about are the ones doing all the damage at Kelso's. Likely one of them is the other bush-whacker that tried to kill him!"

Englund's features betrayed some reaction to that. He frowned, looked over his shoulder at the horses tied to the saloon's hitchrack.

"Which horses you meaning?"

"The gray, the buckskin, and the sorrel with the hair bridle. Can see they forded the river."

The deputy shrugged indifferently. "They's a lot of riders ford the river around here, instead of using the bridge."

"Whoever's riding those three horses are the men I trailed from Kelso's, after they started a stampede."

"You see them—the men forking them?"

"No, were too far ahead of me. I'm going by the fact that the horses had just waded the river—were still wet when I caught up."

"Ain't much to go on," the deputy mumbled. "Maybe I'll see about it."

"You're a fool if you don't," Shawn replied and lapsed into silence. He could see little use in wrangling further with Englund.

They reached the jail. The deputy stepped out ahead, entered, and drew back the doors of two of the three cells. Kitch herded Dallman and his young partner into the first, Shawn into the second. Englund slammed the gratings closed, turned the locks. Tossing the keys onto the desk, he placed his attention on the jailer.

"I'm walking over to the Dagger, see if there's anything to what he's yapping about. Now, mind you—don't go getting yourself tricked while I'm gone."

Kitch's features darkened. He wagged his head. "Ain't nobody ever fooling me again."

"Just be damn sure of it. Stay plumb away from them, hear?"

"I hear," the older man mumbled, and watched the deputy pass through the doorway into the open.

Starbuck, anger undiminished, felt better. At least he'd accomplished that much—persuading Dave Englund to check on the riders. Next thing to do now was consider his own predicament. He must convince the deputy he was not the man the sheriff wanted, and get out of the cell. He was needed at Three Cross—needed bad, he was certain. The stampede had convinced him more than ever that matters for Jim Kelso were drawing to a head.

Mopping at the sweat gathered on his face, he stepped close to the bars, and waited for Englund's return. It would be most difficult to prove his innocence he realized; the entire matter of his being cleared would rest with Sheriff Morrison, and he was absent—days away.

Even if it were possible to find a local resident who had seen Damon Friend, and would declare Englund and Kitch wrong, the deputy would undoubtedly refuse to accept the person's word, and not release him until the sheriff himself approved.

There was only one solution—jailbreak. Englund was planning to make the ride to El Paso and send word to Morrison of the arrest he'd made. That would require the afternoon, possibly most of the evening. Kitch would be in sole charge. He'd watch the old man, see if he could spot a weakness, a carelessness that would lead to an idea.

"Ain't forgetting this, cowboy—"

At Dallman's low voice, Shawn turned to face the man. The heat in the small building was murderous, and he brushed again at the sweat beads on his forehead and the moisture filming his eyes.

"Got you to thank for being in this goddam, two-bit jailhouse. Sticking your nose in my business yesterday, then shooting off your mouth out there today. . . . I'm owing you plenty."

"Any time you're ready to pay off, I'll oblige," Starbuck said coolly. "Doubt if you'll be getting much chance, however—not where you'll be going."

"Hell, way it looks you'll be right alongside me and the Kid—"

"Don't bet on it. Deputy's made himself a big mistake."

Dallman grinned, winked at his partner. "Tried that myself a couple of times. Never did work."

"Will for me," Starbuck said. "Happens to be the truth."

"Well, won't make no difference. No matter whichaway it goes, I'll be laying for you, Starbuck or Friend or whatever your name is—and you can figure on it."

Shawn was barely listening to the threat. He was watching Bud Kitch, remembering the words of caution Englund had spoken to him. The jailer was slouched in the chair behind the desk, his tired, moody eyes on the dusty street. It was near mid-day and the sun was relentless. Indifferently, he brushed at a fly buzzing about his sweat-glistening face.

"You figuring how to bust out of here?"

It was Dallman again. Starbuck only stirred.

A coyness came into the outlaw's tone. "You do, count

me and the Kid in, and I'll forget what I was saying about evening up with you—"

Boot heels rapped against the landing outside the door. As Shawn once more sleeved away sweat he watched Dave Englund enter, hauling up in the center of the sweltering room.

"What about it?" he demanded impatiently.

"Like I thought—was nothing to it."

"What the hell's that mean?" Starbuck shouted angrily. "I trailed those three—"

"Wasn't them," the deputy interrupted calmly. "If it ain't a crock of bullchips to start with, it was somebody else you tracked. These fellows rode in from up Socorro way. Names of Jennings, Palmer, and Duncan. . . . Know any of them?"

"Never heard of them. What'd they say about fording the river?"

"Didn't deny it. Seems they crossed north of town."

"You believe that?"

"Sure. Was some others seen them doing it."

Shawn settled back dissatisfied. It was hard to believe he had made a mistake—even in the face of witnesses.

"Who saw them? It somebody whose word's good?"

"About as good a witness as a man could ask for; Omar Gentry. He seen them. Didn't know them, he said, but he recollected the horses."

Starbuck turned away wearily. He'd been wrong, he guessed. Three men had ridden off Kelso's range after starting the stampede. They'd crossed the river and started for town—but there everything certain ended. Evidently the outlaws had swung off the road somewhere between the point where they had reentered it and the settlement. He had missed that, had continued on, and spotting the mud and water-spattered horses in front of the Spanish Dagger, had jumped to a conclusion.

"Reckon I slipped up somewhere, Deputy," he said. "Followed three men, just like I said. Seems I lost them somewheres on the south road. Might pay you to do some looking down there."

"Be no use. Lot of brush—even an Indian couldn't find nothing in."

Shawn gave it up. "You heard anything from the Kelso place?"

Englund ran his finger along the inside of his collar, easing the sweat band. "Not since Felipe hauled in that dead man last night."

"Was plenty of trouble out there this morning. You

want proof of it, ride down to the bluffs, take a look at the steers piled up at the bottom. Looks like that ought to be enough to bring the law in—or is somebody going to have to kill Jim Kelso first?"

"One of them things," Englund said, refusing to rise to the mockery in Starbuck's voice. "Can't stand around out there and wait for something to happen. Got others folks to look after. . . . I'm ready to step in alone, or with a posse, anytime Kelso's got somebody for me to go after. . . . All we ever hear is a long tale about something after it's done with."

"Sounds like the law around here wants folks to do its job for them, then holler. Put a special deputy on the place, let him hang around."

"Takes money for that—and anyway, that's something Kelso ought to do—hire himself a gun . . . Dammit, Kitch," Englund broke off irritably, mopping at his face, "why don't you prop open that there window? Like an oven in here."

Wheeling, he stamped toward the door, then halted. "I'm going to get a bite to eat. Soon's I'm done I'm lighting out for El Paso. Won't be no hotter riding than standing around here. . . . Think you can look after things while I'm gone?"

"Sure—"

Dallman suddenly rattled the door to his cell. "How about some vittles for us, Deputy? Or maybe this one-horse burg don't feed the prisoners."

Englund favored the outlaw with a contemptuous look, then resumed with the jailer. "I'll have Segura send some grub over for you—and them. That all right?"

"Reckon so. . . . Old woman was expecting me home, but I guess it don't make no difference."

"On my way out I'll drop by and tell her. I ought to be back about dark."

"Take your time," the jailer replied, disinterestedly.

"Just what I aim to do—hot as it is. . . . Now, you watch yourself!"

"Sure, sure," Kitch muttered, and as Dave Englund stepped out into the streaming sunlight, added, "Goddammit, a man stubs his toe once and nobody don't ever let him forget it. . . . Hell of a note."

The afternoon hours passed with frustrating slowness. The heat, trapped inside the jail, was suffocating, and when sundown finally came and the sun's driving lances no longer battered the walls and roof of the squat building, relief was immediately noticeable.

Starbuck, a caged, impatient animal, failing to devise any means for escape, stirred restlessly about in his cell. He felt utterly defeated, yet beneath it all a curious elation flowed; he was finally on Ben's trail. Previously there had been only rumors to go on—vague hints, tips, hearsay, but this was solid—definite. . . . And he had a name.

All he need do was wait until Sheriff Morrison returned, which he likely would now do within the week, let the lawman see that his deputies had made a mistake and locked up the wrong man—and then free, his cash-money reserve built up somewhat, resume the search.

Only he couldn't just sit back and let it work that way. He couldn't afford to wait. He had responsibilities to Jim Kelso, a fine, if somewhat ineffectual gentleman, who was in over his depth, fighting a losing battle against a ruthless, unknown enemy. He had made his commitments to the rancher and he would not welch on them.

Somehow he must break out, return to Three Cross as fast as possible. This could be the very night the final blow would be struck; with Kelso more shorthanded than ever, as well as personally wounded, it offered someone an ideal opportunity.

Dropping onto the hard slat cot, Shawn stared moodily at the door of his cell. The rectangle of bars fit snugly in its frame and there was little chance it could be pried open at the lock—even if he had something with which to pry. His eyes settled on the lock. Hope stirred within him.

Rising, he moved to the front of the cell. In the next cubicle the Kid and Dallman, their faces shining with sweat, snored deeply. In the chair at the desk Bud Kitch also dozed. Shawn glanced toward the street; he must do something soon; Englund would be returning and his presence would make an escape much more difficult.

Bending down, he reached into his left boot, procured the slim-bladed knife carried there in a leather sheath. Opening it, he probed the lock with its point. Satisfaction rolled through him. There was a chance—a good chance, but he'd have to get Kitch out of the way. Concealing the knife, he leaned up against the grillwork.

"Jailer!" he shouted.

Kitch jumped a little, roused, and sat up. "What do you want?" he demanded peevishly.

"Time we ate—"

The jailer glanced to the street, now darkening as night

began to settle over the town. "Got to wait for the deputy."

"Wait—hell!" Starbuck yelled, making a noisy issue of it. "It's supper time. Was only about half enough on that plate at noon to keep a man going. I'm plenty hungry and I'm not about to wait. No reason why you can't get something for us now."

"There sure ain't," Dallman, awake, chimed in. "That deputy ain't apt to get back much before midnight."

Kitch struggled to his feet stiffly, mopped at his face. "Well, you got to eat, that's for certain. Don't see as it makes no difference whether it's now or later."

"It's being hungry now that counts."

The old jailer walked out from behind the desk, and crossing to the door, halted. Looking back over his shoulder, he said, "Don't go raising no ruckus while I'm gone, now—or you won't get nothing. Hear? You do and I'll throw it to the dogs."

Dallman laughed. "Why, grandpa, we'll be quieter'n a mouse. You'll see!"

Kitch spat, then stepped out into the street. Lamps were glowing in windows and a mellowness had spread over Las Cruces, bringing a peaceful sort of suspension, a time at which, it seemed, all things were pausing to rest.

"You wanting him gone so's you can bust out, that it?" Dallman asked as soon as Kitch was beyond hearing.

Starbuck made no reply. Opening the knife, he bent down once more, examined the lock more closely. It was one of the old drop-slide type, activated in the usual manner by key insertion. . . . If he could find enough slack in the framework to wedge his knife point under the tongue, he should be able to flip it back.

Glancing at the doorway to be certain no unexpected visitors or passersby were in evidence, or that the jailer was returning ahead of time, Shawn began to work the knife blade in under the oblong of iron. The lock was heavy, crudely cast, with more thought given to weight than to a fine job of finishing. He found considerable looseness, and managed to find purchase for the blade's point in the rough surface of the metal.

"Getting it?" Dallman asked anxiously.

Shawn paused, looked again to the doorway. All was clear. Careful, he pressed gently, levering the knife. The tongue flipped back into its slot with a dull thunk.

"You done it!" Dallman said in surprised tone.

Ignoring the man, Starbuck slipped the knife into its sheath, once more looked to the street. Kitch would be showing up shortly. There was no time to lose. Opening the cell door quickly, he ducked low to avoid being seen through the window, and hurried to the lawman's desk. Pulling out the top drawer where he had seen Englund drop his pistol, he recovered it and slipped it into his holster.

"The keys—the keys—" Dallman called hoarsely. "Goddammit, throw me the keys!"

"Make it fast," the Kid added, speaking for the first time. "The old man'll be coming."

Shawn, still paying no attention to the pair, crossed to the door, peered cautiously around the frame. Except for three men standing in front of Amberson's Gun Shop, the street was deserted.

"Ain't you turning us loose?" Dallman's tone carried a plaintive note.

Starbuck faced him. "No—you're outlaws, I'm not. You belong in there."

Dallman's features contorted with rage. A string of oaths burst from his lips. "Goddam you—you lousy bastard—I'll remember this! I'll—" Abruptly the harsh words broke off. A change crept into his tone. "Hell, no reason for you to do this to us. We can be friends. ... Tell you what, throw me them keys and I'll forget what I said about squaring up with you. That a deal?"

"You're talking to the wrong man. It's the law you've got to do your bargaining with," Shawn said and turned again to the door.

=== 14 ===

Once more checking the street and finding it empty, Starbuck stepped into the open, and with Dallman's curses following, swiftly circled the jail and gained the alley behind it, where he could not be noticed by Kitch or anyone else who happened to make an appearance.

The outlaw's voice was lost to him here, and walking fast, he went along the littered corridor to a point below the Spanish Dagger. He paused there, threw his attention to the hitchrack. The three horses were gone, he saw—not that it made any difference. Crossing over in the shadow of a large cottonwood, he reached the yard behind the Amador. The chestnut was waiting patiently at the rack where he had been tied, and mounting, Starbuck cut back and rode out of town—a hope burning within him that Dave Englund would not return for a few hours more, at least, and thus stay from underfoot.

He could not shake the hunch that the situation at Kelso's was building to a violent climax, and try as he would, he could think of no decisive way to meet it,—fight it off—and that for the solitary and simple reason that he could find no enemy to engage. It was a frustrating experience, like shadowboxing, where a man lashed out, but found only emptiness.

He came to the point along the bluffs where the steers had thundered over the edge. As he paused and looked down, lean shapes were moving among the carcasses, and faint snarls and growls came to him. The coyotes hadn't had it so good in many a day.

Pulling away, he struck off on a long tangent for the upper end of Three Cross range, where the herd should now be bedded down. He rode steadily but with a certain caution, eyes and ears alert, ready to halt, challenge, draw his weapon at the slightest provocation.

Nothing interrupted the crossing, however, and he came finally to the long, grass-covered ridge lying south of the valley into which the cattle had been driven. Drawing to a halt beside a scrub cedar, he looked down into the swale. Two fires were visible, one on the east slope, one below, and to his left—the south. He grunted his approval. Lambert and the crew were playing it as carefully as they could, setting up their watches on the two sides where trouble, if it came, would first present itself.

Cutting right, he followed along the ridge for a short distance, and then slanted down into a short saddle that connected with the ridge lying along the basin's east side. Gaining that border, he pressed on, the flickering flames of the fire only a short distance away. Relief was flowing through him now; evidently all was well with the herd.

He pulled up short, a faint sound catching his attention. Instinctively his hand swept down to the pistol on his hip—and then fell away as he heard Pablo Mendoza's voice.

"Senor caporal."

Silent, he watched the *vaquero* materialize from the darkness of a cluster of dense catclaw. "Hell of a good way to stop a bullet, *amigo*," he said, weariness and impatience edging his words.

Mendoza's teeth showed white in the murk. "There is no good way for that, my friend—only bad. You have luck in finding the *malhechors* who slaughter the cattle?"

Starbuck shook his head. "A long story. Men I figured were the ones I tracked from here, turned out to be somebody else—according to the deputy. Fellow they call Gentry saw them crossing the river north of town."

"Gentry." Mendoza mouthed the name thoughtfully. "He was the one to give proof?"

Shawn studied the *vaquero*. "He's the one. You know him?"

The Mexican shifted, laid his hand on the oversize horn of the intricately decorated saddle he sat. "I have heard of him. . . . These others—was mention made of their names?"

Starbuck continued to watch the *vaquero* closely. It seemed to him the man's questions carried something more than idle curiosity; they had, in fact, a meaning of importance to him.

"The deputy called one Jennings. And there was a Palmer. Third man's name was—uh—let's see—"

Shawn labored to recall, purposely creating an opening for Mendoza. The man failed to rise to the bait; either he did not know the outlaws, or was too wise to be taken in by the trick.

"Duncan," Starbuck finished. "That's it, Jennings, Palmer, and Duncan. Were supposed to have come down the valley from Socorro. Know them?"

"I do not, *senor*," the Mexican said quietly.

A moment later Shawn dropped his gaze and looked off across the valley. There was no prying anything out of Mendoza unless he wished to give it, that was certain.

"Have any more trouble with the cattle after I left?"

"There was none, and all is good now. We have been in this valley since dark."

"Rest of the crew on the job?"

"The old and the one that limps, they sleep. At midnight they will come that the others may also sleep."

"And you?"

"It is something I have small need for. I have learned to sleep while I am awake—if such is possible to understand. So I was when you came. I sleep but there is enough of me awake to know of your coming."

Starbuck nodded. He had acquired much the same facility himself. "Works for me, too," he said, lifting the chestnut's reins to move on.

"The young *muchacha* asked for you," Mendoza said. "Also the *patron* himself. They were disturbed that you are gone so long a time."

"Was in jail, most of it," Starbuck said.

The *vaquero* leaned forward, peered at him. "In the jail?"

Shawn smiled. "Another long story," he said. "See you in the morning," and rode on.

The ranch was in complete darkness when he entered the yard and halted at the entrance to the barn. Dismounting, he led the gelding through the open doorway, headed him into the first empty stall, and removed his gear. There were grain and fresh hay in the manger, and the big chestnut had previously watered, thus obviating that chore. Retracing his steps to the hardpack, Starbuck made his way to his quarters. . . . So far his hunch had been wrong; both the herd and the ranch itself were untouched and peaceful. He could only hope there would be no change.

He realized how utterly beat he was when he stepped into his cabin. It had been a long, hard day replete with tension, violence, worry, and sapping heat—all of which were dragging at him now, filling him with an exhaustion that overrode even a need for food.

Striking a match to the lamp on the table, he sat down on the edge of the bed, fought with his boots until they came off, and then lay back, stretching himself crossways upon the crackling mattress. He felt his gun digging into his side, realized he had forgotten to remove it. Sitting up slowly, he flicked back the buckle's tongue, stripped off the belt, and hung it on the bedpost.

He sat for a time thinking the smart thing to do was pull off his clothes, crawl into bed properly, instead of waiting, resting—but once more he gave way to the easier course. . . . He'd get to bed right in a minute—just as soon as he—

The door creaked. Unmoving, and instantly alert, he cracked his eyelids. A sigh escaped him. It was Julie Kelso. Patient, he drew himself to a sitting position. The girl, her face angry, was holding a rifle in her hands, had it leveled at his chest. The round O of the muzzle looked as large as a silver dollar.

"Put that damned thing down," he said wearily.

Her eyes flamed brighter, the curves of her lips compressed into a straight line. He considered her for a moment, stirred resignedly.

"What is it now?"

"You've got a lot of gall coming back here!" The words burst from her, lashing him like small pellets.

He moved gently, not at all at ease under the threat of her rifle. She had the hammer pulled back—and the trigger spring could be a worn and touchy one.

"Where'd you expect me to go? I work here."

"Not any longer—not if I have anything to say about it!"

"Which you haven't," Starbuck said bluntly. "It's your pa that I—"

"I know—he hired you and it'll have to be him who fires you—and that's just what he'll probably do. We know what happened. Aaron told us all about the fire and the stampede and the cattle that went over the cliff. . . . Then you disappeared. Going to hunt down the men who did it, you claimed. I want to know one thing—you find them?"

Julie's words were coming out in a rush, trumbling over each other in her haste to say them. She was under a terrible strain and deeply worried, Shawn realized, and a wave of sympathy swept through him.

"Sure didn't. Thought I had them but—"

"What I expected!" the girl cried triumphantly. "It was all just a reason to get off the place, report to whoever it is you're working for, get more instructions."

"Instructions?"

"Don't play stupid! Instructions on what you're supposed to do next. The stampede only partly worked. We lost only a hundred steers. . . . What's it to be now?"

Shawn got to his feet slowly, daring the rifle. Anger born of exhaustion, and the girl's unreasonableness, whipped through him, and he was too tired to care much about anything—particularly what she had to say.

"Now?" he snapped. "I'll tell you straight, I figure to nail up all the doors in the house, set it afire, and then—"

"You would, too!" Julie broke in, tears flooding into her eyes. "It's what I'd expect—"

Starbuck's hand streaked out, clamped about the rifle's action, blocking the hammer and preventing its accidental discharge. Julie relinquished her grasp on the weapon, stepped back, battling a fresh onslaught of tears.

Silent, Shawn released the rifle's hammer, propped it against the bed as he considered the girl. She was bearing far more of the load than she deserved. With an indecisive father, a mother who could not or would not recognize the problems and dangers that faced them, a crew of old men who could be depended upon for little more than tending cattle, and trouble striking from all points, there was small wonder she had no faith in him.

"Know it's been hard on you," he said. "Want you to know I'm doing all I can to straighten things out. You've got to believe that."

Julie didn't look up. "I wish I could—"

"You can. I hired out to your pa to do a job. That's the same as a promise, far as I'm concerned—one I'll keep no matter what comes along."

She shook her head. "Everything's going against us—everybody—even you. Actually it has grown worse since you came."

"Could be another reason that's got nothing to do with me. May be that whoever is back of it all is getting to crack down hard, make his final move."

Julie gave that sober thought. "It's possible, but why? What does he, whoever he is, want?"

"That's the question I keep asking myself. What it is Kelso's got that a man is willing to go the limit to get? There's an answer somewhere but I can't find it."

She had dried her eyes and recovered some of the hostility that had fled under the surge of tears.

"You have a strange way of hunting it—and trying to help. You even hired that *vaquero*. I don't trust him—nobody does."

"You know anything against him?"

She shook her head impatiently, dismissing in a woman-like way the necessity for such facts. "He's a *vaquero*, and that's enough. He's been hanging around doing nothing all this time, and then when he asks you for a job you put

89

him right on. Why would he suddenly want to go to work?"

"Could be he ran out of money. Happens to me every so often. That the only reason you don't trust him?"

"The fire and stampede happened right after he rode out on the range with you. It could be—"

"Mendoza was with me when it started. He couldn't have had anything to do with it."

"He could have arranged it beforehand—had those men start the fire—"

Starbuck shook his head in irritation. "He could have but I'm betting he didn't. There's something that's not exactly clear about him, I'll grant you that, but I don't think he's had a hand in the trouble you're having. And if I did, I would've hired him anyway. Easier to keep an eye on a man working for you than one hiding off in the brush."

"Still think you're wrong," she said truculently.

"All right, go ahead," he replied tiredly, and turned from her. "Now mind getting out of here and letting me get some sleep? Been up since four this morning and I—"

He heard the door slam and looked around, surprised. It was a strange, new experience, having Julie Kelso comply without an argument.

═ 15 ═

Jim Kelso stood at the kitchen window and stared out across the low hills toward the river. In the raw light of early morning the grass had a glazed, silvery look, and the trees assumed a ghostly quality. It was yet an hour or so until daylight, but he hadn't been able to sleep. The wound in his arm had throbbed insistently; however, the discomfort arising from it was much less than that provoked by his own conscience.

How could his world change so swiftly, so completely? Only a few months ago all had been serene. He was a successful rancher, the Three Cross brand was widely known, and held in high esteem by everyone in that part of the land; men, neighbors, his wife and daughter, the hired help—all looked upon him as a person of character and achievement.

But none of them had known the real Jim Kelso—a man who discovered one day that he lacked the courage to face adversity for the simple reason that he did not know how.

Life in the beginning had been pleasant and easy. His share of the family estate in Kentucky had provided money to marry on, move west, and buy up sufficient acreage to start a ranch. Land was cheap, and there'd been enough money to also procure a fair-sized herd of cattle as a nucleus, erect comfortable, weathertight buildings, and start off better than the average would-be cattle grower.

Raising beef had proved a success from the start. The market was good, the first two winters extremely mild, and he'd cashed in handsomely. Everything had gone just right, and it seemed he could do nothing wrong. He had the touch, Myra had declared proudly several times, and so it seemed.

But then came the day of change. He couldn't quite remember exactly when it was—about three months ago he thought. First there was that fire, one of the line shacks on the west range. He really hadn't worried about it. Accidents did happen; a cowhand, or possibly a drifter, careless with a match or a cigarette, or perhaps it had

91

been a party of Mexican *bandidos* crossing the border and venting their spite on a *gringo hacendado*. He'd brushed off the incident.

And then a few days later a water hole had been poisoned, several steers died. He had to face up to it then, admit it was no accident; the act was deliberate. He had known a flash of panic when he realized that, but he'd been careful to mask it from Myra and Julie, who always seemed to think that all he need do was snap his fingers and everything would be set aright.

He'd made a show of talking to the hired help, telling them to keep their eyes peeled, and he'd taken to wearing the pistol he'd bought years ago but hardly knew how to fire. The atmosphere around Three Cross sort of improved and he entertained the thought—a hope, really—that all trouble, as some ancient philosopher once noted, would pass.

It was not to be. A week later a half dozen cattle were driven into an arroyo near the bluffs, and slaughtered. Several of the ranch hands, hearing the shots, had ridden over to investigate. Before they reached the spot guns opened up on them. No one was hit, but the net result was that every man involved quit. They'd not hired out to have lead thrown at them, they declared.

Desperate, a large herd on his hands and only half enough riders to handle it, he'd gone then to sheriff Morrison, and laid the problem before him. It was the natural thing to do, place it in the hands of the law. ... Only Morrison didn't see it in exactly the same light; he couldn't figure out any way he could help, unless Kelso could pin down the source of the trouble—tell him who to go after, and why.

He just couldn't keep a deputy quartered at Three Cross, hanging around drawing wages while he waited for something to happen. The county just didn't furnish that kind of money. ... Find out who was at the bottom of it and he'd damned quick go after them.

Thus the law had proved of no assistance and the depredation and vandalism had continued. More of the help quit until now only the old hands remained—out of loyalty, he liked to think, but he knew it was likely because they had nowhere else to go.

Fortunately he managed to get a large part of the herd sold off, and that eased up on things considerably, and while that portion remaining was still more than the few old cowhands he had working could manage efficiently, they were, with his help, and that of Julie, getting by. One thing good about it, Julie had come to take a great deal more interest in the actual operation of the ranch than she had previous to the start of the trouble.

In a way that pleased him. It was a needed change, yet he secretly regretted it. It would have been a fine thing if she'd been able to retain her illusions as to his infallibility. But he supposed, like all pleasantries, everything must one day end. He only hoped that seeing him in his true light, ineffectual, unable to cope with the reversal of fortune that was plaguing him, she would not turn entirely away.

There was a good chance he could yet pull it all out of the fire. This man Starbuck, the new *caporal*, struck him as one not likely to be pushed around, and if anyone was going to be able to get to the bottom of Three Cross's trouble, he'd probably be the one—assuming he managed to stay alive long enough.

Whoever was gunning for him and the ranch wasn't letting it go at small fires and killing off a few steers anymore. The ambush and the stampede proved that, and he was glad that Starbuck had overruled his suggestion to drive into town, and had instead, insisted that he not again expose himself. . . . Somebody was out to kill him. . . . That was a hard fact now. . . . But who—and why?

Abruptly distraught, Kelso turned away from the window, crossed to the big cooking range that dominated the southeast corner of the room. Earlier he had stuffed a few short lengths of split piñon wood into the firebox, set them to blazing, and now the pot of coffee he'd made was simmering busily. Taking up the gray enameled pot, he poured himself a cup.

He could hear Myra moving about in the bedroom. Julie would be up soon, too. He didn't feel like facing either of them. Walking softly in the wool felt slippers Julie had presented him with last Christmas, he left the kitchen and entered the small room adjoining that he had converted into an office. Closing the door, he slid the bolt and sat down on the edge of the desk. Nursing his coffee, he once again turned his eyes to the yard.

The crew, if it could be called such, had already wolfed their morning meal, were riding out to relieve the men who had been with the cattle during the night. He watched as Candido appeared, apron swept aside and tucked into a hip pocket, dish pan of water in his gnarled hands, and dumped it against the cottonwood growing alongside the cook shack. . . . Candy was getting old, walked with legs crooked, back bowed. He'd not noticed it before.

He was getting up in years, too, he realized—and that

was something he hadn't really become aware of. It was a strange thing, but a man wasn't conscious of that fact until he saw it in his friends.

A gentle tapping sounded at the door, and then Myra's voice asked him what he'd like for breakfast. He passed it off, saying he was not hungry, that he would get something later. He was thankful she accepted that and retired without attempting any persuasion.

His thoughts shifted once more to Shawn Starbuck. He wondered what had happened to him. Lambert said he'd gone after the outlaws who had caused the stampede, was hoping to track them down. Shawn hadn't returned at sundown, and Julie, who for some reason did not trust him, had prophesied they'd never see him again, that he, like all the others, was gone for good. She firmly believed him to be part and parcel to all the trouble they were experiencing.

Julie could be right, he had to admit it—but he was hoping that she was not. Starbuck was the sort of man he liked having around—the kind he wished he himself might be: hard, strong, quick, and not afraid of the devil with both hands full of brimstone. . . . He'd walk over to Starbuck's quarters to see if he'd come in during the night. The prospect wasn't too promising; if he had caught up with the men he was trailing, word would have reached the ranch before then.

Kelso sighed wearily. He'd had high hopes after seeing Starbuck in action there in Coyote Canyon, but now it would appear, as Julie had insisted, all that had been for show, pure window dressing as a means of putting himself in solid at Three Cross. . . . It was hard to believe. He'd always considered himself a pretty good judge of men, but—

The rancher's thoughts came to a stop as his eyes caught sight of a buggy wheeling into the yard. He recognized the light rig immediately—one of the rentals that could be hired at Celso Mondragon's livery stable. The man driving—round, fleshy-face, trim dark suit under a tan duster, rolled brim hat—was familiar. The vehicle drew nearer, halted at the short rack outside the office door. The driver wound the reins about the whipstock, climbed down slowly, stiffly. Kelso remembered in that moment; Blaisdell, the El Paso banker.

Frowning, he stepped to the door, opened it. Blaisdell, smiling in a cordial, businesslike fashion, entered, extended his hand.

"Glad I caught you," he said. "Got in last night. Drove

94

out early this morning on purpose. Wanted to catch you before you rode out, have a little talk."

"Was about to leave," Kelso replied for something better to say. Blaisdell's visit was a surprise. He thought he'd seen the last of him. "What brought you all the way up here?"

"You," the banker said, settling into a chair, "and that client of mine. He plain won't give up. Still wants this place. Insisted I pay you a call, repeat his offer."

"I see," Kelso murmured, leaning against a corner of his desk. Here could be the out he'd secretly, in the bottom of his mind, hoped for—an easy solution—sell. Leave the country, let someone else take on the grief. Myra likely would oppose it—and Julie most certainly would, but they could be won over. All he need do was point out they were not the ones who had to face the bushwhackers.

"Well, could be I'm interested."

"Thought perhaps you might be. Heard at the hotel last night you were having a spot of trouble."

"Other ranchers have seen worse—and it'll pass. Hired myself a new *caporal* a couple of days ago. Plenty sure he'll straighten things out."

"Good. Then I can tell my client you'll consider his offer?"

"Consider, yes. No promise now, mind you, but I'll study on it. Have him put it in writing, send it to me by coach mail—no need you making a trip."

Blaisdell got to his feet. "He'll be pleased to hear you've changed your mind."

"Not definitely," the rancher said, deeming it wise to play it coy. "I'm saying I'll consider it—not exactly take it—not yet, anyway."

"I understand, and I'll make it clear. It's more than I came away with last time. Making some progress, it seems."

Kelso nodded. "Well, man gets older, starts to thinking about a rocking chair, taking it easy—"

"In only three months?"

"In three months," the cattleman said solemnly. "Things can change fast. Folks do, too. . . . You never mentioned that client's name before. Care to now?"

"One thing that hasn't changed—he still wants it kept quiet. Business reasons, he tells me. Seems he's interested in other properties and is afraid his name coming into the open might pose a problem or two."

"Could be," Kelso said, then, as a thought stirred

through the back of his mind, added, "He want my place pretty bad?"

Blaisdell cocked his head to one side, and smiled. "You expect me to answer that?"

Kelso caught himself just in time. He had wondered if the party concerned could desire the property bad enough to apply pressure in such a way as to influence the selling, but he realized in the same instant that he could not possibly voice such a thought.

"Reckon not," he replied with a forced laugh. "Would be worth my knowing though, wouldn't it?"

"To you—but it could cost my client a pretty penny. Sorry I can't give you his name."

"Don't matter. One man's money is as good as another's far as I'm concerned."

"Which is a sound rule of business," Blaisdell said, moving toward the door. "He'll be pleased to know you've changed your thinking about selling—"

"Not for sure," the cattleman cut in quickly. He'd have a job convincing Myra and Julie that it was the thing to do, and while outside events were dictating that he move as quickly as possible, he wouldn't be able to rush matters too much where his womenfolk were concerned. "Want you and him, whoever he is, to understand that. I'll consider his offer—and I'm leaning toward selling. That's as strong as I'll go right now."

"Exactly what I'll tell him," the banker said, climbing into the buggy. "Well, hope to see you again shortly," he said, unwinding the lines he settled back against the cushions. "Good day."

Jim Kelso lifted his hand, but his thoughts were already speeding ahead of the moment. He'd market the herd, turn the beef into cash money. That, with what he had in the bank was more than he and his family would ever need. Then he would accept whatever price for the ranch itself that Blaisdell's client wanted to offer—and be pleased to get it. . . . But first there was the matter of selling Myra and Julie on the idea—and even that required courage.

Julie Kelso had risen early, too. Disturbed by Shawn Starbuck, in a way she had never before known, she sat at the window of her room and looked into the yard, unseeing, unhearing, existing only in her thoughts.

In her mind she knew all the things she had accused him of were groundless, yet her strong pride would not let her admit it even to herself. The life of Three Cross literally rested on his shoulders, in his strong hands, and finally having accepted that truth, she wished now she might break down the barrier that lay between them—and tell him so.

It was folly to think her father would be able to bring an end to the creeping death that was slowly overcoming the ranch. He seemed helpless to fight, to do anything other than stand by and permit it to happen. Shawn was the only man capable of stepping in, setting everything straight, and she was in no way helping, but actually hindering him by accusations, by being disagreeable and opposing him—and by telling him to his face that he was unwanted.

What ailed her, anyway? What perversity of mind caused her to berate and disparage and insult the only man who had ever aroused her inner self—and who likely was the sole hope of the Kelso family and Three Cross?

She saw the door to Starbuck's cabin open, sat up straighter, watched him step out into the yard and swing across the hard pack in that confident, easy way of his. He'd not taken time to shave, and there was a rough, square look to his jaw, while his deep-set eyes—sort of slate gray, she recalled, now appeared dark.

Something within her seemed to convulse, and the inclination to hurry out—robe, nightgown, and slippers be damned—tell him she was sorry, that she regretted all she had said to him, possessed her. And then Rafe Tuttle and Carl Dodd, followed closely by Dan Pierce, came from the bunkhouse and joined him. The impulse faltered.

Later ... she'd make her apology later. She'd wait and watch for him, catch him when he rode in at the end of the day. Or maybe she'd just saddle up and run out to where the herd was being grazed. It wouldn't be hard to talk to him there.

═ 16 ═

No problems developed during the night insofar as the herd was concerned, Lambert told him, and a short time after Ortiz, Mendoza, and the old puncher, who had stood watch the final hours of the shift, had ridden in, Shawn mounted the chestnut and pointed for the valley where the stock was being held.

He couldn't expect to keep the cattle there for any extended length of time, he realized as the gelding loped leisurely across the grassy plains and saddles. The basin simply wasn't large enough and the steers would soon have it grazed over.

Perhaps the emergency would have passed before that time came. ... Emergency. ... He considered that word. What emergency? Certainly there were the baffling incidents that took place periodically, the most serious of those being the attempt on Jim Kelso's life, but actually, when you came right down to hobnails, he was taking precautions against a hunch.

He didn't really know something was about to occur. He had only a feeling, an intuition, one based on perceding events. It could be that matters would rock along now for another month or two before something would break. ... If he could believe that, depend on it, there'd be no use in keeping the cattle penned in the basin. Might as well let them drift as usual, scatter over the range.

But Shawn couldn't bring himself around to where he accepted that. A deep worry, small but persistent, continued to nag at his mind, filling him with a sort of apprehension, almost a fear, for what lay ahead for the Kelsos. He could not ignore it, no matter how hard he tried.

Long ago he'd learned the value of trusting his instinctive insight and the wisdom of heeding its warnings. With matters the way they stood at Three Cross, and that feeling nagging at him now, he suddenly decided he'd be a fool to ignore any premonition, however groundless it might seem.

He drew near the valley, and the bawling of the cattle came to him. But it was a sound of contentment rather than of restlessness and he was not concerned. Reaching the east rim, he rode slowly along the rounded ridge, waving his salutations to the men cruising aimlessly but with effective purpose around the herd.

Kelso had a fine ranch, there was no denying that fact. Plenty of acreage, year-round water, ample grass—all in a country known for its mild winters and not too extreme summers. It was a place some man might conceivably want badly, but there were many other ranches in the valley like it, equal to, possibly even better in some respects.

Why, then, had Kelso's ranch been singled out as a target for so much trouble and disorder? What was it about Three Cross that made it more desirable than all others—so desirable that murder was not to be bypassed? There had to be a reason.

He'd gone over the question countless times before, and now fell to pondering it again as he ranged back and forth across the hills and shallow valleys looking for something, for anything that would throw light on the puzzle and furnish him with an idea.

He had halted at the edge of a small grove around mid-afternoon, and was still threshing the problem about in his mind with no success, when Julie Kelso topped a knoll to the east of him, and came riding up.

Shawn observed her approach with a jaundiced eye, recalling their previous encounters and the bitterness of her words. He'd hoped that she would leave him alone, permit him to do his job as best he could, but he guessed it was not to be.

She was especially attractive today, he noted, watching her draw nearer, sitting the saddle of the gray she rode with a calm, easy assurance. And as before, when he looked steadily at her, the manliness of him stirred and some of the loneliness he had known in the long nights of the past, made itself felt.

But just as on similar occasions before, he thrust such human and personal needs aside; he could never expect to choose a wife, a partner for himself, settle down and have a home, a family as did other men, until he found Ben and squared the matter of their father's estate.

That moment could come that very day—or ten years in the future—there was no way of knowing. Someday, somewhere, he would meet with Ben, or find him dead, and then the quest would be over. But until that time he must deny himself the life other men took for granted.

"Good morning—"

Julie's voice was friendly, had a cheerful quality. Starbuck felt a trickle of relief; evidently she was not here to castigate him. Removing his hat, he stepped from the saddle and walked to the gray's flank, and helped her dismount.

She smiled her thanks to him and crossing to an outcrop of nearby rock, leaned up against it. "I came to apologize," she blurted hurriedly, seemingly anxious to get the words out and have done with it before courage disintegrated.

He studied her, understanding. "Not necessary," he replied in an offhand way. "We both want the same thing. Knew that from the start. Was just that we saw it different."

"I know," she murmured. "But I'm sorry about all the things I've said to you. . . . I've been afraid to trust anybody."

"Natural. Can't blame yourself for that. Three Cross is a fine ranch, and the way things are going—" He let his words trail off, seeing no point in reminding her of the danger her father, and probably she and her mother, were in.

She did not miss his meaning. "We could all be ambushed—killed. I know that."

Starbuck was silent and then shook his head in a show of helpless exasperation. "Trying to prevent anything like that. Spent the whole day so far covering the range, trying to see what's behind it all. Came up with nothing—but there has to be a reason somewhere, and I'm too blind to see it!"

"I know," she said wearily. "I've lain awake nights thinking, hoping to understand. . . . It's all so senseless—and hopeless."

"Not yet. We're still on our feet and we've managed to survive eveything that's been thrown at us so far. If I could just come up with one thought—"

Julie, hands clasped before her, stared out across the flat unrolling before them, a far, distant look in her eyes. A faint breeze had sprung into life, and the tips of the grass were shifting gently to and fro, turning the land into a purple-tinted ocean.

"It may not matter now, anyway."

Starbuck frowned in surprise. "What's that mean?"

"Maybe somebody else will have to worry about Three Cross."

"Your folks thinking of giving up?"

"Not exactly—selling out. Blaisdell, that El Paso banker, came to see my father again this morning. Man he represents is still interested in buying."

Shawn brushed at the sweat on his brow thoughtfully. "You said again—he the one who made your pa an offer a while back?"

"The same. Was about three months ago."

"Thought the name sounded familiar. He mention this time who he was making the offer for?"

"No. My father asked but Mr. Blaisdell said he had to keep it quiet. Something about some other property he's interested in, and this could maybe spoil it for him."

"And your pa's going to accept his offer?"

"He hasn't said so yet. He told Blaisdell he'd think about it. Last time he turned the idea down."

"You think he'll accept?"

"I—I guess so, the way things are going. We have plenty of money and my folks are getting along in years. Why should they put up with all this trouble, this risk of getting hurt—or worse?"

"Can see their point. How do you feel about it?"

"Not my place to have any feelings on this."

"Maybe not, but I'd like to know, anyway."

"I'd not sell—I'd fight. I love Three Cross and I can't imagine what it will be like not to live on it. I don't think any other place could ever be home—but it is my father's decision. He'll do what he believes is best and I'll abide by it."

She drew away from the rock. Starbuck dropped back, allowed her to pass before him and cross to where the gray waited.

"No matter how it works out," she said, halting beside the horse, "I want you to know that I think of you as, well—more than just somebody who came to work for us. I—I only realized that this morning." She paused, color rising in her cheeks. "I hope I'll continue to see you, that we—"

Starbuck stepped into the breach of her confusion, took her by the arm and assisted her onto the saddle. As she settled herself the small rowels of her spurs jingled lightly.

"I hope so, too," he said gravely, and then as if the thought was only then occurring to him, "Blaisdell's first offer, how long ago did you say it was?"

She stared at him with stricken eyes, cheeks mirroring the embarrassment that flooded through her. She had bared her heart to him and he had discreetly ignored it.

"Three months, more or less," she said tonelessly.

His features were void, deliberately betrayed nothing.

101

"Do you remember if the trouble started after that, or did it begin before the offer was made?"

She had regained her composure, and now her dark, full brows arched into a frown. After a moment she said: "I see what you're driving at—that maybe it's Blaisdell's client who is stirring up trouble for my father, trying to force him to sell."

"That's what I was wondering."

"It started before Blaisdell came to see father, I remember. . . . I'm sorry."

He only shrugged. "So am I. Could have been the answer we're looking for, or a step toward it, anyway."

Julie studied him for a long moment, her eyes wide, lips firmly pressed together, and then she said: "Does it really matter now?" and cutting the gray about, started down the slope.

Starbuck watched her ride off, pointing for the ranch while a heaviness filled him. He did not like the role he'd been forced to play, but it was best. He could not permit anything stronger than a casual friendship to rise between Julie and himself. . . . Only after he found Ben would his life be his own.

He started to move back to the chestnut, paused, realizing that the time factor in the offer made to Jim Kelso could mean nothing. Blaisdell's client could have created trouble beforehand in hopes of getting a quick and favorable decision from the rancher. And, that failing, he had simply continued his ruinous activities.

He remained motionless watching Julie fade into the distant trees, and then, wheeling to the gelding, stepped up into the saddle. The chestnut was anxious to be off and struck out at once with no urging, his long, white-clad legs flashing rhythmically as they covered the ride in a proud stride.

An hour or so later Shawn hauled him in once more. His gaze had caught sight of a rider far down the slope, working in and out of the trees and brush. It would not be one of the cowhands working Three Cross beef; the swale where Kelso's cattle grazed lay far to the north and west.

A drifter? Not likely—not in this particular part of the range. This was someone who knew the area, had ready access. He appeared to be searching for something.

Thoughtful, Starbuck watched the rider break from the last of the brush fringing a grove. Sunlight caught at the man, pinned him sharply with its brightness, stirred a sparkle of silver. Shawn stiffened. Mendoza was the only rider on Three Cross wearing such ornamentation. He

102

continued to study the *vaquero,* amending his previous impression; the Mexican seemed to be patrolling rather than searching.

He kept Mendoza in view for a time, and then cutting down into a shallow ravine that slid off to his right, began to follow. He could not see the *vaquero* too well as he rode in and out of the undergrowth and occasional patches of trees, and as the minutes passed, the wonder grew within him as to the man's purpose.

Certainly it was possible for a person to mount his horse and ride across the range for the sheer pleasure of doing so—but Mendoza had been with the night crew and it didn't seem reasonable he'd be spending the day in the saddle, also. Ordinarily most cowhands were glad to pile off their horses, and stay off during their leisure hours, having had all they wanted of a saddle while on the job.

His earlier suspicion of Mendoza surged to the fore. There was something about him that wouldn't stand the light—he was sure of it now. That conviction settled in Starbuck's mind, and being a man who disliked subterfuge in all its forms, plagued with the seemingly unsolvable problems that beset Jim Kelso, he came to a sudden, angry decision. There was some connection between Pablo Mendoza and what was happening to Three Cross, and the way to get at the bottom of it was to confront the *vaquero* bald-faced.

Starbuck's jaw clicked shut, and roweling the chestnut, he set the big gelding to a fast lope, aimed at intersecting the path the Mexican was following a mile or so below.

Mendoza heard him coming, drew in behind a clump of doveweed. Shawn caught the hard glitter of silver through the leaves, as he broke over the last ridge and drove down into the small valley.

Halting at the edge of the growth he said, "You figure to hide from a man, best you trim those silver gewgaws off your *sombrero.*"

The *vaquero* walked his horse into the open, his dark face expressionless. "I do not hide, *senor,* only wait."

Starbuck shrugged. "Call it whatever. . . . Thought you'd be grabbing some sleep."

The Mexican shifted on his saddle, stiffened his legs. The *tapaderos,* thickly scrolled and decorated with leather rosettes, were large as water buckets.

"I am one who needs but little sleep."

"So you told me—now tell me something else."

Mendoza's expression did not change. "What is that, *caporal?*"

"What's going on here at Three Cross? You've got something to do with it. I want the whole story—now!"

The *vaquero's* hands lifted and fell in a gesture of bewilderment. "I know nothing—"

"You have anything to do with that ambush? You in on killing Three Cross beef—burning line shacks—all that hell-raising that's going on?"

Mendoza's face was a sullen image carved in dark mahogany. "I am not a man of that kind," he said stiffly.

"But you know who it is!" Starbuck snarled. "Spit it out, *compadre*, or I—"

"The *muchacha*, she comes. She brings with her the deputy from Las Cruces—"

At Mendoza's interruption, Shawn twisted about. Julie, Dave Englund at her side, was approaching at a fast lope. It could mean only one thing; the deputy was there to arrest him, take him back to a cell. He swore deeply. He had no time for that now—had hoped to avoid the law until matters were cleared up for Kelso. After that he'd be willing to go in and square himself.

"All a mistake," he said to the *vaquero*. "Wants to lock me up, but I'm not about to let him. Important I stay on the job—"

Starbuck paused, the feeling coming over him that he was alone. He turned to the doveweed where Mendoza had been. The *vaquero* was no longer there.

17

Starbuck lifted his gaze, picked up the figure of the
Mexican disappearing into a deep ravine. He swore again.
That was proof enough, he guessed, that Mendoza was
involved.

Angered, he swung his attention back to Julie and the
lawman, now drawing close. If they hadn't showed up
when they did he might have gotten something out of the
vaquero! Stiff, he watched them pull up. There was a shine
of moisture on the girl's forehead and a strained, worried
look in her eyes.

Englund, hand resting on the butt of his pistol, met
Shawn's gaze coolly. "You coming peaceful, or do I have
to take you in?" he demanded with no preliminaries.

Starbuck glanced to the sky. The afternoon was late
and sundown not too far off. With darkness, the trouble
he had been expecting could strike. Mendoza's actions
now heightened that belief.

"Forget it, Deputy," he said quietly. "Do a little thinking about the Kelsos. If it pans out like I think, they'll
need the both of us here."

Dave Englund's mouth drew into a hard grin. "One
thing they sure don't need is a killer hanging around,
making things worse."

"Wrong man, Deputy," Shawn said patiently. "I'm not
who you think I am."

A sort of relief came into Julie Kelso's eyes. Her lips
parted into a smile. "I knew it! I knew you were wrong,
Dave! Shawn's no murderer."

Englund shrugged. "You expect him to admit it?"

Julie nodded. "Yes, I think he would, if it was true."

The deputy favored her with a direct look. "You'd
make a mighty poor judge, but I reckon that goes for any
woman. A bit of sweet-talk and they'll swallow anything."

"Wasn't that," she replied. "Just that I know."

"No matter," Englund snapped, swinging his attention
again to Shawn. "I'm locking you up, Friend—"

"Name's Starbuck—"

"May be what you're calling yourself now, but the real

handle's Damon Friend. Sheriff'll verify that when he gets here next week. . . . Let's go."

Starbuck, glancing at the girl, wished she wasn't there. Making a fight of it would endanger her and this he could not bring himself to do. Locked in a cell, however, he'd be powerless to help the Kelsos if a raid was launched that night.

"I'm sorry, Shawn," Julie murmured, as if reading his mind. "He insisted that I take him to you. My father thought it best, too. . . . He told us you were a murderer, that you broke jail."

"Was in his jail and I got away—that much of it is true. Rest isn't. I'm not the man he thinks I am—and that's what the sheriff'll tell him when he gets here; only I can't lay out a week in a cell."

"Which is what you're sure going to do," the deputy said. "You've got no choice."

"Even if I gave you my word not to leave the valley?"

Englund smiled. "Me take your word—word of a wanted killer? You think I'm loco?"

Starbuck shifted on the chestnut, hand inching toward his gun. "I think you're probably trying to do a job, only you've treed the wrong 'possum. I'm not Damon Friend."

"Just keep on saying it—only I know better. Jailer figures you're him, and he's seen you before. And then there's the way you do your fighting. . . . Everything tallies."

"Size—how about that?"

"Kitch says you look taller, and you ain't as heavy. Makes sense. Man losing weight would seem taller."

He had a name and now a fair description of Ben to go on—but that would be for the future. At the moment he must think of the Kelsos and Three Cross.

"Think the man you want may be my brother," Shawn said, concluding the best course to follow would be one of laying his cards on the table. It couldn't hurt, and very possibly it might set the deputy to thinking.

"I've been looking for him. Heard about a man the sheriff was hunting, came here to see if it might be him."

"But your name—you said it was Starbuck," Julie exclaimed, not fully understanding.

"It is. My brother's real name is Ben—Ben Starbuck. Description and everything you say about this Damon Friend seems to jibe, make me think they're one and the same. . . . Said when he ran off that he was going to change his name."

106

Uncertainty crossed Dave Englund's browned features and then he shook his head irritably. "Maybe so. Up to Morrison to say when he gets here."

Starbuck's level gaze locked with that of the lawman. "No, it's a decision you're making, Deputy. I can't afford to wait."

"Like I said, you ain't got no choice," Englund replied, shaking his head. "What's so all-fired important about a couple or three more days, anyhow?"

Temper flared suddenly through Shawn. "What the hell's the matter with you? Don't you ever listen? Jim Kelso's been shot, probably in danger of getting killed! Cattle are being slaughtered, fires are being set, and the way things are stacking up and—"

"Heard all that stuff, sure, but I can't—"

"And you're doing nothing about it! What's the matter with the law around here?"

"I'm following orders—Morrison's orders," Englund said doggedly. "When Kelso's got something for me to go on, I'll step in—"

"Which will be after it's too late," Julie said bitterly. "After one of us, or maybe all of us, have been killed, and the ranch is ruined. My father asked for help several times. He's never got any."

"Which is why I'm not spending one solitary hour in a cell, Deputy!" Starbuck snapped. "You won't do your job so I'm promoting myself from foreman to hired gun, and standing by these people."

"You get to slamming that iron around and—"

"I'll use it if I have to, and only because I have to," Shawn replied, glancing over the trees. The sun was down and the last light was spraying into the heavens from beyond the hills to the west, creating a vast fan of shifting color. He turned again to the lawman.

"Make you a deal. It's not safe to leave the Kelsos and Three Cross. Got a feeling that something's about to break loose—"

"Just a feeling," Englund cut in disgustedly.

"You bunk in with me for the night," Shawn continued, ignoring the deputy, "and if nothing's gone wrong by noon tomorrow, I'll admit my hunch was wrong and ride in with you."

"That's a good idea!" Julie said. "That way you'll both be on hand and—"

She paused, the distant popping of guns coming to them across the hushed, heated air. Starbuck spun, looked into

107

the direction of the ranch. A column of ugly, black smoke was spiraling into the yellowish sky.

"It's started," he said in a quick, grim voice, and digging spurs into the chestnut's flanks, sent him plunging down the grade.

18

As they drew nearer the ranch the shooting became more intense. The smoke had increased from a single streamer to three.

"Stay back!" Starbuck shouted to Julie when they broke from the trees to the south of the yard.

He drew his pistol, and threw a look at Dave Englund. The deputy had his weapon in hand, was crouched low over the saddle. Shawn glanced again to the girl as the horses pounded on. Lips compressed, eyes filled with anxiety, she gave no indication that she would obey his command.

Gunshots began to dwindle, the smoke to thicken, as they raced across the wide flat. Starbuck could see riders curving in and out of the murk that lay over the yard. The barn was blazing furiously, as were several of the small sheds. He couldn't tell if the main house or the crew's quarters had been set aflame yet or not.

He turned again to Julie, hoping she would slow, hold back, allow Englund and him to go in first. She refused to meet his eyes. Abruptly they topped the little ridge bordering the clearing in which the structures stood, and rushed into the yard. All was in chaos, utter confusion.

Four masked men were lacing back and forth, firing pistols indiscriminately. A dozen fires blazed—but Kelso's house and the low structure where the crew bunked were as yet untouched. Several Three Cross men had taken a stand inside their quarters and were returning the raiders' shots.

Starbuck saw figures lying in the swirling dust and smoke at that moment—Kelso near the kitchen shack, Aaron Lambert midway between the barn and the corrals. He heard Julie scream, was aware of her spurring past him toward her father.

Towering anger swept through him in a wild gust. Throwing himself from the chestnut, he went to one knee, leveled his pistol at the nearest shadowy figure wheeling through the pall. The bullet went true to its mark. The raider caught at his chest, then slumped forward as his horse disappeared into the gloom.

Englund opened up somewhere off to his left, and almost immediately a riderless horse trotted by, head up, ears pricked forward, eyes bulging with fear. Shawn, searching now for the two remaining riders, began to retreat in the direction of the house—to where he had seen Kelso sprawled. Julie would be there. He'd best get her inside and out of harm's way. He wondered where Mrs. Kelso was.

The shooting ended abruptly and a hot, pungent stillness, broken only by the crackling flames, settled over the yard. Straining his eyes to locate the outlaws, Shawn continued to back slowly for the looming bulk in the half dark that was the ranchhouse.

Shortly he saw Julie. She was to his right, her mother with her. Both were on their knees beside Jim Kelso. Even from where he crouched, several strides away, he could see that the rancher was dead. The broad stain on his chest was all the evidence needed.

He crossed hurriedly to the two women. Roughly shouldering them aside, he bent down and gathered up the rancher's body.

"Place for him's inside the house," he said, and started for the structure at a staggering run. It was the only way he knew of to get the girl and her mother under cover.

Myra Kelso hastened to get ahead of him, opened the door, and then showed the way to a corner room where Starbuck deposited the cattleman's body on a bed. He turned at once, came face to face with Julie. He studied the grief in her eyes briefly, and then with anger again soaring through him, strode for the doorway.

"Sorry—" he murmured as he brushed by her.

He neither heard nor expected an answer, simply rushed on, gun in hand, into the open. Grim, he started across the yard. Smoke and dust were beginning to dissipate, and he could make out three or four figures running back and forth from the horse trough, carrying wooden buckets filled with sloshing water as they endeavored to halt the flames threatening the cook shack.

The barn, the wagon shed, with its adjoining blacksmith's shop, several small tool and feed sheds, were still burning steadily, had been abandoned as lost. The air was hot, choking, filled with bits of floating soot and glowing sparks. He saw two men bending over Lambert, watched them pick up the old rider, start for the bunkhouse. A moment later Dave Englund, his left arm bloody and hanging stiffly at his side, appeared, followed unsteadily. One of the raiders lay nearby; there was no sign of the others.

Holstering his weapon, Shawn stepped quickly to the deputy's side, helped him into the smoke filled building. It had not been caught up by the flames but the open windows had permitted layers of drifting smoke to enter.

Ortiz, his face smeared with soot, clothes smoldering where live coals had dropped upon him, stepped back as they came through the doorway. Beyond him Pierce was working over Lambert, but there didn't appear to be much anyone could do.

Dave began to struggle with his vest and shirt, trying to work with his good arm. Shawn helped him remove the garments, and then as Pierce turned to have a look at the deputy's arm, he moved to Lambert's side, stood for a long minute staring down into the slack features of the old rider.

"Jim—they get him?"

It was Pierce asking the question. Shawn came about, nodded.

"How about his missus?"

"She's all right. Julie, too. . . . Expect we'd better get the doctor out here."

"Already sent Fermin for Ed Christie," Pierce replied, forcing Englund to a sitting position on the edge of a bunk.

Bitterness and anger suddenly overwhelmed Starbuck. "Who were they? Masked—saw that, but somebody must've recognized one of them! Was Mendoza there?"

The usually expressionless features of Isidro Ortiz tightened, and then he shrugged in a hopeless sort of way, as if decrying the all too ready practice of the *Americanos* to blame the Mexican people for such things. Shawn laid a hand on his shoulder.

"Asked that because I was talking to him earlier. He ducked out on me."

"Didn't spot him," Pierce said then. "Sure would've recognized him from what he's wearing. You saying he's mixed up in it?"

"Don't know for sure, but there's some connection," Starbuck answered, watching the old puncher dab at the puckered hole in the deputy's arm with a wad of cotton soaked in disinfectant. "Think I'll have a look at that one—"

"No need," Englund said, pushing Pierce away. "I know him. He's one of them three you claimed you'd tracked into town after the stampede. He's the one they called

Duncan. Expect a couple of the others were his sidekicks—Palmer and Jennings. Fourth man was Vern Ruch."

Shawn stared at the lawman as the full import of the information drilled into him. He'd been right about the three riders from the start, but that wasn't all; the fact that Omar Gentry had lied to protect them meant that they, as well as Ruch, were in his employ. Those four carried out the raid on Three Cross; it would have been at Gentry's direction.

Did that mean that Gentry was the party wanting Three Cross so badly? Was he the mysterious client that the El Paso banker, Blaisdell, represented? If so, why, why all the violence, now even death, to bring about the sale? What was the urgency, the need—the big attraction?

Starbuck stirred irritably. He was back to the puzzling question that had galled him before—only now certain things had clarified, had become definite. Gentry was a part of it. So also were Vern Ruch, Jennings, and Palmer—one of whom was badly wounded, possibly even dead. Pablo Mendoza fit into the picture somewhere, but in just what way he could not be sure.

Regardless, he knew now where to look, who to call to account not only for all the trouble that had descended upon Three Cross, but for the more serious crime of Jim Kelso and Aaron Lambert's deaths. Wheeling, he moved to the door and paused.

"Want the bunch of you to move to the main house, fort up. Don't think there'll be any more trouble but best we not take a chance."

"This here place is pretty tight for making a stand," Pierce said.

"Maybe so, but there should be somebody with the women—and it'll be better if you're all together."

Englund glanced at Starbuck's set features. "You riding into town after Ruch and the others?"

"I am—"

The deputy pulled himself to his feet. "You hold off a bit, I'll go along."

Shawn considered the lawman. He'd lost a lot of blood, was far too weak to undertake even the ride, much less a confrontation with gunmen. . . . And he knew he'd have his own hands full without being burdened with the care of the deputy.

"Be better if you stay put—"

"That's for certain," Pierce agreed. "You ain't in no shape to do much of nothing."

Englund settled back, wagged his head. "Don't hardly

112

seem right, you taking it on yourself to go after them. . . .
Job for the law. Still figure you ought to wait."

Job for the law! The words echoed in Shawn's memory,
reminding him of the thought voiced only a short time
earlier by Julie Kelso, that help from that same law, when
and if it came, would be too late.

"Can't wait," he said. "Chance they may pull out, make
a run for it. . . . Best I move in on them now."

19

Not long after midnight, Shawn Starbuck rode into Las Cruces. The glowing anger that had gripped him was undiminished, and there was no uncertainty in his mind as he guided the chestnut toward the Amador Hotel.

During the crossing of the silver-flooded flats and shadowy hills that lay between Kelso's and the settlement, he'd had time to assemble his facts and place them in orderly fashion; he was entirely convinced that Omar Gentry was the man solely responsible for the rancher's troubles—and now for his death.

It would have been Gentry who made the offer to buy Three Cross, who had hoped to speed up and guarantee the acceptance of his proposal by making matters untenable for Kelso. He doubted Gentry had intended for the rancher to be killed; it was likely an accident. There was room for consideration there, however. Gentry could have desired Three Cross so intensely—reason why still unknown—that he had sanctioned the murder of the rancher feeling it would be much easier to deal with a distraught widow.

Reason unknown. . . .

Starbuck considered that as the gelding walked softly through the ankle-deep dust of the deserted street. He could still find no answer to that puzzling factor, just as Pablo Mendoza's place in the scheme was yet in darkness. But he'd solve both questions soon; the time for settling was at hand.

He reached the Amador, drew up to its hitchrack. The adjoining Spanish Dagger was dimly lit, but the muffled sound of voices and occasional bursts of laughter coming through the open doorway attested to the presence of a goodly number of patrons.

The hotel was dark except for a solitary lamp in the lobby, and a lighted window on the upper floor where a guest was apparently keeping late hours. Elsewhere the roadway lay silent and in deep shadow—even the remaining saloons having closed for the night.

Dismounting, Shawn walked quietly to the entrance of the Dagger. Halting in the blackness outside the door, purposely propped open to trap the cooling breeze slipping down the valley from the north, he probed the faces of the men lined up at the bar, and those at the tables that fell within his range of vision.

Neither Gentry nor Ruch were to be seen. If Palmer or Jennings—whichever was alive—was there, he would have no way of knowing, since he'd never seen them except as masked riders moving in and out of the smoke and spinning dust of Kelso's yard. Jaw set, he hitched at the pistol hanging on his hip, stepped inside.

Arnie, his ruddy features drawn by a broad smile, nodded a welcome and said, "Beer, Mr. Starbuck?"

"Make it rye," Shawn replied, leaning up against the counter. Half turning, he swung his gaze over that part of the room he'd been unable to see from the street. The two he sought were not present.

The bartender slid his drink into his hands, leaned across the counter in a confidential manner. "You get all squared up with the law?"

Starbuck nodded. "Was a mistake. Deputy thought I was somebody else. . . . You see Gentry tonight?"

The saloonkeeper frowned, drew back. "Well, yes. Was in early."

Starbuck downed his drink, glanced about casually. "Don't see him now. Happen to know where he is?"

Arnie refilled the shot glass. "Couldn't say. His room, maybe, late like it is."

The bartender moved off to answer the call of another patron. Shawn emptied his glass, felt the liquor jolt some of the weariness from him. Dropping a coin on the counter, he turned away, catching Arnie's eyes on him. Nodding, he crossed the room and moved through the archway that led into the hotel. There was one room in the Amador that was lighted. Unless he was completely wrong, there was where he'd find Omar Gentry, along with Ruch and the third man, who were likely reporting the results of the raid on Three Cross.

The lobby was empty, the desk deserted, there being only a small sign next to a tap-bell, with the words *Ring For Clerk* lettered upon it to greet late arrivals. Shawn crossed to the stairway, mounted it, and made his way down the corridor until he came to a door under which a streak of light was visible.

Putting his ear to the thin panel, he listened. The clink of coins and a low mutter of voices came to him. A fresh wave of anger washed over Starbuck. Kelso dead, Aaron Lambert dead, Three Cross in charred ruins—and the men responsible callously playing cards! Drawing his pistol, he grasped the door's china knob in his right hand, and in a single movement flung the panel wide and lunged into the room.

The men at the table came to their feet in surprise. A chair overturned noisily, money clattered to the floor. Ruch reached swiftly for his weapon, froze when he saw the leveled gun.

Shawn surveyed the party coldly. Gentry, Vern Ruch, a rider who was either Jennings or Palmer, and a flashily dressed individual—one of the local gamblers, probably. Omar Gentry was the first to break the stiff silence.

"What's this all about?"

"About a raid on Three Cross—and a couple of killings."

Gentry's expression did not change. "Killings? Who?"

"Jim Kelso—and an old timer named Lambert—"

Only then did Gentry betray reaction. He flipped his cold eyes at Ruch. "You fool—" he began, and then smoothly recovered. "Wrong place, cowboy. You're looking for the deputy sheriff."

Shawn smiled quietly. He'd been right. Ruch and the others had overstepped themselves. Kelso's death had not been a part of the plan.

"I know where the deputy is—at Kelso's with a bullet in him. I'm here for you and your gun hawks."

Gentry shook his head. "Not for me. I don't know—"

"Don't play cozy with me," Starbuck cut in. "Duncan's dead. Ruch and your other hired hand there were spotted, along with the one that got a bullet in his belly."

The tall man's facade cracked slightly. "Somebody's making a mistake—"

"You've already made it," Shawn snapped. "From the start. Trying to force Kelso to sell out to you was bad enough, but killing him was the worst. . . . He was ready to accept the offer your banker friend was making for you, but you couldn't wait."

Omar Gentry said nothing, and in voicing no denial where Blaisdell was concerned, Shawn knew he'd guessed right once more.

"Want you to keep your hands up high—all of you. And turn around slow. I'm taking your guns, then we're walking over to the jail."

Alarm spread over the features of the gambler. "You got no call bringing me in on this! I don't know nothing about what you're saying. . . . Come up here to play a little stud, that's all."

116

"Tell it to the deputy," Shawn answered. "He'll be around in the morning. Get your hands up—"

"Maybe you'd best raise yours, Mr. Starbuck," Arnie's voice said from the doorway.

Shawn felt the hard muzzle of a gun press into his spine, saw relief slip into the faces of the men in front of him. Ruch immediately circled the table, a hard grin pulling at his lips. He wrenched the pistol from Starbuck's fingers and stepped back, his own weapon now out. The bartender came on into the room.

"Obliged, Arnie," Gentry said, picking up a handful of the coins lying on the table and dropping them into the saloonkeeper's vest pocket. "Appreciate this."

Arnie smiled fawningly. "Glad I could help, Mr. Gentry. Seen when Mr. Starbuck come in that he had something on his mind—asking about you and such. Then when he headed up stairs I figured I'd best have a look-see."

"Was a big favor—and I won't forget it. . . . Better get back to your customers now."

"Yes, sir, Mr. Gentry," the saloon-man said, and hurried for the door.

As he stepped into the corridor, Gentry pivoted to the gambler. "You, too, Harley—get out! And keep your mouth shut. You know what'll happen to you if you breathe one word about what happened here tonight!"

"I sure do," the gambler replied, and crossing the room quickly, also disappeared into the hall.

Ruch, Starbuck's pistol tucked under his waistband, toyed with his own weapon while keeping it pointed. "What's next?"

Gentry, features suddenly taut, whirled on the gunman. "What's next? Goddam you—I'll tell you what's next! That stupid bungling of yours is going to force us to act now!"

"Couldn't be helped. The old bastard came out shooting—"

"You should've helped it! Instead of being able to sit back, take our time like I'd planned, we'll have to grab what we can and make a run for it tonight."

"Does it make a lot of difference?"

"Makes one hell of a lot of difference. Kelso's dead— thanks to your bungling. Cat's out of the bag now. By daylight tomorrow everybody in the country'll know who did it—"

"Not if Palmer and me take this joker down the river a piece and put a bullet in his head."

"What good will that do? You heard him say the deputy

117

was at Kelso's and was in on the whole thing. And there's others besides him alive and able to talk—the women for instance. If you had to kill a couple, then you'd have been smart to kill them all so's there'd be nobody left to do any finger pointing."

Ruch was unruffled by the tongue lashing. He shrugged. "So, like I was asking—what's next?"

"We go out there tonight—right now, get what we can, and move on."

Shawn listened, realizing he was getting close to the answer he had been seeking—why Three Cross was wanted so badly by Gentry. . . . But the way matters were shaping up, there was a good chance he'd not live to make use of the information.

"You want I should tie his hands?" Palmer said.

"No," Gentry replied, pulling on his hat and reaching for a leather-trimmed corduroy coat hanging against the wall. "Somebody in the saloon might notice, start wondering. Just keep up close to him—the both of you."

Starbuck, alert now for the slightest opportunity to escape, took a half step back. Ruch moved in beside him, seized him by the arm, shoved him toward the door.

"Do what you're told, *amigo*—unless you want me bending this gun barrel over your head."

Starbuck, off balance, stumbled into the corridor. Palmer and Ruch closed in beside him, and preceded by Omar Gentry, flanked by the other two outlaws, he started down the hallway. Reaching the stairs, Gentry motioned for them to wait while he took a quick glance. Finding all was clear, he beckoned them to follow, and shortly they were in the darkness of the street.

"Get the horses—the rest of the stuff, too," Gentry said, facing Palmer. "We'll wait here."

The rider turned for the stable. Shawn glanced along the row of silent buildings. There was small chance of there being anyone up and around at that hour who could help. He brought his attention back to Gentry.

"Whatever this is all about, you won't get away with it. You said it yourself—the deputy and a half dozen others know all about what happened at Kelso's. They'll be after you by daylight."

"After us, sure—but a long ways behind us. Time the sun comes up we'll be far from this burg."

"And plenty richer," Vern Ruch added with a grin.

It was the wrong thing to say. Gentry spun to the gunman. "Not rich as we ought to be—thanks to that thick skull of yours! If you'd used some common sense, not acted like a stupid—"

"Easy," Ruch murmured, Gentry's lashing words finally beginning to rile him.

"It's the truth! Had it set up just right—took months— then you bungle it! Should've known you'd make a slip!"

"We can always come back—"

"With a murder charge hanging over our—my head? Stupid's not the word for you, Ruch. Ought to be a stronger one."

The gunman stiffened perceptibly. "Back off, Captain," he warned again.

Gentry, touching the outlaw with a calculating glance, shrugged, sighed deeply. "Well, no point bitching about it now. It's done, and the thing to do is get what we can." He hesitated, eyes toward the stable. "Here comes Palmer. Get this bird's horse. It's that chestnut, Vern."

Holding his own pistol on Shawn, the tall man allowed Ruch to move off, and then, smiling humorlessly, said, "You know, cowboy, I'm personally taking on the job of putting a bullet in your head. Going to be a lot of satisfaction. I worked up plenty of sweat putting this plan of mine together—and then you horned in and queered it."

"Maybe so, but mostly it was your own man, Ruch."

"Sure, but if it hadn't been for you he'd not have pulled the stupid stunt he did. You horning in got him all shook up, jumpy. . . . Wasn't for you—and him—I'd've ended up a rich man."

"Understood you already were," Starbuck said, prying, still searching for that elusive answer.

"Far from it. All show—part of the plan. You ever see an army man end up rich?"

Shawn shook his head, continued to press for the missing piece of the puzzle. "And you figured raising cattle on Kelso's place—"

Gentry snorted. "Cattle? You think that's why I was after his ranch?"

"What else?"

Omar Gentry leaned forward slightly. Light filtering from the Amador's lobby lamp glinted against his features, pointed up the strange glow in his eyes.

"Gold—"

Starbuck came up sharply. "Gold!" he echoed.

"Yes, sir—Jesuit gold," Gentry said in a taut voice. "Three chests of it buried on Kelso's property."

20

Jesuit gold!

Shawn stared at Gentry. That was what lay behind the man's ruthless determination to possess Three Cross! It was a bit hard to believe. He'd heard tales before of treasures buried in the New Mexico hills by priests called back to Spain by superiors who no longer trusted them, and had often wondered how much truth was in such reports. Very little, he had been assured several times.

Omar Gentry, however, didn't strike him as a man who would move on fantasy. He would be more than half sure of his information before he invested time and money in such a venture—particularly in a project where he had planned to purchase an entire ranch in order to own the property upon which the treasure was supposedly cached. His reasoning there was easy to understand; as owner of the land anything found on it was legally his.

"Mount up," he heard Gentry say.

Moving to the chestnut, he went to the saddle, noting the two shovels and several pairs of saddlebags Palmer had brought with the horses.

"Best we get right along," Gentry continued. "Not much time left before daylight, and we want to be gone by then."

Ruch nodded, jerked his thumb at Starbuck. "What about him? Ought to shuck him somewheres so's we won't be bothered."

Omar Gentry grinned. "Got plans for him. Being big and strong—he'll do the digging for us. Can get rid of him after that."

The gunman signified his approval of the idea. "Glad to hear that. These here hands of mine never did fit no shovel."

They moved out at once, striking due west for the river, fording it almost directly opposite the settlement. There, with Palmer forging out to take the lead, they angled off through the short hills, keeping to a trail that ran parallel to, but was somewhat above the road Shawn and Jim Kelso had taken that first day.

As they rode steadily on through the cool night, Starbuck tried to look ahead, prepare for an attempt to escape. Chances weren't good, he had to admit. Palmer was in front of him, Gentry and Ruch, riding side by side, were at his back. At any effort to make a break they could easily shoot him out of the saddle.

But to delay until they reached their destination would be pressing his luck to the limit. He had no inkling of where the gold was buried, but there was little doubt in his mind that any opportunity to get away would be served best along the brush-lined trail. . . . He must somehow distract the two outlaws behind him, buy a fleeting moment of chance.

"Heard about Jesuit gold," he said, twisting about on the gelding. "Always figured it was just talk."

Gentry shrugged. "Most tales are. This isn't."

"Expect every man who goes looking for it feels the same way."

"Not every man gets his hands on what I did—a letter telling all about a treasure. Even the Mexican government's heard of the one I'm—we're—after. They just didn't know where the cache is."

"A letter—not a map?" Shawn was putting the question to Gentry but his eyes were on Vern Ruch. The gunman appeared to be dozing.

"What I said. Maps are usually not worth the paper they're scribbled on. What I got my hands on was a letter from some family in Spain to an old *padre* living near Chihuahua. Was a relative, I suppose. Told all about the treasure three Jesuits had buried. He was to turn it over to the government, help pay for the war Benito Juarez had been fighting against the French."

"But he gave it to you instead—"

Gentry smiled, obviously enjoying the recounting of his ingenuity. "Not exactly. Might say I relieved him of it. . . . I'd been down there, helping Juarez run his army ever since our war ended in sixty-five. Was no problem for me."

"Then you came up here, located the treasure, and when you found out it was on private land, started trying to buy it. That about three months ago—when you had Blaisdell make Kelso that offer?"

The tall man laughed. "You've got yourself in the wrong calling, friend. Instead of a cowhand you ought to be a detective—like one of those Pinkerton agents. . . . Yeh, I had Blaisdell make an offer—legitimate and on the level, too. Just good poker playing to lay out a couple of thousand dollars to win back twenty or thirty times that much—in gold."

"Kelso would have never sold that cheap."

"When I got through with ragging him, he'd likely have sold for less. Got a feeling he'd just about reached that point—only Ruch, there, had to go and foul everything up with that damned gun of his. . . . Have to grab what I can of the gold now. Maybe I can come back in a few years when it's all forgot, dig up the rest."

"If it's there at all."

Gentry spat. "It's there. No if nor ands about this treasure. Fact is, the Mexican government's got a man here right now, watching me, hoping I'll tip him off. The old *padre* wasn't dead as I thought, seems."

"A *vaquero* by the name of Mendoza—he the agent you mean?"

"That's him. Poor bastard—sure have led him a long chase, and he's no closer right now to getting that gold than he was in Chihuahua."

That accounted for Pablo Mendoza, Shawn thought, settling back. A representative of the Mexican government; it explained his hanging around, watching, waiting, patrolling the valley. He was simply keeping an eye on Gentry, hoping the man would make his move.

"Ought to be about there," Ruch said, shifting on his saddle. The gunman had not been as unaware of things as he had wanted others to believe, apparently. "Good thing. We sure ain't going to have much time."

"Thanks to you—" Gentry snapped.

Starbuck was looking over the shadowy land, striving to recall the terrain, the location of the arroyos, the deeper ravines, but his knowledge of the area was scant. If he were to make a move toward escaping, however, it should be soon; the brush bordering the trail would afford him excellent cover—if he could reach it before a bullet cut him down.

Palmer, quickening the pace despite the roughness of the path, began to veer right. Shortly the shaded depths of a small, steep-walled canyon came into view. Shawn strained to see the floor of the declivity, to determine the nature of its floor. If it was smooth and sandy, he could risk jumping the chestnut down into it. Cluttered with rocks and brush, it would be foolhardy—and fatal.

After a few moments he gave it up. It was impossible to tell what lay below. He'd have to come up with something else.

"Rider coming—"

At Palmer's low-pitched warning, Gentry stopped. Instantly Vern Ruch spurred to Starbuck's side, jammed a pistol against his back.

"One sound, cowboy, and you're dead!"

Shawn heard it then, the light but steady *tunk-a-tunk* of a horse coming down the trail toward them.

"Some drifter," Ruch murmured.

"Maybe," Gentry answered at low breath. "Pull off into that brush ahead of you. We'd best wait and see. Can't afford any more mistakes."

Ruch dug the pistol's muzzle deeper into Starbuck, kneed the chestnut into a thick stand of false mahogany immediately to their right. Palmer dropped back, joined them.

"Mind what I said," the gunman again warned Shawn.

Starbuck barely heard. Ruch was close. He could see the handle of his own pistol sticking up from the outlaw's waistband where it had been thrust. It was less than an arm's length away—available and tempting.

"Here he comes," Palmer whispered, and then added, "It's that Mex—"

In that fragment of time, Shawn Starbuck elected to gamble, make his try. His hand shot out, jerked the pistol from Ruch's waistband.

"Mendoza—look out!" he yelled, and firing point blank at the gunman, threw himself backwards into the brush.

The gelding reared in sudden fright, long fore legs striking out, slashing at the horse Ruch was riding. Gentry yelled something. Two quick gunshots crashed as Shawn hit the solidness that was the slope of the little canyon, and went plunging on to the bottom.

Instantly he veered to the side, began to claw his way through a band of scrub oak, knowing that he must get away from the point where he had dropped from the outlaw's sight. He could see the chestnut outlined against the sky above him, along with another horse. Ruch's likely. Nothing else was in view—and there was only silence.

He paused, began to proceed more cautiously. What had happened to Gentry and Palmer? And Mendoza? Ruch was down, undoubtedly dead; he couldn't have missed a fatal shot at such close range. . . . Those two other reports—did they indicate an exchange between the *vaquero* and Gentry, or possibly Palmer? Had any of them been hit?

He gained the top of the deep slash. The trail was only a step or two ahead in the open. It looked like a silver band in the starlight—soft and deadly. Crouched, he waited, listened, swinging his attention from right to left. The chestnut, and Ruch's bay, were now off to one side grazing amiably on the clumps of bunchgrass.

Where the hell was everybody?

He sweated out another long minute and then, impatient but careful, flat on his belly, he began to crawl toward the horses.

"Senor—"

Mendoza's hushed summons came from the brush on the opposite side of the trail.

"Here."

"You are not injured?"

"No. . . . How about you?"

"A bullet in the leg. It is nothing."

Shawn remained silent for several moments, listening into the night. There was nothing except the cropping sound the horses were making. Evidently they had not been overheard.

"There's two of them left," he said then. "You happen to see which way they ducked?"

"Into the brush, I do not know exactly where. The man Gentry is one."

"Yeh, Gentry and Palmer."

The outlaws were simply waiting for them to show themselves, Starbuck realized. . . . He'd oblige them but not in the way they hoped.

"Can you walk, *amigo?*" he called in a whisper.

"Oh, yes. The wound is small. You wish for me to come there?"

"No. . . . Expect they're hiding in that thick brush to the left of the horses, hoping we'll step out and give them a couple of easy pot shots. You keep low, work in from that direction. I'll do the same on this side. . . . Ready?"

"Si, caporal, I am ready."

At once, Starbuck began to make his way through the tough oak bushes, keeping as flat to the ground as was humanly possible. Across the way he could hear a faint scraping as Mendoza kept abreast.

He paused, sweating even in the night's coolness, brushed at his eyes to clear the moisture. Careful, he raised his head. The gelding was only a few strides away. He saw Ruch then, stretched out at the edge of the trail, face down. Dropping low again, he continued.

Abruptly a shadow raised up before him. Starlight glinted off metal. Instinctively Shawn threw himself to one side, triggered a shot from a prone position. Almost in the identical breath, two quick reports blasted along the opposite side of the trail.

Rolling to one knee, Starbuck hung there in the darkness while the echoes bounced through the night. A groan came to him through the pungent, drifting wisps of smoke.

"Mendoza?"

"Here, *senor*. I—I have had the bad luck again. Come— there is no danger. I see the *cabrones*. They will trouble no man again."

Starbuck leaped to his feet, crossed the path, and hesitated. Glancing about he located the *vaquero*, quickly knelt beside him. Mendoza had taken a bullet in his chest. An arm's length away Omar Gentry lay on his back, sightless eyes staring up into the star-spattered sky. Evidently the two men had all but collided in the dark, and both had fired together. ... A short distance to the left Palmer, the shadow that had risen in his path, lay draped over a fallen tree.

"Best I get you to the doc," Shawn said. "Like as not he's still at Kelso's."

Mendoza gestured feebly with his hand. "There is no need. I rest well here and would stay. We are men, *compadre*. We know death has come for me."

Shawn lowered his head. "Afraid so. . . . I'm sorry."

"Do not be. I am pleased for I have finished the job my government sent me to do. I have prevented this man Gentry from finding the gold that belongs to my country, the *Gorgojo* treasure."

"The what?"

"*Gorgojo*—a word that makes little meaning. It is the name given to the treasure by a dying man—a priest slain by Gentry for a letter he carried. It was one that told of the gold."

"There an English word for it?"

"This I do not know. In the language of my people it refers to a small worm, one found in meal."

"A weevil," Shawn supplied. "You're right, it doesn't make much sense. We were going after the gold when we ran into you."

Mendoza stirred hopefully. "Then the location of this treasure is known to you?"

"Afraid not. Gentry never told me. Don't think the others knew either. Somewhere on Kelso's ranch is about as close as I can get."

The *vaquero* settled back. For a time the only sound was his labored breathing and then, managing a shrug, he said: "It is sad. My people are very poor, starving from the time of the war. They are in need of the simplest of things, and have great need of the gold which was taken from them by the Jesuits."

Mendoza paused, breathing hard. He clutched at Starbuck's arm, lifted his head slightly. His eyes were bright. "A promise, *senor!* Tell the *senora*—the woman of Kelso of the treasure. Beg of her in the name of sacred charity to find this treasure of Gorgojo, return it to my people who are the rightful owners. ... Do this for me, I ask it of you!"

Shawn clasped the *vaquero's* hand firmly, nodded. "You've got my word on it."

"It is enough," Mendoza sighed, his lips parting in a faint smile.

"If she's willing, I'll do some scouting around the hills, see if I can turn up—"

Starbuck's words drifted into nothingness as a sudden thought, like a shaft of penetrating light, ripped into his mind, sent a tremor racing through him. ... Three graves that, perhaps, were not graves at all; three crosses on a hill that could have been meant to serve as markers for men who planned one day to return but never did—and a strange word—*gorgojo*—that lacked meaning.

Could the mumbled words of the dying priest been misunderstood? Could he have, instead, muttered the name, *Golgotha*—another hill in a far away land where centuries ago there also had stood three crosses? That must have been the way of it! The Jesuits had designated the location of their buried treasure by drawing an obvious but unsuspected parallel.

Shawn bent over the dying man. "Mendoza—listen to me. ..."

The Mexican stirred weakly. His eyes opened and the smile again crossed his lips. *"Adios, compadre."*

Starbuck looked more closely at him. It was too late. "So long, my friend," he said quietly.

"Vaya con Dios," the *vaquero* murmured and fell silent.

Pablo Mendoza would never know that the treasure he sought, and wanted returned to his people so badly, had been found.

21

The chests were there, as Shawn had been certain they would be, buried deep beneath the piles of stone that marked the location of each cross. He had explained it all to Myra and Julie Kelso and they agreed it rightfully belonged to Mexico and should be returned.

To avoid political complications, Starbuck, with a dozen special deputies under the direction of Sheriff Abel Morrison, transported the treasure—mostly jeweled church vessels, chalices, crosses, and crucifixes inlaid with precious stones, and a good-sized amount of gold coin, to the border, where it was handed over to a small army dispatched to meet them by Pablo Mendoza's superiors.

Now, astride the chestnut gelding, Starbuck paused on the summit of a hill east of Three Cross, and in the clean, crisp sunlight of New Year's Day, looked back to the ranch. He raised his arm in farewell. Julie Kelso, standing in the center of the yard, lifted her hand in reply.

Everything had worked out. Morrison had cleared him of the murder charge the deputy had lodged against him, had in addition supplied him with all the information he could muster concerning Damon Friend—who unquestionably was Ben. The accusation against his brother would stand, however, the lawman told him; but it was a matter that could be cleared up if Ben would return and face trial.

The Kelsos, mother and daughter, had recovered from the loss of Jim as well as could be expected in that short time, and were planning to continue raising cattle.

Sitting motionless there on the saddle, eyes roving moodily the broad swale in which the ranch lay, now a pale, sage green under winter's touch, Shawn sighed regretfully. . . . He could have remained as foreman, run Three Cross as if it were his own, but he knew it wasn't possible. It would never be until he found Ben.

Thus he was moving on, just as he had told Jim Kelso he would when the first day of the new year came. He had gained far more than needed wages during his stay; he had a description of, as well as a name for his brother. And while the frontier into which Ben had disappeared was no smaller than it had been in the beginning, he now possessed that first link with which to build a chain. Perhaps he'd find the second in Texas.

Deputy
of
Violence

☆ 1 ☆

Shawn Starbuck swung his horse down into the brush-filled cup behind a shoulder of rock and dropped silently from the saddle. He didn't know if the oncoming copper warriors were Comanche or Kiowa. He'd been warned he'd likely encounter both in that blistered, hellish waste-land of west Texas, and that he'd best keep a sharp eye out if he hoped to stay alive.

Crouched, feeling the fiery lash of the sun on his back and neck, praying the sorrel would make no sound, he watched the painted riders wind slowly up the hill. Four-teen in all. . . . About half carried rifles—mostly single-shot, Army Springfield carbines. Evidently they were re-turning from a raid. Several exhibited wounds, all ap-peared dog-tired, were slumped heads low, legs dangling loosely, as they sat their lean ponies.

Halfway up the grade one of the braves buckled, fell to the scorched sand. The column came to a halt. The Indian behind the fallen brave rode in closer, stared at his com-rade. After a time he dismounted, and saying something in quick Spanish, nudged the man with his toe. There was no response. Others then moved in, and for a time all carried on a conversation in the seemingly angry but normal manner of their kind.

A decision was reached. The brave *was* dead, and the question, obviously, had been whether to leave him for nature to dispose of or take him on to the village. The latter proved to be the choice. They draped the limp shape over a horse, tied feet to hands under the animal's belly, and moved on.

Slowly, painfully, the sun hammering relentlessly at their glistening, sweaty bodies, they made their way to the crest of the ridge, topped out, and dropped over to the yonder side. Shawn waited until the last bowed figure had disappeared, threw a long, searching glance to the trail up which the party had come to be certain there were no more, and then sighed heavily. He had almost blundered into the braves. If he hadn't turned off, headed for a knoll from which he intended to have a look at the surrounding country, he would have.

Mopping the sweat from his face and neck, he swung to the saddle, wincing as his backside came in contact with the sun-scorched leather. Roweling the big horse lightly, he rode up out of the pocket behind the rock, gained the summit of the hill for which he had been pointing, and shading his eyes, looked around.

He swore softly as his gaze swept over the shimmering, heat-blasted hell. He'd as well admit it—he was lost.

Not that he didn't know where he was—generally; deep in that seared, desolate land north of the Mexican border, which now lay miles to his right on the far side of the Rio Grande. . . . He was aware of that much, and it was of no help. Mexico was the last place he wanted to go at that moment.

His hoped for destination was the Hash Knife Ranch owned by a man named Hagerman. It was in the Carazones Peaks country. That was the rub; where the hell was the Carazones Peaks country? He had no sure idea of its location, and there was no one within miles—save that band of blooded braves—who could head him into the right direction, and he wasn't about to ask them.

There were peaks at about every point of the compass, smudgy, indefinite looking through the layers of dancing heat, and the map he'd scrawled into his mind back at Fort Davis didn't seem to fit in anywhere.

All he could say was that he was in deep, southwest Texas—a vast, formidable world of glittering rock, pitiless heat, starved cactus, withered shrubs, and little else. There were no roads, no definite trails—only untracked flats and slopes and vague, unreal formations lying dead under a blinding, steel sky. The Hash Knife Ranch could be anywhere.

He had hoped to reach Hagerman's the day before and by that high-noon hour have satisfied his reason for going there—that one of Hash Knife's riders was or was not his brother Ben for whom he'd been searching so long.

The tip that such was a possibility had come to him in El Paso. He'd gone there after first journeying to Fort Worth and investigating a clue turned up in the small New Mexico town of Las Cruces. It, like all the others he'd pursued with such faithful persistence in the past, had proved false. Then, a stagecoach driver, in answer to the inquiries he routinely made wherever he happened to be, mentioned a passenger he had carried.

The description Shawn gave was a necessarily meager one as it had been well over ten years since Ben, in a burst of temper, had rebelled against the iron-fisted ways of their father, Hiram, and run away from their farm home in Ohio. But the driver felt his passenger fit and suggested that if Starbuck didn't mind the long, hot ride to the Carazones Peaks, it might prove worth his while.

Old Hiram Starbuck, in his will, had made the provision that before the estate could be settled equally between his two sons, Shawn, the younger, must find his errant brother. Until such was accomplished the thirty-thousand-dollar residue lying in the bank could not be touched—not even for expense money needed by Shawn to finance his quest.

In the beginning it had been a different and welcome change for him, still several years short of legal manhood. He had ridden away from his boyhood home filled with high hopes and the firm conviction that he would encounter no great difficulty in finding Ben and returning him to Ohio.

The months that followed proved otherwise. The small amount of cash the family lawyer had seen fit to advance him on his own initiative soon played out. Shawn was compelled to take a job, work for a time, and rebuild his capital in order to continue the search.

The pattern was thus established, and steadily and surely through the tedious days that followed, the farm boy who had never ventured more than a mile or two from the fieldstone house on the Muskingum River, changed into a tall, cool-eyed trail rider far older than his years, and one quick of mind and hand—a man others hoped would side with but never stand against them. . . .

Pulling off his hat, he forearmed the sweat from his face, stared moodily across the baked ground through eyelids narrowed to cut the intense glare. Reason told him the Carazones Peaks would lie to the east—but would he find them due east, or considerably to the south? He swore feelingly. In this empty sameness a man couldn't tell much about anything. It sure wasn't a country to go wandering aimlessly about—no towns, no ranches, no living persons, only transient Indians. It was a world abandoned to the cruelest, immoderate elements.

He could always turn around, head back north. There were a few small settlements that way, he thought, but he wasn't absolutely sure. He reckoned Fort Davis was his best bet if he decided to double back, but he disliked the thought of doing that after coming this far. If he did, he'd just have to swing back again as soon as he got his bearings. There ought to be some other answer.

One thing certain, he'd have to do something. Trail supplies were low and while he still had one full canteen of water, it wouldn't last indefinitely if he continued wandering about in this blistered slice of hell. He swore again, once more mopped at his face. The damned heat must be a hundred and ten or more.

Lazily, he came off the saddle, feeling the burn of the horn as he hooked his hand about it, and swung down. He grunted as his heels hit the solidness of the butte's crest, and immediately he felt the fire of the castigated soil spearing through the soles of his boots.

Ground reining the sorrel, he walked slowly to the edge of the formation. Off a few paces to his right a long-eared jackrabbit watched him indifferently from the filagreed shade of a snakeweed clump. No other living thing was to be seen; no birds overhead, no companion varmints to the jack—only the long-reaching, burning plains and hills and ghostlike peaks scattered helter-skelter in the distance as if the Power, in a moment of frivolity, had flung a handful of pinnacles across the scorched, level surface to relieve the monotony.

Shading his brow with a hand, he scoured the country with a painstaking probe, pivoting slowly to encompass a full three hundred and sixty degrees. At northeast he paused, interest whipping suddenly through him. . . . Smoke. . . . Or was it a dust devil whirling its wild way across the desert?

He brushed at the moisture beading his lashes, squinted hard. It wasn't dust. The thin banner twisting vertically upward was dark, not tan or yellow. He lowered his head, blinking to ease his aching eyes. . . . Smoke meant fire— and fire indicated a ranch or a town. It could also mean an Indian village, he thought wearily, or possibly a grass fire. The grama was dry enough to burst into flame of its own accord. But it was a streamer and that would tend to rule out a range fire.

He resumed his contemplation of the smoke. It now appeared to be growing thicker, and not dissipating. . . . A ranch or a town—it had to be one or the other. Hope lifted higher within him. The source of the twisting column was on the far side of a distant bank of hills, near the base of a soaring peak. It looked to be an area lying in the hollow of several high formations.

No matter, it was his one chance—and the only solution. He'd go there, which would actually amount to doubling back over his own tracks to some extent, except that he would be farther east, replenish his grub and water, and find out how to reach the Carazones Peaks. It would cost him at least a day, perhaps two, but it beat riding all the way back to Fort Davis or just wandering aimlessly about and ending up nowhere.

Coming around, his movements slow, utterly restricted by the driving heat, he returned to the gelding, stepped to the saddle, remembering this time to ease himself into the stove-hot leather hull gently, bit by bit. Finally settled, he threw another look to the wisping smoke, established its location with reference to several prominent landmarks, and rode down off the bluff.

Hours later, with endless miles of nothing but glittering sand, cat's-claw, saltbush, snakeweed, and cactus behind him in a glowing pit of invisible flame, he topped out a low ridge and looked down into a wide, shallow wash. A thin band of gray-green lay along its opposite bank, and relief stirred through him as his eyes caught the faint sparkle of silver—a creek.

The sorrel picked up the smell of the water at once, tossed his long head anxiously. Shawn let him move off immediately, dropping down onto the sandy floor and crossing at an eager walk until they came finally to the stream.

It was barely a trickle, but there was shade provided by a stand of stunted trees and a thin-leafed shrub unfamiliar to Starbuck. He halted at the creek's edge, climbed off, and with his foot, scraped out a hollow that filled slowly. Leaving it for the gelding, he unhooked his canteen, and while the horse sucked noisily at the small pool, had a swallow of the tepid water in the container.

The smoke was due north. The streamer seemed larger, darker now, but he guessed it was only because he was nearer. The presence of the creek cheered him, added credence to the belief there was a settlement or a ranch in the offing. Water was a scarce commodity—meant life in this desert world that seldom felt the kiss of raindrops, and the availability of the precious liquid in whatever quantity was a surefire guarantee that somewhere nearby humanity would be found.

A quarter hour later he was again in the saddle, refreshed somewhat by the brief interlude in the comparative coolness along the stream and by the feeling that his problem would soon find a solution. One thing was certain, he'd do his traveling at night and during the early mornings from now on. A man was a damned fool to punish himself and his horse by moving about under that sun.

Looking ahead he could see the arroyo in which the creek flowed and that he was following, was narrowing sharply and graduated into a steep-walled canyon. Abruptly he slowed as something else caught his attention. A short distance in front of him he saw the deep-cut ruts of wagon wheels crossing the stream at right angles. And then a bit farther on there were the hoofprints of cattle, a small herd, running parallel with the ruts as they also forded the stream. All ran east, aiming for a gap in the irregular horizon.

It would be a ranch, not a town, Starbuck concluded as he continued on. The cattle tracks were old, likely several weeks. The rancher would have been making a drive to market—a long journey from that location. He would be forced to take them east to where he'd hit the old Western Trail, as many called it, then swing north along its course to a final halt in Dodge City. . . . A long, hard drive. . . .

Starbuck, eyes on the breech in the skyline, felt the sorrel hesitate in stride. He looked around quickly. A frown pulled at his features. There no longer was a creek or a path skirting it; both had disappeared at the base of a towering rockslide.

Puzzled, Starbuck considered the vertical slab of granite. The stream simply went underground at this point; he understood that—but what had become of the path? Wheeling the sorrel, he backtracked to where the cattle and wagon had crossed, swung onto their trace. Urging the reluctant gelding with his spurs, Shawn headed him into the dense brush that lay west of the creek.

Staying on the ruts left by the broad, iron-tired wheels, he guided the sorrel through the tough growth. The vehicle had moved on no regular course, had simply carved a way through the sage and sand willow, straddling the clumps, forcing a passage that left little mark. A dozen yards farther on the prints veered from direct west to north. Starbuck kept the horse in one of the now faint tracks, realizing shortly that he was circling the rock formation.

Again the gelding slowed his step. A ragged wall of tall weeds, brush, and scattered rock once more blocked his way. Starbuck swore irritably. What the hell was it all about? He leaned forward, easing his aching muscles, eyes on the tangled growth. There was something not exactly right about the brush—something unnatural. It came to him what it was—the brush was neatly interlaced. Here and there he could see small bits of rawhide string beneath the gray leaves.

Dismounting, he stepped up close to the wall. It was an improvised gate. Grasping it near what looked to be center, he pulled. The entire section came back with a dry rattling sound, disclosing an entrance into a short canyon. He could see the wagon-wheel ruts again along with the hoofprints of the passing cattle.

Lifting his gaze, he threw it beyond the narrow cleft. Far ahead lay a sprawling valley, green with grass and shaded with trees.

Shawn scrubbed at his jaw thoughtfully. Someone was taking great pains to keep the valley's location a secret, that was sure. On casual observation a passerby would think the wagon and the cattle came from somewhere to the west, had simply forded the creek at that point. Had he not been following the path along the stream it was likely he would have drawn the same conclusion.

Turned silent, he stood motionless in deep concentration—a tall, serious boy who became a man too early. In repose the leather-brown skin of his face was still smooth, showed only traces of fine lines at the corners of his eyes, blue now but cold gray in certain light. He had but a thin beard and his hair was dark, and when somewhat long, as it was now, inclined to curl along his neck.

There was a confidence and an ever ready alertness to Shawn Starbuck that marked him as one who had ridden the uncounted miles of many trails and encountered all that accident and design had thrown at him—and survived. The mark of such was upon him, definite, and was there for all to see—and heed.

He'd not be welcome at that ranch, or whatever lay at the upper end of the distant valley. The brush-covered entrance made that a foregone truth. But he had no choice; he must have trail supplies and he needed information. He could not be on his way without both.

Reaching back he took up the sorrel's reins, led him through the gate, and pulled it back into place. Mounting, he continued, now on a well-defined trail.

The canyon broadened and the stream again was evident. More gentle growth became apparent and the stands of Christmas cholla, lechuguilla, and cat's-claw disappeared. Clusters of yellow-blossoming groundsel, clumps of jimson, white flowers folded against the sun, cluttered the receding slopes.

But shortly he saw he was coming to the end of the canyon. The valley, of which he'd been afforded but a small glimpse, lay farther still, somewhere beyond a hogback rising ahead.

He reached that level, halted, breath quickening at the sight of the wide, green expanse that stretched before him. That first look had surprised him, but he was totally unprepared for what he now saw. . . . Grass, trees in profusion, myriads of blue lupine, wild marigold and other flowers ablaze on all sides. The bright sparkle of not one but several streams met his gaze. . . . It was a scene wholly unexpected in the desolation across which he had come—

and it was not difficult to understand why someone was most anxious to keep its location unknown.

But there was a strangeness to it all, a hushed restraint, a stillness that differed from that he felt on the flats where the very force of the remorseless sun and the vast emptiness of sheer space called down a coercing hush upon all things.

He became more conscious of the repressiveness as he pushed steadily toward the now more distinct column of smoke rising from beyond a second ridge near the valley's midway. When he finally gained the summit of that last roll and looked down upon a cluster of a dozen or so weathered shacks and buildings, he was even more aware of it.

It was a small settlement, he saw, and not a ranch. It appeared to be deserted, but the smoke rising from one of the structures belied that. Farther up the valley he could see farms lining each side, their plain, unpainted buildings squatting, bleak and forlorn, in the foreground. As near as he could tell the small plats of land, bountiful with fruit trees, corn standing tall and green, carpets of vegetables, extended the full length of the swale—twenty miles at least, possibly more.

Wiping at the sweat on his face, he urged the sorrel on, starting him down the easy grade at a brisk walk. Regardless of the welcome he might receive, it would be good to get off the saddle, wash up, have a meal cooked by hands other than his own: . . . And he'd sleep that night on a springs and mattress—give himself a treat.

That was a new thought, more than he had planned to do. He'd figured to just get supplies and directions and ride on. But the day was growing late. As well stay the night, start fresh in the morning while it was yet cool, make as far as he could before it got too hot, then pull up. He'd not lose much time.

He reached the outskirts of the village, again conscious of that strange restriction that seemed to hang over everything; it was as if he were entering some sort of void and it set up within him a faint disturbance. Once more he was struck by the abandoned appearance of it all. No living soul was in sight. Yet there were the rows of cultivated fields, the smoke winding up from a rock stack—the blacksmith shop, he noted—the curtained windows of the houses, a washing hanging on a line.

The first structures to his immediate right were vacant,

13

the door of the second one sagging drunkenly from a single leather hinge, windows gaping open. To his left stood a livery barn, but he was unable to see into its dark recesses and could not tell if there was man or beast inside.

A general store, judging by what he could see behind the windows, was at the end of the dusty street; some distance back of it was a steepled church, its once whitewashed walls now a neglected gray. Close-by were several smaller houses and huts.

On the opposite side of the street from the store was what looked to be a feed and seed merchant. Next to him, and coming back up the narrow separation, was the blacksmith shop that had sent up its guiding plume of black for him to follow. Next to that lean-to building was the two-story bulk of what served as a hotel. Beyond and around these major structures were more smaller houses—residences, Starbuck assumed.

He drew up across from the hotel, a curious fact dawning on him; none of the business places bore names or any lettered indication as to the nature of the establishment. It was as if the owners did not wish their identities known, nor care to divulge the nature of the trade they were engaged in.

Evidently it was up to any possible customer to ferret out the source for his needs. . . . That would be the case, Shawn reflected, where a stranger was concerned—and because no strangers ever visited the hidden valley with its bleak settlement, it posed no problem.

He dismounted slowly, digesting this all as his eyes covered the street, the windows of the buidings and houses, the doors that stood open in most instances to gather in any vagrant, cooling breeze.

No one had appeared—no man, no woman, no child. Not even a dog contested his arrival—an event that one could ordinarily expect to encounter upon riding into a town. Somewhere he could hear chickens clucking, and that homey sound did something to break the tension that, unknowingly, had built within him.

There were people—somewhere. They were simply avoiding him, keeping out of sight, afraid for one reason or another to make their presence known.

Why? Did it have to do with the carefully hidden entrance to the valley? He shrugged. There was a reason, a good one, no doubt—but it didn't concern him. Come daylight he'd be on his way, leaving them to their secret paradise.

Walking stiffly, bathed in sweat, he crossed the street to the hitchrack fronting what he was assuming to be a hotel. Winding the sorrel's leathers around the bar, he took his saddlebags and rifle, mounted the two steps to the porch. Pausing there for one more look up and down the street, he entered the open doorway.

☆ 3 ☆

The lobby was fairly large. It was stuffy with motionless, heated air; and light, entering through the doorway and a single window fronting on the street, only partly relieved the gray shadows streaking the area.

A bench and a few straight-backed chairs stood against the walls. A long, narrow table built from rough lumber was near the center and supplied surface for several yellowing almanacs.

Opposite the entrance a counter arrangement had been constructed. Half a dozen pegs, with keys dangling on rawhide string, protruded from a whitewashed board that was affixed prominently to the wall behind the improvised desk. It was as if the management wished to convey the impression that privacy was available on the premises—if little else.

Still conscious of the disturbing, eerie quiet, and wondering at the absence of life, Shawn crossed to the counter. There was no tap bell on the dusty board, and after a few moments he rapped sharply.

A door at the end of the lobby opened. A balding, cadaverous man, with the left sleeve of his butternut shirt hanging empty, reluctantly entered, made his way in behind the counter. He had small, dark eyes that peered out from beneath a shelf of ragged, graying brows in which Starbuck could read suspicion and mistrust.

"Need a room," Shawn said.

The man glanced beyond him to the street. "You alone?"

"I'm alone."

The hotel man frowned as if disbelieving. "You looking for somebody then—maybe figuring to meet them here?"

Sweaty, worn from the long hot day, hungry, Starbuck stirred impatiently. "No, I'm not looking for anybody. I'm by myself—and I don't expect to meet somebody. All I'm after is a good meal and a room for the night. Can you oblige me, or not?"

16

The man's shoulders lost some of their tense rigidity. Reaching back he took one of the keys from its peg, laid it on the counter.

"Room at the head of the stairs. I'll see you get some fresh water."

Shawn picked up the key. "There a stable out back? Horse of mine needs—"

"I'll see to him."

"He's the sorrel," Starbuck said, and then shrugged. There was no necessity for being so specific; the gelding was the only horse on the street. He turned for the stairs, paused, curiosity piquing him. "Town's deserted, seems. Something wrong?"

The clerk's face blanked, his eyes became expressionless. "Oh, folks are around somewheres," he said vaguely, and then manner changing, he came out from behind the counter. Extending his hand, he said, "Name's Simon Pierce. Yours?"

"Starbuck—Shawn Starbuck."

"Glad to meet you, Starbuck. Shawn. . . . That got something to do with the Indians?"

"Shawnee tribe. My ma took the name from that."

"What I figured. . . . Just passing through?"

"Be riding on in the morning. Want pay for the room now?"

Pierce wagged his head. "Morning'll be fine. Can settle up for the horse, too."

"You want me to register then?"

"Register? Oh—well, I don't keep no regular book like that. No need for it around here. Just forget it."

Starbuck hung the saddlebags over his shoulder, grasped the rifle by its action, moved for the steps. Again he hesitated, looked to Pierce, now heading for the front door.

"Soon as I put this gear in my room and wash up, I'll be wanting a meal. There a place to eat?"

Once more a stilled, thoughtful expression claimed the one-armed man's features. A strong flow of doubt seemed to tear at him, possess him, and then he shrugged as if dismissing it all.

"Ain't no restaurant, but we've got what you'd call a dining room." He pointed to a door at the south end of the lobby. "In there. The wife and daughter'll take care of you."

The room was dark, choked with stale trapped air.

17

Shawn tossed the leather pouches onto the bed, stood the rifle in a corner, and thinking of Pierce's strange actions, crossed to the single window. Throwing up the oilcloth shade, he drew back, absently watched the fine dust filter down onto the sill in a filmy sheet.

The hotel enjoyed few patrons, it was clear. He doubted the room had been occupied in months; and from the reaction of the townspeople to his arrival, it appeared they hadn't seen a stranger in years! Such was possible, he had to admit as he tugged at the window in an effort to loosen it in its frame, considering the hidden entrance to the valley.

There was a knock at the door, and propping the window open with a short length of wood provided for the purpose, he crossed the room and drew back the panel. No one was there but a bucket of water was waiting for him. Picking it up, he filled the china pitcher, poured the remainder into the companion bowl.

Washing his face and neck, hands and arms, he dried himself with the threadbare towel hanging from a hook above the washstand. . . . Later he'd strip, clean himself properly because there didn't seem to be much hope of getting a real bath in a tub at a barber shop.

Fact of the matter was, he hadn't noticed a barber along the street. He scratched at his jaw; there were quite a few odd things about the town—whatever its name was.

Pulling on his shirt, he hitched at the low slung forty-five hanging on his left hip, and leaving the room, descended to the lobby. There was no sign of Pierce, and walking to the front door, he glanced out. The sorrel was gone. He grunted in satisfaction at that. The big red horse needed looking after. He'd had a hard day. Wheeling, he recrossed the lobby to the door Simon had indicated, opened it, and entered.

He paused just inside. The room, smaller than the lobby and at the rear of the building, had four or five tables with accompanying quartets of chairs placed here and there. Three roughly dressed, hard-looking men occupied a corner position. All looked up at his entrance, studied him with calculating coldness.

A bottle of whiskey was on the table before them, and this, too, brought a realization to Shawn; there had been no saloons on the street either.

Briefly nodding to the trio, he turned to the opposite corner, sat down back to the wall so that he faced the entire room. It was a subconscious habit, one acquired possibly as a need always to be aware of his surroundings and of those who moved about him. It also satisfied a need to simply watch people and observe their ordinary actions. . . . A man riding an endless trail finds loneliness an ever present companion.

He felt the critical gaze of the hardcases still on him, and easing back in his chair, he returned their stare with unblinking assurance. At once all looked away. One, a dark man with a scruffy black beard and fish-cold gray eyes, reached for the bottle. The remnants of the meal they had just eaten were still before them.

The rider tipped the bottle to his lips, took a long pull. Immediately the man to his left, a thin, quiet individual with a scar tracing from the corner of an eye to the edge of his mouth, extended a hand for the liquor.

"All right, Abe, you don't have to hog it. Could save me and Bobby Joe a little."

Bobby Joe appeared to be the youngest of the three. He, too, was dark, but with a scanty growth of hair, and a way of nervously flipping his eyes about.

Shawn considered the men from hooded eyes. He wondered if they were local residents or if they, too, as had he, stumbled onto the hidden valley and its small settlement. Likely such was the truth. Somehow they didn't seem to belong. . . . A second thought came to Shawn; could they be the cause of the paralysis that gripped the town?

He shifted wearily, swung his glance to the wall to his right in which was the door that evidently led into the kitchen. Whatever—it was of no interest to him. He was there by accident, wished nothing but food, rest, and information as to how he could reach the Carazones Peaks country.

The kitchen door swung open. A girl, seventeen, possibly eighteen years of age, face flushed with heat, round, blue eyes bright, her lips set to a firm line, entered. Casting a sidelong glance at the three men in the corner, she started across the room for Starbuck.

This would be Simon Pierce's daughter, he guessed, and she was frightened. There was no doubt of that. He watched her approach, noting that she was pretty in a doll-like way, and had a neatly rounded figure that was not entirely concealed by the voluminous garment she wore.

As she passed the table where the men were, a laugh went up. Bobby Joe half rose, reached for her, saying

19

something in a low voice. The girl jerked away, cheeks flushing, the shine of fear brightening in her eyes.

She came to a halt before Starbuck, glared down at him. "Well?"

He studied her, faintly amused by the anger she was directing at him, and then said, "Supper, if it's all right with you. Steak, potatoes—plenty of both—and whatever else is handy. Like some light bread, but biscuits will do. Pot of coffee. Can talk about pie later."

The girl bobbed her head. "If you're wanting whiskey, we don't have any."

"Never mix my eating with my drinking," Starbuck drawled. He swung his glance to the men. "They giving you trouble?"

"No more than I can handle," she snapped, but she plainly was reluctant to recross the room and return to the kitchen.

"Expect you can. You'd be Simon Pierce's daughter."

"Yes, I'm Hetty. Why?"

"No reason. Took a room for the night and he mentioned you and your ma ran the dining room. This town got a name?"

Hetty Pierce slid a sidelong glance at the corner table. Bobby Joe was still hunched forward on his chair watching, waiting. Abe and the scar-faced one were slumped in their seats, heads slung low as if dozing.

"No, I guess it really hasn't," Hetty said, coming back to Starbuck. "This is what folks call the Hebren Valley. I suppose you could call the town that, too—only it's not exactly a town."

"Was wondering about that."

"We call it a Community—we're sort of a sect. Everyone works together, like a family. Combine our labor and share equally the fruits—that's the way Oram Grey—he's our Senior Elder—likes to put it."

"Those aren't regular stores along the street?"

"No, sometimes we call them that but they're more like warehouses or storage depots. Everything we produce is put into them, and we all draw what we need as time goes along."

Shawn nodded understandingly. He knew now why there were no names on the buildings, why there was so little activity.

"Noticed where a herd of cattle had been driven out. You raise beef, too?"

20

Hetty looked again at Bobby Joe. He still faced her, his hot, bold glance raking her continually.

"Some. The men—all the younger ones—drove our herd to market over a month ago and they're not back yet. First time we've ever sent cattle to market. We do more farming than anything else. How did you happen to come here?"

"Got myself lost looking for the Carazones Peaks country. Saw smoke and tracked it down. Was coming from your blacksmith shop. . . . Getting powerful hungry. You want me to walk you back to the kitchen?"

Hetty's lips tightened. "Never mind," she murmured, and turned away.

She walked straight at Bobby Joe and then, when almost upon him, veered suddenly, reached for a chair at an adjoining table. Sliding it toward him, she effectively blocked him off, and hurried on.

Bobby Joe's eyes flashed with anger, and then he laughed, slapped the top of the table. Settling back, he reached for the bottle, took a quick drink. The man with the scar stirred, looked up.

"What's biting you?"

"That there priss of a gal!" Bobby Joe replied, taking another swallow of the liquor. "Keeps waltzing me off."

The older man rubbed at his chin. "Was you smart, you'd leave her be—"

Bobby Joe snorted. "Rollie—the big know-it-all about women! When'd you get to be so smart?"

"Long time ago—and I've seen her kind before. Once knew a cowpoke that took a fancy to a girl like her. Just kept warting her all the time but she plain wouldn't have nothing to do with him. Then one day she got real sweet like and baked him a mistletoe pie—only she told him it was a gooseberry. Well, she wasn't bothered none by him no more after that 'cause it killed him dead. . . . You keep messing around and something like that's going to happen to you."

"Not her. She's just honing for me to take her. Playing it cozy, that's all."

"Acts to me like she don't favor you none a'tall."

"That's because you don't know nothing about women. Anyway, whether she's willing or not, it ain't nobody's business but mine. . . . Didn't hear you hollering when Abe took on that yellow-haired gal he keeps meeting up with."

"Different. She's a growed woman and looking to be

21

took. Plain she's been needing a buck young enough to do her some good for a long time, seeing as how she's got a husband more'n twicet her age. But this here Hetty, she's only a kid—"

"Kid—hell! And she's sure ready. Was watching her go to bed the other night and—"

"So that's where you was! Dammit, Bobby Joe, you cut out that tomfoolery—leastwise until Con gets here. Then if he says it's all right, then all right—but I ain't letting you mess things up until he does! Hear?"

"Sure, I'm hearing. . . . There ain't no chance of stirring up nothing."

"Hell there ain't!"

"You'll see. First thing you know I'll have her eating out of my hand like a little kitty cat. . . ."

Starbuck was listening idly. It sounded as if the men did belong in Hebren Valley, that Bobby Joe was endeavoring to make up to Hetty Pierce and was having no luck. But their words were harsh and they seemed not in character with the sort of persons he figured would populate the area. . . . Too, it had been fear he saw in Hetty's eyes—as well as those of Simon Pierce.

The kitchen door opened. Hetty, a platter heaped with food in one hand, a cup and saucer in the other, appeared, began to make her way warily toward Starbuck.

Bobby Joe came to his feet, a wicked grin on his lips. He lunged forward, caught the girl around the waist, and settled back onto his chair, drawing Hetty, precariously balancing the platter and the coffee, onto his lap.

"I think I'll just eat that there steak myself, honey-bunch," he said, laughing. "And you can feed it to me, whilst I tell you what you and me are going to do—"

Starbuck, anger rising within him at the abuse the girl was being compelled to endure as well as seeing his supper snatched away from him, rose quickly. In two long strides he crossed to where Hetty struggled to free herself of Bobby Joe's strong, roving hands.

Snatching the platter from her, Shawn jerked the rider's stained hat down over his eyes, wedging it tight to the nose, and pulled the girl free. Wheeling, he started back for his table, hearing the enraged cursing of Bobby Joe, the surprised questions of Abe and Rollie, once again aroused from their stupor.

On beyond the entrance to the kitchen Shawn could see the strained, worried face of Simon Pierce, and next to him a thinner, older edition of Hetty, her features also taut with fear.

The truth of the situation dawned upon Starbuck in that instant as he caught the look in the eyes of Hetty's parents. Rollie, Bobby Joe, Abe—they weren't local residents, members of the Hebrenite sect; they were outsiders, outlaws undoubtedly, who had moved in, probably during the absence of the settlement's younger men who were away on the cattle drive.

That they had terrorized the people was evident by the very fact that all were remaining hidden, unseen. The Pierces, being the operators of the hotel and the only place where meals could be obtained, were bearing the brunt of their presence. Such was particularly true where Hetty was concerned.

Shawn sighed inwardly. Regardless of where he went there was always trouble of some sort. It was impossible, it seemed, to move through life without encountering it, and try as he would to not become involved, he always ended up in the entanglement.

This time it would be different. This time he was going to stay out of it, come blizzard, blasphemy, or the rebuilding of Babylon. He'd eat, go to bed, sleep, and in the morning get the grub and information he needed—and ride out. The sooner he could get to Hagerman's Hash Knife Ranch and find out if Ben—or he guessed he should call him Damon Friend because that was the name that he was going by in New Mexico—was there, the better. If need be he'd—

"Look out!"

☆ 4 ☆

At Hetty's shrill warning, Shawn pivoted. Bobby Joe crashed into him from the left side, jarred him solidly. The plate of food slipped from his hand, fell to the floor.

Biting back his anger, mindful of his determination to not become involved, Starbuck righted himself, fell back a half step.

"No need for this," he said. "Was my supper—"

"The hell you say!" Bobby Joe shouted, and rushed in once more.

Shawn sidestepped easily, and then abruptly furious, he caught the rider by the arm, swung him around. Off balance, staggering, Bobby Joe rocked forward. Starbuck's knotted fist caught him with a down-sledging blow to the jaw, drove him to his hands and knees.

Rollie yelled something. Shawn glanced up quickly. Bobby Joe's two friends were on their feet but showed no indication of participating, only of shouting advice and encouragement to their champion, now shaking his head in an effort to clear it.

Shawn drew back, almost slipping on the mess underfoot. Still simmering, he leaned over, clamped strong fingers on the back of Bobby Joe's neck, and with a sweep of his booted foot, kicked the man's supporting arms from beneath him.

Bobby Joe flopped forward. Starbuck, dragging him around, shoved his face into the scramble of meat, gravy and fried potatoes, ground it about thoroughly.

"You wanted my supper," he snapped. "Now eat it!"

Bobby Joe, choking and spluttering, yelled a smothered oath, fought to escape the inexorable pressure of Shawn's grip on his neck.

Finally satisfied, Starbuck released his hold, stepped back. His anger had cooled somewhat, and after a moment he drew a chair from an adjoining table, sat down, and motioned to Hetty.

"Be obliged if you'll bring me another order of the same."

The girl, wide-eyed, a frozen smile parting her lips,

nodded woodenly. "Yes, sir," she murmured, and wheeling, hurried off into the kitchen, brushing by her stony-faced parents without a word.

Shawn slumped in his chair but at coiled-spring alert, watched Bobby Joe pull himself to his knees. Bits of potato clung to his thin beard and crumbs of mashed biscuit plastered his forehead and cheeks. Grease smeared over his face gave it a dull shine.

Twisting his head, he brought his burning eyes to bear on Starbuck. Hate throbbed in their depths as he scraped the mess from his features with a cupped hand.

"Goddamn you—you son of a bitch!" he mouthed. "I'll kill you for that! I'll—"

Starbuck shrugged. "Get some help," he said indifferently.

Instantly, without rising, Bobby Joe threw himself at Shawn. Arms outflung, he encircled Starbuck's legs, and pushing hard with his feet, toppled man, chair, and all to the floor.

Starbuck kicked free as he crashed to the hard boards. Catlike, he rolled to his feet. He heard a sound behind him, jerked to one side, took the butt of Abe's pistol aimed at his head, on a shoulder. Spinning, he drove a rock-hard right fist into the older man's belly, sent him stumbling and retching for breath back into his chair. Instantly he wheeled to face Bobby Joe surging in.

The young outlaw staggered him with a good, roundhouse right to the jaw. Subconsciously, he dropped back two steps, fell into the cocked stance of a trained boxer—just as he'd been taught to do by his father.

Be smart. You get hurt, throw up your guard, and stall—give your head time to clear. That was what old Hiram, who had received his training from an English champion, had told him. And Hiram Starbuck knew well the art; while never boxing professionally, he had prided himself on the weekly exhibition matches he had put on in the town near their Ohio farm.

So proficient was Hiram and so appreciative his admirers that they one day presented him with an ornately decorated silver belt buckle upon which was imposed the ivory figure of a boxer in the familiar fist-raised stance of the expert. It was now one of Shawn's prized possessions and worn constantly by him.

"Well, hi-di-hi!" Rollie yelled from the table as Bobby Joe paused. "Would you look at what we got here!"

Starbuck continued to circle, backing carefully, allowing his faculties to return to normal, maintaining a close watch on his rear to be certain no one would slip in behind him again.

"One of them fancy-dan fighters we been hearing about!" Bobby Joe shouted, taking up the derision. He was making a great show of it, projecting it not only to his companions but also to the Pierces gathered in the doorway of the kitchen.

"Here's where I show you folks how a real fighting man does a job—and does it without all that running and dancing!"

Shawn considered the outlaw with taut amusement. His head had cleared entirely and he awaited only an opening to step in, finish off Bobby Joe, and have done with it. Abe and Rollie had pulled back, seemingly confident now that their partner could take care of himself.

Abruptly Bobby Joe pushed in, fists swinging. Shawn feinted neatly, crossed with a slashing left that brought quick blood to the corner of the man's mouth, followed with a right that smacked solidly into the side of the head.

Bobby Joe yelled, halted flat-footed. He shook himself as if in disbelief. He hadn't touched Starbuck, yet had taken two shocking blows. Wheeling, he swore loudly, came in fast.

Once more Shawn, shifting like a fleeting shadow in sunlight, moved in, smashed a combination left and right to Bobby Joe's face, again danced away. The young outlaw bellowed his frustration, spun, threw himself at Starbuck. Shawn, taking several wild, aimless blows that did no harm, ducked low, began hammering the man mercilessly about the head, the belly, and the ribs. He kept at it for several seconds, driving like the pistons of a locomotive. Bobby Joe began to wilt. Shawn moved lightly away.

Wiping at the sweat clothing his face, sucking for wind, he watched the outlaw narrowly. The man's knees were trembling, seemed hardly able to support him. He'd had about enough. Slowly then Bobby Joe sank to hands and knees. His head came forward, hair stringing down over his glazed eyes. Rollie was yelling at him to get up, to show the fancy dan a thing or two—to fight.

Bobby Joe seemed not to hear. He remained motionless. Shawn moved forward. Raising a leg, he placed his foot against the outlaw's shoulder, shoved hard. Bobby Joe went over sideways onto his back, arms and legs outflung.

Rollie cursed, came in fast. Starbuck, not expecting the charge, attempted to sidestep, slipped on the grease-smeared floor, half fell. He took a sharp blow to the ear from the scar-faced man, another high on the head.

He winced as Rollie drove the toe of a boot into his belly. Pain roared through him as a second kick found his groin. Buckling, he pivoted away, felt the outlaw's weight come down upon him as the man threw himself upon his back, looped an arm around his neck.

Furious, struggling to keep his footing, Starbuck finally got himself firmly stanched. Reaching up he grasped Rollie's forearm, locked tight against his windpipe, tore it loose. Bending in a quick, humping motion, he swung his weight forward, threw his strength into his hands. Rollie went soaring over his head, crashed into the nearby wall.

A clattering of dishes sounded as shelves on the opposite side of the partition spilled their loads. Shawn, thoroughly aroused, wheeled to face Abe, saw the outlaw, gun in hand, rising from his chair.

The outlaw's features still had a pasty color, effects of the blow he'd taken, but there was a hard, murderous glint in his eyes. Shawn's hand swept down for the holster on his hip. Alarm rocked him. The forty-five was not there. He'd lost it sometime during the scuffle. He looked hurriedly about, spotted the weapon under the table to his left—two long strides away.

"Don't try it!" Abe muttered.

In that same instant Shawn heard Hetty shout, saw motion from the corner of his eye as she threw the cup and saucer she held straight at the man. Instantly he lunged for his pistol, snatched it up, and rolled away, upending the table, sending several chairs skittering across the floor.

Flat on his belly, forty-five leveled, he faced Abe. The rider, pistol hanging at his side, was mopping coffee from his eyes with a forearm. Rising slowly, he nodded at the man coldly.

"Put that iron away—unless you figure to use it."

Silent, Abe slid the weapon back into its holster. Starbuck waggled the barrel of his pistol at Bobby Joe, now struggling to his feet, and then at the scarred Rollie, who lay motionless against the base of the wall.

"Get 'em out of here—"

Abe turned reluctantly, knelt beside Rollie, and shook the man to half consciousness. Rising, he beckoned to Bobby Joe for assistance.

Somewhat unsteady the younger rider crossed to where his friend had pulled the scar-faced Rollie to a sitting position, and draping one of the man's limp arms about his neck, assumed a share of the burden. Together they got him upright and started for the door.

Hetty barred their way. "I'll have a dollar pay from each of you," she said, eyes flashing. "This is one meal you're paying for!"

The outlaws came to a halt. Abe groaned, glanced to Bobby Joe. The young outlaw's lips drew back into a sneer.

"The hell you say! We ain't paying for—"

"You are this time—and from now on, else you stay out!"

Bobby Joe stared at her, shook his head. "Go to the devil," he said, and nodding to Abe, resumed the slow march for the lobby door.

Shawn, hand resting on the butt of his holstered weapon, moved toward them. "You heard the lady. Pay up."

Again the three men came to a stop. Bobby Joe's face was taut, and his dark eyes glittered as he swung them to Starbuck.

"Mister, you're sure bucking for the graveyard!"

"Maybe," Shawn replied quietly. "Meantime, you'll pay what you owe."

Abe shrugged, dug into his pocket with a free hand, and produced several coins. Dropping three silver dollars on the table beside him, he touched Starbuck with a hating glance, and then again the outlaws moved on.

Silent, fingers still hooked lightly about the handle of his pistol, Shawn watched the men pass through the doorway into the dark lobby. He did not stir until he had seen their dark silhouettes block briefly the street entrance to the

28

hotel and then disappear into the open. Only then did he turn and resume his seat at the table.

"Like that meal now," he said tiredly to Hetty and her parents, standing quietly to one side.

He was beat, hungry, and uncomfortable from the dried sweat plastering his body. He ached dully in several places from the blows delivered by Bobby Joe and Rollie, and there was a stinging along his jaw where a ring one of the outlaws was wearing had etched a deep scratch.

What the hell was wrong with him? Was he trouble prone—as some people seemed to be accident prone? What sort of freak luck forever attended him, drew him into someone else's problems? For once—just once—he'd like to be left alone to go about his business and—

"Mr. Starbuck—reckon I ought to thank you."

It was *Mr. Starbuck* now, Shawn noticed as Simon Pierce's voice cut into his thoughts. The art of courtesy drilled into him by his schoolteacher mother and the need to employ it when dealing with others, regardless of circumstances, pushed the sardonic irritation from him.

"No need," he murmured, not missing the thread of disfavor in the tone of the one-armed man—and misinterpreting it. "Whatever the damage is, add it to my bill."

He fell silent again, watched Hetty gather up the silver dollars, move toward her father, hand extended.

"Damage won't amount to anything," she said, catching the last of his words. Her eyes still glowed from the excitement. "Worth it anyway. It's the first time they've been taken down since they rode in here—weeks ago!"

Simon Pierce cupped the silver coins in his hand, studied them with no expression. "Sorry this had to happen. . . . Afraid it'll mean more trouble for you."

Starbuck smiled wryly. Through the kitchen doorway he could see Mrs. Pierce busy at the stove. The smell of frying potatoes and sizzling steak wafted to him, further whetting his appetite.

"I'll hear from them—no doubt of that. Their kind never let things lie. Have to get in their licks, somehow. . . . But it's nothing to fret over. Who are they?"

"Outlaws—army deserters. There's more of them coming here. They're hanging around, waiting for them."

"This a regular thing?"

"No, first time for these three. Seems Kilrain—he's one of them they're waiting for—was here during the war.

Army patrol or something. They stumbled onto the valley by accident."

Shawn nodded absently. "Same as I did."

"Reckon so. Name of Kilrain's sort of familiar. May recognize him when I see him again. He's the head of a gang of outlaws. He decided our valley, being hid away like it is, would make a fine hideout. Going to use it for their headquarters. The three that you run into tonight came on ahead, are waiting for him and the rest to show up. . . . Leastwise, that's the way we figure it from what they've told us and the scraps of talk we've picked up."

"Sounds like you don't want them around. Why don't you run them out?"

"With what—and who?" Hetty demanded in a bitter voice before her father could speak.

Simon Pierce frowned, glanced to his daughter reprovingly. "Never mind, girl. . . . What she means is, there's not a weapon among us—in the whole valley, unless you want to call axes and tools like that, weapons. You see, we don't believe in violence."

"And if we had guns there's nobody around to use them," Hetty added. "Every man able to ride a horse— even the larger boys—are on the cattle drive. We couldn't run them off even if we had the means."

Starbuck shifted on his chair. "When the others return, you can straighten it all out."

"Likely," Simon Pierce said, "but that won't be for a couple more weeks, maybe longer."

"And by then," Hetty finished, "those cutthroats will have settled in good and we'll never be rid of them! They'll own the valley and everyone and everything in it."

"Looks like you'd best change some of your thinking," Shawn said, glancing hopefully toward the kitchen where Mrs. Pierce was removing a pan from the oven of the stove. "Hardcases like Bobby Joe and his pals only understand force. You can't go easy on them or they'll run you right into the ground."

"We've been folks who've lived without violence for generations," Pierce said slowly. "And we've survived, even those who set themselves against us and oppressed us. Expect we can do so again where Kilrain and his gang are concerned."

"Generations?" Starbuck repeated. "You been here that long?"

"Not exactly right here all that time. Our Family, as we

30

call it, got started in Pennsylvania about a hundred years ago."

"Probably would've been smart to stay there. Better chance for your way of living than here where a man has to depend pretty much on a gun."

"It wasn't exactly a single group then—just several different families all living in one part of the country. Floods hit every summer, Indian troubles, now and then droughts—always something that kept wiping them out.

"Was a man by the name of Hebren—Malachi Hebren who was sort of the leader. One day he got the idea of them all banding together, throwing what they owned into one basket, so to speak, and then pooling their labor so as to stand up against misfortune as a single party instead of as individuals. Thus, sharing, nobody would ever want. Idea worked, and later on they got to calling it Hebren's Family, and those who were in it—my folks at that time—Hebrenites.

"Family soon got pretty big and some of them moved to Missouri, but that state got all torn up by the talk of war, some folks being for the Union, some siding with the South. Came down to where a man had to decide where he stood and declare himself.

"That's when we picked up and moved out. Hetty was just a little one then, two, three years old. Leader of our Family, the Senior Elder he's called, was and still is Oram Grey. He'd heard of this country and about this valley. Didn't know exactly where it was, and we spent the best part of a year hunting it, but we finally come across it, moved in and settled down to living the way we figure folks ought to live—at peace with each other."

"We can't look at it that way any longer, papa," Hetty said impatiently. "They've spoiled it—these outlaws—and we're either going to have to fight them or pick up and move on again—just like the Family did in Missouri and Illinois and Pennsylvania, and all the other places where we've been set upon and hounded into leaving."

Simon Pierce nodded sadly. "If we have to move on, that's what we'll do. Be hard this time, however. This here's a beautiful valley and it's been mighty good to us. We've prospered—crops, cattle, our people—"

"What's left of them," Hetty said scornfully. "The young ones, leastwise the boys, run off as soon as they're big enough. . . . I would, too, if I could."

"Hush, girl," Pierce said. "Your day will come, your time to marry, have your own—"

"My time's come and gone! There's no men left my age that I can take as a husband. They've all gone, and there's only old Ezrah Vinsent and—"

"Hush!" Pierce said again, more sternly. "Time will take care of your needs, and you will be provided for."

"Not with a husband—that's for sure! Youngest unmarried man in the Family now is Ezrah and he's near seventy. The oldest boy is thirteen. . . . What kind of a choice is that?"

"Time will provide," Pierce insisted doggedly. "Problems are solved by patience and understanding. Always have been. Yours will be also."

"Maybe, but before all the younger men weren't leaving as soon as they were big enough."

Starbuck, weary of the bickering that had nothing to do with him, looked again to the kitchen. The Hebrenites and Hetty had trouble, but there was nothing he could do to help them. And as Simon Pierce had said, matters had worked themselves out in the past, likely they would do so in the future. One thing did stir interest within him, however.

"How've you managed to keep this place a secret all these years? Know you keep the trail blocked and the entrance hidden, but expect you have to send out now and then for some supplies, things you can't make or grow, like coffee."

"Mostly we get along without the things we can't provide, but you're right, there are a few items we must buy in the outside world. . . . Window glass, iron, a few other things. Oram Grey sees to it, and only those appointed by him are permitted to leave the valley for such purposes."

"It's—it's like a prison," Hetty murmured, biting at her lower lip. "A terrible prison!"

"We have two men who do what freighting is necessary," Pierce continued, ignoring the girl. "And the cattle drive—our first—is led by Tolliver Grey, Oram's son. The men and the boys with him, and the freighters, will never speak of the valley. It is bred into them—and they know the value of secrecy. Nobody will ever learn of the place from them."

"Those outlaws found it."

"An accident, Kilrain's coming here. Those are the

32

things we can not protect ourselves against—and it may cause us to move once more."

"Was that army patrol the first to stumble onto your valley in all the years that you've been here?"

"The first and last until Bobby Joe and Abe and Rollie rode in—and you, of course. Their coming was no accident. Kilrain told them how to find it."

Shawn could understand why the valley had gone unnoticed. The surrounding country, wild, desolate, and heat ravaged, extended no invitation to travelers. To the contrary, likely all avoided it as they would the plague.

"It'll make a good hideout for Kilrain and his bunch," Shawn commented. "You won't find any posses wanting to hunt the country around here for them. Might call your valley an outlaw's heaven."

"Especially when they'll have the whole town waiting on them hand and foot, looking after their needs even when it comes to women like Esther Grey—"

"Hetty!"

The sharpness in Simon Pierce's voice stilled the girl's tongue for the first time. Suddenly downcast, she turned away.

"I'll see if your supper isn't about ready," she murmured to Shawn, and moved off toward the kitchen.

Pierce watched her go, shook his head. "Sometimes I think being young is the hardest time of life. There's so much to do, but so little permitted. I'm often sorry for them."

"She's right about one thing," Starbuck said. "Sure no business of mine, but you won't be able to keep your young people much longer under your thumb, the way you have. Losing them already, in fact. Know I'd find it hard to stay cooped up in one place all my life, no matter how fine everything was."

"Even if you had no worries about where your meals would come from, where you would sleep, or how you would get clothes to put on your back or boots on your feet? We have our own schoolteachers who work from the best books we're able to get. Our women—all of them— are expert in medicine, better than many doctors, and can handle any problem. Every need of our people is cared for.

"In the world outside, a man's got to have money to live and to support his family with. In our Community there is no such thing as want—or worry over it. The

33

Family shares equally all that is possessed. Nobody has any need for money, just as nobody ever suffers or goes without."

Shawn leaned back. He could see Hetty dishing up his food, heaping a platter high.

"Don't think your way's exactly new," he said. "Indians've been doing it that way, more or less, for a long time."

"And you don't agree that it's good—better than the hard scramble to stay alive that outsiders have to face?"

"Can't agree to anything that keeps a man tied down against his will. If he likes your way—fine. It's his life, his business. But I can't see penning him or any of your folks here unless they want it that way."

"You were raised different, taught the kind of life most people face—slaving to make a living, sometimes starving and suffering and never knowing the quiet, peaceful paths that men are supposed to enjoy. . . . The sort of life you speak of is a struggle—one where a man is actually at war with another in his fight to provide for himself and those who depend upon him."

"Which, to my way of thinking is how it ought to be," Shawn replied. "Man should stand on his own two feet, rely on himself and nobody else."

"The old way," Pierce said wearily. "It's not the right one simply because it was what you were taught, what others you know do. . . . That it is what others have always done don't make it right."

Hetty emerged from the kitchen bringing the platter—well filled as before with meat, potatoes, string beans, and thin slices of onion—in one hand. In the other she carried a tin of biscuits smeared with honey.

Brushing aside her father, she set the food on the table in front of Shawn and moved away, making room for her mother.

"My wife, Patience," Simon said, remembering no introduction had been made.

The older woman nodded to Starbuck, waved him back into his chair as he half rose to acknowledge her.

"I'm thanking you for what you done—whether the men folk like it or not," she said smilingly. "And this is my own special way," she added, placing a saucer with a thick wedge of hot apple pie capped with melting butter near his plate. "Hetty, bring the coffee."

The girl turned away at once. Patience, bulky in her

Mother Hubbard garment, swung about to face her husband.

"And Simon, you've done nothing but nigh talk Mr. Starbuck to death. Now you can do something good for him. He'll be wanting a bath soon's he's finished with his vittles. You get yourself busy and lug the tub and some buckets of water up to his room. Hear?"

☆ 6 ☆

Shawn grinned his approval of Patience's crisp words, glanced at the appetizing food, and rose.

"Something wrong?" Hetty asked anxiously.

Starbuck moved for the door and into the lobby. "Figured I'd best have a look, be sure I'm not about to have visitors. Like to eat this meal in peace."

The girl followed to the entrance of the hotel. A few persons were now in the street, conversing, casting glances furtively in their direction. Others were coming. Looking around Shawn could see no signs of the outlaws.

"Bobby Joe—and the others, they camped in town?"

Hetty pointed to the lower end of the street, to the three vacant shacks Shawn had noticed as he rode in. "Last house—the Mason place. Living in there. Use the middle one for their horses."

Starbuck settled his gaze on the end structure. A lamp burned somewhere inside, and after a moment he saw movement behind the dirt-streaked window. He grunted, satisfied.

"Looks like they're set for the night," he said, and turned back into the lobby.

Hetty hesitated. "If you like, I'll stay here, keep watch."

"No need," he replied. "They'll be looking for me, but I expect they've had enough until morning."

Hetty Pierce laughed, and together they returned to the dining room. Simon had disappeared and Patience, on her hands and knees, with scrub brush and bucket of soapy water, was cleaning the mess on the floor. She straightened up as they entered.

"Everything all right?"

"Everything's fine," Shawn said, and with a thankful sigh, sat down and began to eat.

Hetty fell to helping her mother, first assisting with the cleaning chore, then removing the dishes and scraps from the table the outlaws had used. The food was excellent, done to perfection, and Shawn, after days on the trail eating his own cooking, made the most of each bite.

Halfway through, muted voices in the lobby snared his attention. Immediately he got to his feet and crossed to the connecting doorway, a quick caution laying itself upon him. . . . He could have figured wrong about the outlaws. Perhaps they weren't waiting until daylight after all.

It was Simon, along with several bearded men and a few elderly women. They ceased their talking when he appeared. Pierce, stepping forward, lifted his hand for attention.

"This is Mr. Starbuck," he said. And then turning to Shawn, "Like to have you meet these folks." He pointed to a lean, very erect man with a sharp, heavily lined face, alert black eyes, and snow white hair and beard.

"This is Oram Grey, our Senior Elder."

Grey extended a horny hand, gravely clasped Shawn's fingers in a surprisingly strong grasp. The man would be at least eighty—possibly more, Starbuck thought.

"Glad to meet you, Mr. Starbuck."

"My pleasure," Shawn replied, thinking of the wedge of apple pie cooling all too rapidly on his table. He shifted his attention to the next man, one of only a few years less age. He was small, had an apple-round head, craggy features, and long trailing moustache to match a spade beard.

"Jaboe McIntyre. He looks after our feed and seed warehouse. Runs our grist mill."

His grip, too, was strong. Starbuck looked to the next individual.

"Micah Jones, our blacksmith, and jack-of-all trades. Can make just about anything a man wants, and does—including the hide shoes we wear."

There was no difficulty in determining Jones's calling; large, thick torso, powerful shoulders and arms, he could have been nothing else.

"Ezrah Vinsent, the storekeeper where supplies are kept."

Hetty had spoken of Vinsent, Shawn recalled. Something about him being the only available bachelor in the valley. . . . Seventy years old, she'd said. He had an odd shade of blue eyes, sandy hair, and a ruddy complexion. Short and squat he could be no taller than Hetty herself.

"There're a few more Elders but they ain't around right

now. Oram's son, Tolliver, and Charlie Crissman, to mention a couple."

Starbuck bobbed his head. "My pleasure to meet all of you. Now, if you'll excuse me, I'll—"

"We've been told of your encounter with the men who have moved in on us," Oram Grey said in a deep-toned, carefully modulated voice. It was evident he had received better than an average education—a tribute apparently to the quality of the Hebrenite schoolteachers. "I fear you have let yourself in for great trouble."

Shawn's shoulders stirred indifferently. "Something I've gotten used to. . . . Now, if you'll excuse me, I'll finish my supper. Was a pleasure to meet you all."

Wheeling, he returned to the table, sat down. Shortly the talking in the lobby resumed.

He finished his meal, superbly topped off by the apple pie and a second cup of coffee—which undoubtedly was something of a luxury in the valley because it was an article that had to be brought in—and rising, looked expectantly toward the kitchen. Neither Hetty nor her mother were in evidence to accept his pay for the meal. Dropping a dollar on the table, he pivoted on a heel and made his way through the lobby to the street.

A coolness had settled over the land and the pale glow of a three-quarter moon was lighting the fields and softening the harsh, square lines of the buildings, and transforming the country beyond into a silvered, undulating sea. . . . Far up the valley a cow lowed mournfully.

The warm, velvet quiet of the night, the good smells of the earth, the muted noises—it all made him think of Muskingum, of the farm along the river, and of the times long ago.

His mother, Clare, tall, her gray eyes filled with those shadows that lent them a mysterious beauty, would be finishing up in the kitchen after the evening meal. His father—strong, iron-willed yet strangely sentimental— would be smoking his pipe in serene contentment as he sat in the chair he'd built under the apple tree that shaded the house.

And Ben—solemn faced, intent, and stubbornly independent—likely he'd be off to himself, dreaming the dreams that were to take him away soon after their mother died.

It would have been a quiet hour there, too. Cool and pleasant, with the kindness of night closing in silently to bring an end to day. Chickens would be murmuring sleepily on their roosts. The cows and big-hoofed thick-bodied work horses—animals with bottom, his father would say—could be heard munching solidly at their rations of grain in the barn. Overhead the last crows would be stringing raggedly across the dark sky for their night's perch in the tall sycamores growing along the river.

It had been a good life despite the hard labor and the occasional violent clashes of will between Ben and their father. . . . And then one day it was all over; it was of the past. He was grown, footloose, searching the length and breadth of the land for a brother who was never there.

Was there any use, any point in continuing such a seemingly hopeless quest? Should he heed those who often told him that he was wasting his life away, frittering the young years into old age, to awaken suddenly one day and find life gone and he with nothing to show for it? Should he—

Motion inside the old Mason house at the end of the street drew his interest. Lamplight lay against the window in a yellow sheen, filled the rectangle of the doorway and spilled out into the small front yard. Bobby Joe stepped into the open, stood quiet in the deepening night, face turned toward the hotel. Shawn, not certain if the outlaw could see him, held himself still.

Something was said by one of the outlaw's companions inside the structure. Bobby Joe wheeled lazily, sauntered back through the doorway, and was lost to sight. . . . Could the outlaws be planning to seek him out, square accounts that very night after all? He still doubted it. They would wait, pick a better time, hoping for a moment when they would not be expected.

As if to verify that conclusion, the light in the shack winked out. Shawn continued to watch the place for another five minutes, both the front and a portion of the building's rear being visible in the moonlight, and when he saw no movement, concluded he had nothing to fear until morning. Coming about, he entered the hotel.

There was still no one in sight as he crossed the lobby, mounted the stairway, and entered his quarters. Simon had been there. A large wooden tub stood in the center of the room. It was filled to half capacity. Alongside stood two buckets of additional water. Several thick towels and a bar of soap lay on the bed.

The Pierces—at least Patience and Hetty—had gone all

out to show their appreciation for what he had done. When it came to Simon, he wasn't so sure. Nor could he be certain about Oram Grey and the other Hebrenite Elders. He saw no thanks in their eyes and heard no words of praise when he met them in the lobby.

It didn't matter. Tomorrow he'd be gone, and the Hebren Valley would be behind him—just a recollection. Shrugging, he pulled off his clothing, stepped into the tub. The water was cool, refreshing, and taking up the small brick of soap, he began to scrub himself. After a thorough going over, he reached for one of the buckets, poured its contents over his head, and settled back, enjoying the pure luxury of the moments.

An ease crept in, possessed him, relieving the tension, the stiffness of sweat and dust, the dull ache of muscle and bone put to test during the encounter with the outlaws. ... It was good to just soak, let his mind lie idle, not think.

He remained in the tub for a good half hour, then rising, toweled off with the coarse cloths provided, and drew on a clean pair of light drawers. After that he dug out his razor from the depths of the saddlebags, and despite the lack of hot water, scraped the stubble of whiskers from his face.

He took the next few minutes to check over the contents of his pack, rearranging for convenience's sake as well as taking note of the things he needed and that, hopefully, he would be able to obtain from the settlement supply store in the morning.

Finally satisfied, he sat down on the edge of the bed, pleasantly tired, relaxed, and at peace, and thought about the Pierces and the rest of the persons living in Hebren Valley. That they faced a serious crisis was undeniable.

It boiled down to simple facts; they could not retain possession of the valley, continue the pacifist way of life they fancied unless they were willing to fight to preserve it—and this they could not and would not do. Violence was no part of their creed—even if the avoidance of such cost them home and all possessions.

And regardless of the outcome of the problem with the outlaws, the day was coming when the secret of the valley's location would be out. The word would leak somehow, and in a land spreading westward hungrily, with thousands of hopeful souls seeking land and a new life, it would be impossible to preserve the immunity.

The quiet rap of knuckles on the door brought Starbuck to his feet. He remained motionless for a time until the careful knocking sounded again. Quietly, he drew on his pants, and lifting the forty-five from its holster hanging from the bedpost, he crossed to the door.

Once again the rapping came, insistent but cautious. Shawn laid his hand on the knob. "Who is it?"

"Oram Grey," a low voice replied. "Important that I talk to you."

Shawn turned the key in the lock, drew back the door. Oram Grey, his lean face bleak and drawn, stepped inside quickly, closed the panel with his shoulders.

Starbuck, irritation showing in the tightening muscles of his jaw, eyed the man narrowly and dropped his pistol back into its leather sheath. He was tired, was looking forward to a much needed rest—and in no mood for a dressing down over the encounter he'd had with the outlaws. He hadn't asked for it; it had simply come to him and it wasn't in him to back off when pressed. If that went counter to the Hebrenite way of life, it was simply too bad.

The elderly man crossed to the washstand, reached up to the lamp bracketed above it, and turned up the wick, brightening the flame. He nodded to Shawn.

"Eyes are not what they used to be—and I like to see a man good when I'm talking to him. Can read the truth in his face sometimes when you can't hear it."

Starbuck's shoulders stirred. Crossing his arms, he leaned against the wall, features patient.

"Know it's late," Grey murmured, "and that you're tired. But this is important to me—to everyone in the valley. I hope you'll listen."

With no particular show of interest, Shawn said, "What's on your mind?"

Oram Grey reached deep inside himself for a full breath, squared his slight frame. "I need your help."

"Mine? Don't see how I can help."

"Way you handled those outlaws is proof that you can—if you will. Simon Pierce told me—all of us—what you did. Came to me that you were the answer to the problem that threatens my people."

A stir of suspicion moved through Shawn. "Meaning what?"

"You can rid us of them."

Surprise jolted Starbuck. He studied the older man

42

closely. "Thought you were against a thing like that. Way Simon talked, you'd do anything to avoid violence."

"Simon told you what is true—and you'll get no thanks from the other Elders, or even the Family—"

"Then how is it you, the leader of them all, can ask me to fight—kill, actually, because that's what it'll take—for you?"

Oram Grey turned about slowly. Drawing aside the curtain, he stared into the paleness outside the window.

"Comes a time when a man must make a choice for the good of those who trust in him. We are against violence, yes. Our history is that we have often moved, forsaken all we owned and held dear, to avoid it."

"Then how can you justify asking me to fight for you now?"

"Before the others, I can't. To myself I can. I feel, honestly in my heart, that it is best. I am going against my own principles, and those that I teach and advocate, and that have been drilled into us all from the beginning—but for the good of all I believe it must be done."

Starbuck considered in silence. Then, "Nobody else knows about this—your coming here, I mean?"

The old man shook his head. "No one. And should you agree to my offer, no one must ever know what I did, that I hired you to do this job."

Shawn again leaned back against the wall. "I'm not a gunslinger."

Grey's black eyes were small points beneath their shelf of shaggy brows. "Even if it meant saving the lives of many fine people?"

"Hardly come to that—"

"Afraid it will before it's done with. This Kilrain who is coming will take his advantage of us and our beliefs. He knows we are pacifists, that we will knuckle under and not oppose him and his men. Thus they will be able to do with us as they wish."

"Answer to that is to send word to the nearest lawman, have him come in, take care of them for you."

Grey said, "No," quickly, as if alarmed. Then, "That would prove as fatal to us as the outlaws themselves. It would reveal the location of the valley, and we would soon be overrun by outsiders—"

"Most outsiders, as you call them, aren't like this Kilrain and his bunch. There're a lot of fine people around looking for a place to stop, build a home, who'd be a credit to your valley."

Oram was silent, reserving whatever thoughts he had on the matter to himself. Then, "Will you listen to my offer?"

Starbuck moved away from the wall, the weariness riding him, dragging at his tall frame. Nodding patiently, he sat down on the edge of the bed.

"Already told you how I feel about it, but go ahead."

"Thank you," Grey said. "As I've pointed out, we'll be helpless before a man like Kilrain and the ones who'll be with him. Not that we're afraid; fear has nothing to do with it. It's simply that we have no understanding of violence and it's against our nature and upbringing to involve ourselves in it.

"However, with all that is happening—our young folks leaving, our people growing old, dying out—I feel that I should take steps to preserve our way of life. . . . I owe it to all those who have gone before me, and to those who now look to me for guidance."

"Meaning you would sanction violence in order to preserve a sect that is against violence?"

"In plain language, yes. That is where you could help. The need is to rid the valley of the outlaws—those who are here now as well as Kilrain and the others he is bringing with him. Once here, they must not be permitted to leave. If we let them escape, they will tell others of the valley and it will no longer be a haven for us."

"Which adds up to killing them all—every one of them."

"I'm afraid so. It's the only solution."

Shawn considered the old man, feeling a thread of compassion course through him. Oram Grey, the trusted leader, the infallible teacher and chief advocate of the peaceful life, recognized the inadequacy of this belief when threatened by the presence of a ruthless outlaw gang; and so dedicated to his people and their faith was he that he was willing to compromise himself and his ideals to preserve that faith.

"You must understand that the others in the valley can never know that I came to you—the reasons undoubtedly are clear. For your services, you will be paid well. I don't know how much money you would expect. The amount is entirely up to you—and it will be met. Cash will be available when my son and the others return from selling the cattle."

Starbuck shifted wearily. "I'll say it again, I'm no hired killer."

"Not like I was asking you to rid us of men, but of scum-rats the country'd be better off without."

"Not questioning that, but a man's a human being regardless of whether he's good or bad."

"But if the price was high enough—"

"Got nothing to do with it!" Shawn exclaimed angrily, rising. "You don't have enough money to turn me into a murderer! Nobody has."

"Even when it means so much to many—to half a hundred honest, hard-working, God-fearing people—who without your help will be at the mercy of these outlaws?"

"Don't put it on my back. Go to the law."

"You can be the law. I'll appoint you as our town marshal. Nobody must know, of course—"

"Still be murder—and I'm not about to pin on a paper star and masquerade as a lawman to cover it up. Be willing to help in any other way you want. . . . Somebody said you thought Kilrain and the others were army deserters. When I ride out, I can swing by the nearest post, advise the authorities, and have them send a detail to pick them up. Or I'll find a sheriff or federal marshal for you."

"No—we'd be no better off. The valley would be overrun. It no longer would be ours—a secret place where we can live in peace."

"You're going to lose that secret anyway, no matter how it works out, same as you need to make some changes in your thinking. Backing away from trouble won't work in this world today. Everything's changed."

"I realize that, but after all that's been taught the Family, the—the code we've learned to live by. I just can't suddenly turn my back on the faith and tell them it's all wrong."

"You're only fooling them, making it harder when you don't. Faith's a fine thing, but it won't keep others from coming here, and it sure won't keep outlaws from running over you. Best thing you and your people can do is face up to the facts—in one way or another you've got to fight to live the way you want."

Oram Grey again looked through the window. Off in the distance a light moved slowly, jerkily across a field; someone with a lantern.

"There's no chance of you changing your mind?"

Shawn shook his head. "No—not to do what you're asking."

Grey moved slowly toward the door, a bent, very old man under the massive burden that had abruptly fallen upon his frail shoulders. He paused, one hand resting on the knob.

"Obliged to you for listening. Somehow I feel better."

"Only wish there was a way I could help. The army or some lawman—that's the only answer. They'd keep it quiet if you'd tell them."

"Perhaps, but there'd be nothing for sure. And Kilrain and the others—they'd talk if only to spite us."

"Expect you're right there."

Grey turned to the door, drew it open a small crack, once more hesitated. "My coming here—talking—you won't mention it to anyone?"

"You've got my word," Starbuck said, and watched the man look right and left and then step out hurriedly into the hallway. "Good night."

There was no reply from the leader of the Hebrenites.

☆ 8 ☆

Starbuck closed the door, turned the key. He wished there was some way he could help Oram Grey and his followers—short of accepting an under-the-table job as a killer—but there appeared to be nothing he could do. His suggestion to Oram that he get in touch with the army or the law had fallen on deaf ears, and beyond that he could see no way in which he could be of service.

Hiring out as a gunslinger was not his idea of a job. During his search for Ben when it had been necessary to find work, he had done many things—stagecoach driver, shotgun guard, deputy sheriff, trail boss, plain everyday cowhand, wrangler, and many others, but never had he contracted to be an assassin—and he wasn't about to begin now.

Coming about, he reached for the lamp to turn down its wick. Weariness was dragging at him with leaden weights, dulling his thoughts, slowing his movements. It would be good to crawl into the bed, get a full night's sleep. He'd head out in the morning as soon as he could get supplies together and straighten out his directions.

He paused, rubbed at his jaw, wondered if anyone in the valley would know where the Carazones Peaks lay; it was possible no one would because the members of the Family, as they were called, were never permitted to leave. He shrugged. Someone, surely, would at least have an idea where—

He halted dead in the center of the room as again a knock sounded on the door. He frowned, wondered if Oram Grey had returned, had a different proposition in mind. . . . The answer would be the same; he was not going to let himself get involved.

The knocking came again. Wheeling angrily, he took up the forty-five once more, crossed to the door, and flipped back the lock. Pulling open the panel, he stepped back, surprise hitting him hard. It was Hetty Pierce.

47

"Shut the door—hurry!" she said in a quick, tense voice and brushed by him into the room.

Starbuck did not move, simply stared at her. She was clad only in a nightgown and some sort of light cotton wrapper, had it pulled about her body. Her hair—freed from the severe bun into which it had been gathered—now cascaded about her face and neck and down onto her shoulders in dark glistening folds.

She gave him an impatient glance, stepped past him, and taking the door in her hands, closed and locked it herself.

"I've got to talk to you," she said, facing him. "It's important."

It seemed to be a night for talking, Shawn thought, continuing to study her. He shook his head. "Hardly the time or the place—or the way to come dressed for that."

"Had to wait until ma and pa were asleep. . . . Anyway, I'm eighteen, or almost. I don't think you're much older than that."

"Maybe not in years but where I've been and what I've seen makes me about twice your age."

"No difference," Hetty said airily, sinking onto the edge of the bed. "I was listening outside—a little. I heard you and Oram Grey. Why didn't he want you to say he'd been here?"

"Reasons of his own," Shawn answered, wondering just how much the girl had actually overheard.

She made a gesture of dismissal with her hand. Then, "You're leaving in the morning?"

He felt a thread of relief. Hetty evidently had caught only Grey's last words. The old man's secret was safe.

"My plan. Could be Bobby Joe and his friends will have other ideas."

She took a deep breath, squared her small shoulders. "I'm going with you."

Starbuck did not permit his reaction to her words to show. He considered her quietly, impassively. The yellow lamplight touched her cheeks, creamed them to a softness, and made her eyes much darker. She was a pretty girl, he thought again.

"Not that easy done," he said, moving toward the window. There had been a note of desperation in her tone and he feared to be blunt with her.

"Why not? I can ride—and I'll be no trouble. Just let

48

me go with you until we come to some town, then I'll look after myself."

"Doing what?"

"I can cook, or maybe I can get myself a job as a waitress in a restaurant. I could clerk in a store. I've heard the freighters say there are big stores in the towns where they have a lot of clerks. . . . Why, there's a hundred different ways I could support myself!"

"You've never been in a town so you can't know what it's like. Take my word for it, it's not that easy."

"I don't expect it to be, but others manage it. I can, too."

"Life's plenty hard. Country's never yet recovered from the war—and that's ten years ago—eleven actually. Every job has a dozen people standing around waiting for it. I know—I have to hunt one up pretty often—and it's a lot easier for a man to find work than a woman."

"I'll make out," Hetty said stubbornly. "I've just got to get away from here! I'll go stark mad if I don't!"

"May seem that way to you. Best you remember that here you've got a roof over your head, people to look out for you—and you always know where your next meal is coming from."

"And that's all! There's nothing more! I heard you tell papa yourself that you couldn't live like that, all penned up. Do you know what's in store for me if I stay?"

Starbuck's shoulders stirred heavily.

"I'll end up wedding Ezrah Vinsent, that's what. He's the only unmarried man in the valley—and he's seventy years old. That's almost four times my age!"

"You won't have to marry him. They can't force you."

"Oh, yes, they can! It's a sort of rule. A girl must marry, produce children. It's the only way they can keep the Family going. And since there aren't any boys my age—they're all years younger—it leaves only Ezrah."

"You've been told it's to be that way?"

"Oram Grey's mentioned it to papa—that I'm of marrying age and that Ezrah needs a wife and me a husband. Next time he talks to him he'll ask that a date be set and want to know if the honeymoon rooms are ready for us."

Shawn frowned. "Honeymoon rooms?"

"That's about all the hotel's for. It's the custom for newly married couples to have a week here. They're given their choice of the rooms and move in right after the ceremony. Everything's brought up to them, and they don't leave—just stay put. Then when the week's over, they go to live in the house the Family has provided for them."

The Hebrenites had it figured down to a fine point, Starbuck thought. Nothing was left to chance.

"What happens if you refuse to go through with the wedding?"

"Nobody ever has, but they'd have it their way eventually. The Elders've got the say-so over everybody. They're never opposed—not in anything they decide. And papa's one of them."

"You mean he'd go along with what Oram Grey and the others ordered whether you liked it or not?"

"He'd have to. He's got no choice either. Sometimes I think I'd be better off to just give in to Bobby Joe, let him have me."

"Bobby Joe—the outlaw?"

"That's who I mean. He keeps trying to catch me when I'm off by myself. A couple of nights ago he tried to force my bedroom window. I threw a bowl of soapy water in his face. . . . I'm afraid of him but it could be I'm wrong about him. One of the women has taken up with Abe, another of the outlaws—"

"Esther?" He was merely mentioning the name she had dropped.

Hetty looked at him in surprise. "Yes, Tolliver Grey's wife. How did you know?"

"Something you said earlier. Her husband is the one heading up the cattle drive."

"That's him, only don't make it sound like he was a young man. He's sixty or better, and Esther's only thirty-five. . . . Everyone around here is so old—the men, I mean."

"Don't Oram and the Elders know she is living with this Abe?"

"She doesn't live with him—she just sneaks out whenever she can, day or night—and meets him. I'm sure Oram doesn't know about them. I don't think anybody does except my folks and me. We've seen them meet and then watched her come home at all hours."

Shawn rubbed at his jaw. "Your pa being an Elder, it's a wonder he doesn't say something to her about it."

"I expect he has but he'd never mention it to us. . . . I—I'm sorry for Esther. I understand how she feels and I

50

think I know why she has to do it. We're all in a trap here."

"Can't say she was very choosy about who she took up with."

"How could she be? They were the first outsiders many of us had ever seen. And they're young and strong. I'm grown woman enough to know that's what Esther needed. Tolliver may be younger than his father, but you'd never know it. He seems every bit as old."

"What happens when her husband returns?"

"Who knows? Esther'll probably go right on meeting Abe Norvel every chance she gets—could be she'll run off with him. And Tolliver won't do anything about anything. He won't put up a fight for her, I mean. The men are forbidden to do anything like that. They're supposed to just sit back, talk things out in a peaceful way."

"Beats a shoot-out, I expect."

Hetty looked at him closely. "Would you agree to such an arrangement?"

Starbuck shifted his eyes to the window. "Well, no, not my idea of—"

"You see! It's not my idea either! If I ever have a husband, I want him to love me and want me enough to fight for me—even kill for me if he has to. I'm not going to be a piece of livestock to be bargained over, parceled out. . . . That's why I've got to leave here, Shawn, get away, make a life of my own, and find the kind of man that suits me.

"My folks—and the Elders—they don't realize that the Family is dying out, that there soon won't be any of the sect left. They'll pass on and all of the young people will have gone away—and there won't be anybody left.

"And I can't stay here and become the wife of an old man I hate! That would mean I'd be trapped here for the rest of my life with nothing to think about but dying. I'll do like Esther before I'll let that happen!"

Impulsively Hetty came off the bed, moved up to where she faced Starbuck. She was very close and he could hear the quick pound of her breathing, smell the warm womanly sweetness of her.

"I've got to go with you, Shawn. . . . I'll die if I can't! Will you let me? I'll pay any price you ask—any."

He was silent for a time, thinking of many things, thinking, too, of what the future held for Hetty Pierce in the valley, and was understanding her hopelessness.

"What about your folks?" he said then, breaking the hot stillness. "Wouldn't be right for you to run off without telling them."

"Papa will never agree," she said dispiritedly, looking away. "He has to stick by the rules. Mama will say I'm right—I'm sure of that. She can see what is happening and she'd want me to go because of the outlaws and what will happen when they take over."

Starbuck swore silently. The last thing he wanted was to be burdened with a girl when he pulled out in the morning—assuming he was able to do so. But he was finding it difficult to refuse her. It meant life itself to Hetty Pierce. She was like a caged bird frantically seeking to escape, and he could not deny that freedom. But he'd not do it under a cloud.

"It'll have to be all right with both of them," he said. "You get them to agree and we'll pull out together first thing in the morning—unless Bobby Joe and his bunch stop us."

Hetty's lips parted into a smile and her eyes brightened. "We won't have to worry about them! There's a path behind our barn. Runs west, clear to the foot of the mesa, then turns south. We can get to the gate by taking it—and nobody will even realize we've gone."

"You know this trail? You've been over it?"

"Dozens of times! Everybody has—except the outlaws, of course."

"It leads to the mouth of the canyon?"

She nodded. "I've been there, rode there by myself several times, intending to leave. I always got scared and changed my mind. I didn't know what I should do once I was outside the valley—no idea of where to go."

"It's the one we'll use—and I'm glad you mentioned it. Like to avoid making trouble around here if I can."

"Well, you can easy, unless they just happen to be looking and see us leave, or for some reason, miss us. If that happens, it could be a problem because the trail down the valley is a lot shorter. They could ride on ahead, cut us off."

"Up to us to be careful then, and starting early is a good guarantee."

"I'll be ready when you say—"

"*You'll* be ready if your folks agree to it. I'll want to hear it with my own ears. Also, I've got to gather up a few supplies—grub."

"I'll put what you need in a sack, have it all fixed for you. Save time. Expect you ought to have bread, meat, pickled fruit, things like that. Don't think there's any coffee left, not much anyway."

"Forget it. I've a few beans left. Main thing's food—what you listed."

"I'll add whatever else I think you can use. There was something else you said you had to do—"

"Find out how to get to the Carazones Peaks country, and a ranch owned by a man named Hagerman."

Hetty shook her head. "There's nobody around here can tell you that. The freighters might, but they're both away on the cattle drive."

Starbuck only stirred. He'd half expected that. It appeared he'd be forced to cut north to one of the forts or settlements after all, if he was to get his sights lined up right. It would be better now, anyway; he'd be able to get Hetty settled and off his hands that much quicker—assuming the Pierces allowed her to go.

"About five o'clock, that be when you'd like to start?" she asked.

"Be fine."

"Everything will be ready—"

He considered her narrowly. "It's understood now, isn't it? No point your being there waiting unless your folks tell me it's all right."

"I'll tend to that. Mama will agree, I know, and I'm sure she'll be able to persuade papa."

"But you said, him being an Elder—"

"Don't worry, mama can do most anything with him once she sets her mind to it," the girl replied, and reached for the top button of her wrapper. Her face was intent, her eyes shining bright. "I made you a bargain, Shawn, said I'd pay whatever price you asked. . . . I'm ready to pay now."

Starbuck stood wholly still. He had realized to some extent how important escape from the valley and freedom was to Hetty, but it had not occurred to him that it meant this much. Dark, hard-cornered face expressionless, he took her fingers into his hands, stopped their fumbling with the wooden buttons.

"You're one hell of a lot of woman, Hetty Pierce," he said gently, and leaning down, kissed her on the lips, and stepped back. "There—now we're square. You've paid off in full. . . . Good night."

Stepping by her, he unlocked the door, held it open. She stood in the center of the room as if transfixed, staring at him in disbelief. Suddenly tears flooded into her eyes, and cheeks flaming, she hurried past him and disappeared into the hall.

☆ 9 ☆

Alone in her barren room, Hetty stood at the window, and staring into the pale lit night, sobbed for a reason she could not exactly explain to herself.

She had lied to Shawn, lied for the first time in her life, and that, she sought to assure herself, was the source of her tears. But she knew better. He had refused her—had treated her as a child—and that cut deep. And then like a shaft of light, the truth came to her. He had refused her not because she was less a woman but because he was more a man. Had Shawn been Bobby Joe or someone like him, the situation would have ended differently.

She felt something deep within her stir at that realization, and immediately her thoughts flew back to those moments when they had been together, and a warmness flowed through her. . . . She knew now—and Shawn must be made to understand, to recognize the feeling that had sprung up between them.

Turning from the window, she dashed the drying tears from her cheeks and crossed to the row of pegs on the wall from which her few pieces of clothing hung. Choosing the one dress she considered her best, she folded it carefully, laid it on the bed.

Then gathering up other bits of personal apparel, she put them and the dress into the handbag she'd knitted and lined with a remnant of flowered percale someone had given her, and hung it on the bedpost.

Going to the doorway, she entered the hall, quietly made her way past her parents' bedroom to the porch on the back of the hotel. Opening the closet where her father kept his spare work clothing, she selected a butternut shirt, a pair of pants—faded and shrunk from many washings to a size that would come nearest to fitting her—and a ragged-brimmed, hand-woven hat of straw. Folding all into a bundle, she returned to her quarters.

There she donned the rough garments, finishing off the garb by pulling on a pair of the thick-soled work shoes made by Micah Jones and provided by the Family for members to use when they did their periodic stints as field hands.

Taking up the knitted bag, she went back into the hall and headed for the kitchen. She spent a good quarter hour selecting and assembling the food items that Shawn wanted for the trail, placing them in a muslin sack used for grain, and left it on the table. After that she let herself out the side door and made her way to the barn.

Resolute, she entered the stable and singled out one of the four horses standing in their stalls. She backed the animal, a thick-bodied, heavy hoofed black used by the teamsters, into the runway where the light was better, and saddled and bridled him.

Affixing the knitted bag with her belongings to the patched hull, she led the horse to the doorway. She started to mount up, was taken by a second thought. Leaving the black, she returned to the hotel, slipped quietly down the short hall to her parents' room. It wouldn't be long until time for them to be up and about, she knew, and she was taking a bit of a risk, but it had to be done.

Entering, she crossed in the darkness to her mother's side of the bed. Placing a hand on the older woman's shoulder, she shook her gently. Patience opened her eyes at once. Hetty held a finger against her lips for silence.

"Just want to tell you I'm riding up to the lake to pick berries. Going early before it gets hot. Tell Mr. Starbuck I put the things he wanted in a sack. It's on the kitchen table."

"Things?" Patience echoed drowsily.

"Food. He asked for it. . . . Tell him good-bye for me."

Simon stirred restlessly, partly awoke. Patience nodded, settled back.

"I'll tell him," she murmured thickly.

Hetty drew off, studied her mother's slack care-lined face for a long breath, resisting the urge to place a farewell kiss upon the older woman's cheek for fear of rousing her again and possibly creating a quick suspicion. Wheeling, she returned to the hall and to the waiting black.

Satisfied with the charade that she felt would allay all questions relative to her absence when the morning came, she climbed onto the saddle and swung the horse toward the trail that led into the west. The hull was much too large for her and the stirrups too long, but she'd not worry about that now. She'd adjust them later. At the moment her mind was soaring with the thoughts of what lay ahead for her—beyond the valley.

A town—a street with rows of stores running down each side, filled with things she'd never dreamed of, peopled with smiling, friendly folk who waited to welcome her. There'd be clean, neat little homes scattered about on green hillsides, brightened with flowers, shaded by huge trees, all lived in by happy, laughing couples who loved each other and who married because of that love and not as a bounden duty arranged by dried-up, bearded old men who cared only that children be the result of their union.

It would be heaven living in such a world, Hetty was sure. She'd never actually seen what it was like outside Hebren Valley, but she had looked at the pictures in the magazines the freighters brought in—or did until Oram Grey put a stop to it because he said it gave the young members wrong ideas and made them dissatisfied.

Oh, it would be truly wonderful to be free, to live in such a glorious world!

☆ 10 ☆

Starbuck was awake and dressed well before first light. Moving to the window, he glanced at the sky. . . . Another scorcher of a day coming up. Motion in the street caught his eye. A woman on a small pony was just moving into the shadows near the feed warehouse. Esther Grey, he guessed idly and turned back into the room. Collecting his belongings, he tucked them into his saddlebags, entered the hall, and quietly made his way below to the kitchen. He found the sack of provisions Hetty had prepared for him, and leaving several silver dollars on the table to settle his bill, hurried to the stable. Saddling and mounting the gelding, he located the path the girl had spoken of, moved off, secretly pleased that he had disturbed no one and that Hetty had not been there, waiting for him.

The sorrel, frisky after the night's rest and feeding, pranced show-horse style along in the cool, half light. It was with difficulty that Shawn restrained him from breaking into a lope and setting up a hollow beat on the baked ground that would be heard in the settlement.

The land was no different here from elsewhere in the West, he noted. The moment he pulled up out of the valley with its cool springs and streams and gained the flat sandy heights above, his surroundings changed.

The grass lost its lushness, turned from rich green to grayish thin clumps. Large trees became nonexistent, replaced by cedars and other scrub growth designed by nature to survive the heat with a minimum of moisture.

The fertile, dark soil was loose now, studded with rock; and the metamorphosis of the country itself was from one of tranquil, prosaic farming to a friendless, rugged world of wild, fierce grandeur. He was only a short distance from the floor of Hebren Valley, yet it was as if he had removed himself a thousand miles.

Such was no novelty to Shawn. In his search for Ben, he had whipped back and forth across the impatiently stirring West, from the Mississippi to California's Russian River, from the sleepy *pueblos* south of the Mexican border to the frozen plains of Montana. He'd come to accept change and difference as part of life, just as he had learned all men vary not only in appearance but in thought and ideals and in their estimation of values.

He thought of Oram Grey at that moment, of his lonely despair, his need to do what he felt was necessary for his followers even at the cost of his ideals. To the leader of the Hebrenites any means to an end evidently was justifiable as long as it compromised only him.

Starbuck looked ahead. The trail, having followed an almost due west course, was beginning to veer south, meander along the shale-cluttered base of a line of red-faced bluffs. The valley, deep green and shadowy, was below and to the left.

The villagers would be up by that hour, preparing for a day's labor in the fields or whatever communal duties had been assigned them. Shawn stared thoughtfully at the faint band of pearl showing along the eastern horizon. Was that the way men were intended to live—as Oram Grey and his Hebrenites believed?

Was living as a single family, each person having no more and no less than another—with all delegated and sharing labors that contributed to the welfare of the whole rather than to the individual—was that the way it was supposed to be? Was that the true and satisfying life?

It hardly seemed so to him. A man was nothing in that sort of arrangement, no more than a cog in a machine, a solitary straw in a broom. What was there to an existence such as that?

Gently, he eased back on the gelding's leathers, mind suddenly cleared of all thought, finely tuned senses keenly alert. A short distance along the trail, behind a shoulder of rock, his eyes had caught a hint of motion. An animal of some kind, perhaps—or it could be a man.

Reaching down, he moved the holster on his left thigh more to center, let his hand rest on the weapon's smooth walnut butt. The pearl in the east had changed now to a rose-orange flare, and around him the land was losing its softness and the harshness of reality was reclaiming the starved brush and heat-blasted rock.

Slowly he drew abreast the slab of sandstone. Above it was only the steep barren slope. If it was a trap, there would be only one rider involved; the shoulder was not large enough to conceal two. . . . He grinned faintly; the thought of Bobby Joe and his friends waiting somewhere along the trail was making him unduly edgy. Likely it was a deer—or possibly a cougar. The big cats liked those rock ledges.

But Starbuck was not a man to accept probabilities. Guiding the sorrel in close to the formation, he drew his pistol and halted.

"You—back of that rock! Move out where I can see you."

At once he heard the dry creak of leather, the slow thud of hooves. The head of a pony appeared, and then its rider. Shawn swore softly in surprise. It was the woman he'd seen crossing the street earlier that morning—the one he assumed was Esther Grey.

He considered her coldly, slid the forty-five back into its holster. "Good way to get shot. What were you doing there?"

She raised her head, looked directly at him. She was an attractive woman with a wealth of hair that was the color of panned gold, full curving lips, and large, light eyes that, being somewhat slanted, gave her a faintly Oriental appearance.

"Waiting for you."

Starbuck sighed quietly. "Expect that means you're wanting to leave the valley, too."

Her brows lifted. "Too? Is there someone else going with you?"

"Wanted to."

"Who?"

"Don't see as it matters. You're Esther Grey, I reckon."

She nodded. "I'd like to ride with you to the next town, if you don't mind."

Starbuck shrugged. It appeared he was slated to have company whether he wanted it or not. First Hetty and now Esther—and he couldn't very well refuse her.

"Expect you know there's a chance I might not leave the valley. Your friends could be aiming to head me off."

"I don't think they know you're gone," she said.

"What I was hoping. Surprised to see you. Thought you were all set to go with them—leastwise, with the one called Abe."

Esther looked off into the valley. "I—I decided to go on now—with you."

Shawn gave her words passing consideration. She and Norvel had evidently quarreled, causing her to change her ideas and plans.

"Is it all right—my riding with you? I have my own food and water, and I'll not be in the way. I have to go. I just can't stay in the valley any longer."

He could understand that to remain there as the wife of Tolliver Grey and the woman of Abe Norvel would create an impossible situation for her, but he had his doubts about her future just as he'd had for Hetty's.

"You realize what it'll be like on the outside?"

"I haven't been out of the valley since my parents brought me here—a long time ago. We came by wagon train from Nebraska, but we never stopped at any of the towns, always avoided them, so there's very little I know of things."

"You'll not find them the way you think they are."

Esther Grey stirred dispiritedly. "I don't expect to. They never are."

"What can you do—what sort of work, I mean?"

Like Hetty Pierce she probably planned to work as a waitress or a cook—the jobs there were always more than enough applicants for.

"I can teach school," Esther said. "That's what I was trained to do in the valley."

"Fine," Starbuck said, relieved. "Chances are you'll make out. And you're old enough to know what you want—and what you're doing."

"I do—for years. It's just been a matter of waiting for someone to help me—to take me, really—out of that prison."

"What about your husband and children?"

"He's part of the prison—and there are no children. There's no reason why I should stay. I don't fit. I never have and it's doubtful I'll be missed—even by the man who is my husband if he were there. . . . Are you letting me ride with you? I'd go on by myself only I wouldn't know which way to turn once I was free."

"If that's what you want," Starbuck said, and glanced to the east. A small edge of the sun was breaking over the ragged skyline.

"Best we get started. Going to be a long, hot day."

He touched the gelding with his rowels, sent him trotting on down the trail. Esther swung in behind him, and shortly they were moving steadily along the gentle grade.

They rode in silence, Esther wrapped in her own thoughts, Shawn looking ahead, weighing the probability of trouble at the mouth of the canyon guarding entry to the valley. If the outlaws had discovered that he had pulled out and were determined to stop him, they would make their play at that point.

There was no assurance it mattered enough to them one way or another whether he rode out or not. They would always carry a grudge for him, of course, but it wasn't likely they'd go to any great lengths to settle it. And as for his departure from the valley, they would probably view it as good riddance. Maybe luck was still with him.

Again he reined in the sorrel, a quick, sharp oath springing from his lips as they rounded a bend. Waiting in the center of the trail was Hetty Pierce.

☆ 11 ☆

Clad in a man's clothing several times too large for her slight frame, Hetty greeted him furiously.

"So this is why you wouldn't let me come! You were bringing her—and you didn't want me tagging along!"

Starbuck, temper on a short fuse at being saddled with one woman and facing the prospects of a second, swore angrily, said, "The hell! Found her waiting on the trail, same as you."

Hetty glared at Esther suspiciously. "A likely story— and I'm noticing that you didn't make her turn back."

"She's a grown woman, old enough to know what she's up to."

"And I'm not—"

"No, by God, you're not!" he replied bluntly.

Hetty recoiled slightly from the sharp impact of his words. She folded her arms across her breasts, settled herself stubbornly on the outsized saddle girthed to the plow horse she was riding.

"Well, you're taking me, anyway. If Esther can go, I can, too."

Shawn sighed helplessly. "Expect the best thing we can all do is turn around and go back, forget this day ever started. If we ride fast enough, maybe we can get there before either one of you is missed."

"Only one who'll miss her," Hetty said acidly, glancing at Esther, "is her outlaw lover."

The tall woman smiled patiently. "I'm afraid that's all over—ended."

"Good! You ought to be ashamed—"

Again Esther smiled. "Why should I be ashamed of something that was good and natural? To Abe I was something besides another pair of hands to work in the fields, someone who wasn't a teacher or a cook or a drudge to take care of a house—I was a woman."

Hetty's eyes spread indignantly. "You've got the nerve to talk about it, to flaunt—"

"No, I'm just trying to explain, but it's something you'd never understand."

"No, I never will! You had a husband and you were carrying on with that outlaw—"

"I was married to Tolliver Grey. He was never a husband, at least not what I think a husband should be. And after we learned I couldn't bear children for him, it became worse—less a marriage. I might as well have been dead."

"You were still married, no matter what," Hetty insisted firmly. "You ought to've remembered that."

Esther stirred listlessly. "I couldn't expect a child to understand—"

"I'm no child!"

"Of course you aren't," the older woman said coolly. "What price did you offer to pay Mr. Starbuck if he'd take you with him?"

Hetty wheeled to Shawn. "You told her!" she cried, cheeks flushing wildly.

"He told me exactly nothing about you—not even that you wanted to leave," Esther said. "But I know my kind—and I know what hopelessness can do to a woman caught in its trap."

Her voice broke. She turned her head, looked off to the south. Freedom lay in that direction and her resolve to find it was mirrored in the brightness of her almond-shaped eyes, the firm set of her lips.

Shawn rode out the silence that had fallen between them for a full minute, then nodded. "If you two've got all the poison out of your craws, we'll do a little sensible talking. . . . Still think you'd both be smart to turn back."

"No," Esther said at once. "I'll ride on alone, take my chances, before I'll go back to the valley."

"So will I," Hetty declared.

"All right," Starbuck said resignedly. "We'll go on. Keep remembering this, though. We're still not out of here. Hard to say what could be waiting at the mouth of the canyon."

"He means your outlaw friends," Hetty said, glaring at Esther. "They're all worked up because he had a fight with them—beat them—"

"No only them," Shawn said. "Could be your pa and a few of the Family Elders—if they've found out you're missing."

"They won't," Hetty said promptly. "Told my ma I was

going berry picking. They won't expect me back for hours."

Starbuck looked away, surpressed a smile. Hetty had done a lot of figuring. Turning back to her, he said, "Don't pay to be too sure of something like that. Could be they weren't fooled."

Hetty wagged her head stubbornly. "They won't be there. . . . I know."

Shawn was silent for a moment, then glanced up to find Esther studying him. The sun was out in full strength now and its light caught at her hair, turned it to the color of the marigolds that grew so profusely on the slopes.

"When you were around Abe and his friends, they mention anything about me, like keeping an eye on me, things like that?"

The tall woman said, "No, nothing. But I didn't see the others last night—only Abe."

"I see. . . . You happen to know their last names?"

Esther's eyes showed some surprise. "Why, yes. Bobby Joe's is Grant. And it's Rollie Lister and Abe—or really Abraham—Norvel. Why? Is there some reason—"

"Nothing special. Just wondered if I'd ever heard of them. Seems not."

He wondered at the relief that flashed across her features, and then riding forward a few strides, raised himself in the stirrups and looked off toward the end of the valley. The small, narrow canyon that lay at its beginning would be just beyond the ridge he could see looming up hazily in the distance. It would be wise to avoid the valley entirely by swinging wide and coming in to the canyon from below the ridge, he decided. They would then be only a short distance from the exit.

Wheeling about, he explained the situation to the two women, and finished with, "Important we go quiet so let's have no more of this wrangling between you two. We keep to the brush and stay off the high spots on the trail. Once we're in the canyon, we'll have to be twice as careful. Understood?"

Esther nodded. Hetty said, "We'll be careful," and then, "Shawn, everything will be fine once we're out of the valley, won't it? I mean, there'll be no more trouble—no need to worry—"

"Nothing much," Starbuck replied, heading back onto the trail. "Just Indians—Comanches and Kiowas both—a sun that'll fire up to over a hundred, short water rations, and no idea of where the nearest town is. Outside those few minor items, we'll have no problems. . . . You both ready? Let's go."

Under his breath he sighed heavily. How the hell could he have gotten himself jockeyed into a situation like this? Two runaway women—one fleeing from a husband who meant nothing to her, the other escaping her parents and a marriage to a man she feared and despised—both desperate to abandon a life they could no longer bear. And to top that off there was the possibility of having to fight his way—and theirs—through the guns of three outlaws.

All he'd wanted was information and a small stock of provisions so that he could continue on his way. How did it end up? As usual, with someone else's troubles on his shoulders—two quarreling women at that!

He reckoned he could stand it. Such occurred in one form or another, it seemed, from time to time, and he always managed to survive although there'd been a few occasions when there'd been doubt. . . . But two contentious, perverse women. . . . He grinned wryly at the realization. If they weren't at each other clawing and scratching like a couple of bobcats disputing territorial rights, he'd be plenty surprised.

Twisting about on his saddle, he gave the pair a long look, noting Esther's set, resigned features, Hetty's stubbornly defiant expression.

"If you two are smart," he said, "you'll cut out that feuding and get together. Thing to do is find a good town, get yourselves jobs, and share a house. Won't be so hard or so lonesome if you'll do it that way."

"I'll never get lonesome for the valley!" Hetty declared immediately.

Shawn plucked at his ear. "You'll be surprised how soon you'll start thinking about all the good things and wishing maybe you could live them over again. Happens to everybody when the nights get long and it's quiet and you can't sleep. . . . Can even happen in the day—the remembering how it was."

"I'll never feel that way—never! Will you, Esther?"

The tall woman brushed at her eyes. "I don't know. Right now I don't think so. I think only of the bitterness I found there."

"Well, you can bet I won't be sorry. I hate the valley. I'll be so glad to be far away from it that I'll welcome anything—everything!"

Starbuck made no further comment. He slid a careful glance to the sun, now well on its way to the midday mark in the empty sky. Heat was rising steadily. They would be forced to halt soon, let the horses rest.

There was little shade of consequence to be seen on the slope they were crossing, but at the foot of the ridge that separated canyon from valley, he could see a dark band of growth. There could be a spring. If so, it would be a good place to call a halt.

They reached the tiny oasis late in the morning. The spring was small, furnished water only for the horses, which Starbuck led up, one at a time.

He drank sparingly from the half-filled canteen he carried. It was still some distance to the larger creek below the canyon where he planned to refill both containers, but he was unworried. There was water in the area and that was a satisfying knowledge. Too, Esther had provided herself with a gallon jug that was full and which she offered to share with Hetty. The girl accepted it without hesitation, seemingly forgetting her acrimonious feelings for the yellow-haired woman for the moment.

They took advantage of the shade to rest and eat a little of the supplies Shawn had brought; and an hour later were again in the saddle, following a faint path that climbed steeply to the top of the ridge.

Once there, the trail as steeply dropped off onto the yonder side, and in short time they were down in the narrow canyon with Hebren Valley, at last, behind them and lost to view.

That realization seemed to visit each of the women, and both were abruptly silent as if for the first time they were facing up to the fact that they were leaving the past behind, had crossed, finally, a river of no return.

It was their problem, Shawn thought, singling out the mouth of the canyon with its improvised gate now visible in the distance. He would suggest once more that they change their minds, return to their sheltered havens in Hebren Valley—and let it drop. If they decided to go back, all well and good; if they chose to continue with him, he'd do what he could for them and make the best of it. He wouldn't lose any large amount of time, anyway; he was forced to cut back to one of the settlements for directions, regardless. He'd leave Hetty and Esther there.

The trail angled sharply to the right, began to follow the edge of a deep arroyo that sloped down from the higher plateaus to empty into the stream flowing along the floor of the canyon.

The gate was definite now. The brush lashed to the framework, long since dried, was a flat sage-green; and from where they were, it stood out in stark contrast against the still growing shrubbery. Looking back, he pointed to it.

"That's the way out. You're free once you're on the other side of it. Either one of you wants to back out, now's the time to do it. Be your last chance."

Esther Grey, features expressionless, shook her head. Hetty, toes pushed into the stirrup loops instead of the too low wooden bows, lifted herself, looked to the north.

"Not me. . . . I'll never be sorry. . . . Never."

Shawn resumed his position. "Sure hope not," he said. "Leaving home's a big jump. I know because—"

Stiffening with alarm, he hauled up on the sorrel's reins as three riders burst from the dense brush dead ahead.

"It's Bobby Joe—the outlaws!" Hetty Pierce screamed.

"Down into the arroyo—jump!" Starbuck yelled, drawing his pistol.

Gunshots rattled through the hot stillness. He felt the gelding shudder, stumble, was suddenly leaving the saddle in a soaring arc as the big horse went down. A white hot force slammed into the side of his head—and then blackness engulfed him in a vast, soft cloak.

☆ 12 ☆

The brutal, penetrating lances of the noon-day sun brought consciousness back to Shawn Starbuck.

Face down in the arroyo bed, he opened his eyes slowly, caution stilling any outward movement of his body until certain he was alone.

He could hear nothing but the drone of insects, the far-off mourning of a dove. Sweat bathed him completely, and there was a stinging along the left side of his head, an uncomfortable stiffness to the skin. His left shoulder ached with a persistent throb. It must have borne the full brunt of his fall.

Where were the others—Esther and Hetty, the outlaws?

A shaft of panic hit him, sent a stream of fear coursing through him. Hetty—in the hands of Bobby Joe and his partners. . . . And Esther—she'd be no better off if she was no longer of interest to Abe. Moving only his eyes, he stretched his vision to encompass as much of the immediate area as possible. He saw only the glistening sand, the thin weedy growth, and a gray mottled lizard panting rapidly beneath a rock at the edge of the arroyo.

He sucked in a long breath, winced at the pain the effort evoked. . . . He couldn't just lie there, wait for darkness. That was hours away. He'd not survive the heat, and the two women—he groaned, thinking of them. He'd have to gamble—hope luck was with him.

Twisting his head slightly, he turned his face an inch at a time to the opposite side, straining to catch any sounds that would indicate the nearby presence of the outlaws.

He was alone in the arroyo. A few feet away the head and neck of the sorrel hung over the lip of the wash, the remainder of the gelding's body still on the flat above. The big horse had been dead when he hit the ground, Shawn guessed.

Slowly he sat up, making no sound. The outlaws could be in the lower end of the arroyo. Flat on his rump, legs extended in front of him, Starbuck paused. A wave of nausea swept over him. He held himself rigid until it passed and was replaced with a steady stabbing pain in his head.

He raised a hand, gingerly touched the burning, aggravated area above his ear with fingertips. . . . Dried blood and a tenderness such as he'd never known. . . . He lowered his arm, sat there thinking. He remembered then. A bullet had slammed into him, striking a glancing blow just as the sorrel had started down. He'd been pitched off the saddle, thrown hard into the arroyo ten feet below.

Starbuck muttered an oath. It was a wonder he was alive. The bullet from the outlaw's gun had missed being a killer by the merest fraction of an inch. And the fall—there was no good reason why it hadn't provided him with a few broken bones.

He continued to sit there, motionless, still somewhat stunned, with the sun beating down upon him while he waited for a second spasm of giddiness to pass and a degree of strength to return to his enervated body. Then, easing forward, he got to hands and knees and slowly crawled to where the head of the sorrel hung into the arroyo. The gelding's lips were pulled back, revealing his broad yellow teeth. It was as if he were snarling defiance at the sudden death that overtook him.

Pausing for a long minute, still listening, striving to pick up any signs of life close by, Shawn drew himself upright. Again the nausea claimed him while a host of needle points dug into his brain.

He ignored it all as best he could, hanging on patiently, doggedly, knuckles of his hands showing white as he clung to the rocks in the arroyo's wall, until the sickness once more passed. Slowly then, he drew himself up as far as he could. He was unable to see over the edge of the wash.

Worn from the attempt, he glanced around seeking a break in the wall or a lower area. He could see none and moved back then to where he was directly below the dead sorrel. A fairly large rock jutted from the gravelly soil offering a foothold, while a clump of groundsel—yellow flowers blooming raggedly—suggested purchase for his hands. . . . If he could manage to reach that far up, he should be able to grab a part of the sorrel's saddle—a stirrup, perhaps—pull himself to where he could look onto the flat.

There was no saddle on the gelding.

Balancing on one foot, clinging grimly to the slowly

yielding clump of brush, sweat streaming down his face, he stared at the horse. The outlaws had removed his gear. He looked down at his middle hastily, swore vividly. Belt, holster, gun—all were gone. He guessed he would have noticed it sooner except he was still a bit thick from the rap he'd taken from that grazing bullet.

But he was alone. He got that much satisfaction out of the effort expended in climbing up halfway. The flat to the east of the wash with its stand of brush, out of which Bobby Joe, Abe, and Rollie Lister had come, was deserted in the hot sunlight.

Again ignoring the shocking stabs of pain, he threw himself forward on his belly, clawed to catch the sorrel's mane. He felt the coarse strands between his fingers, locked tight upon them. Then, digging toes into the arroyo bank, he drew himself over the lip of the deep cut onto the level of the flat.

Panting from exertion and pain, drenched with sweat, he sprawled alongside the sorrel. Flies were buzzing around the ragged wound in the animal's chest where the lead slug had ripped its way, and he unconsciously brushed at them with a hand, sent them pulling back in a dark swarming cloud. Whoever had fired the bullet that killed the gelding had got in a lucky shot; the lead slug had missed bone, gone straight to the heart.

Shawn felt a stir of regret and pity, and then relief for the sorrel. The red had carried him over a lot of country, had been a fine, dependable mount. He hadn't suffered, and if death was to come, that was the best way—fast and unexpected.

Breathing normally at last, he got to his knees, to his feet, and looked around, moving his head slowly to prevent a resurgence of the nausea. Evidently the outlaws had figured him for dead. They had noted all the blood on the side of his face, and as he was totally unconscious from that as well as the fall, they'd simply assumed they'd killed him, had appropriated his gear, taken the women captive, and moved on.

He felt the stir of fear within him again as he thought of Esther and Hetty being in their hands. Esther, of course, was older, wiser, could probably take care of herself pretty well. . . . But Hetty Pierce—and with Bobby Joe hungering for her the way he had— He rubbed at his jaw, tried to think.

Where would they go?

Back to the valley—that seemed logical. But again, there could have been a change in plan, and with the two women at stake, he couldn't afford to be wrong. No one knew exactly what the outlaws had in mind, he had just drawn conclusions from scraps of information picked up here and there. For all he knew they could have left the valley or have decided upon another place nearer the entrance to hole up. . . . He had to be sure.

Starting forward, eyes on the ground, he began to search for tracks. Giddiness overcame him and he caught himself, turned, and stumbled toward the darker green shrubbery that marked the location of the stream. He'd get some water, wash his face good. Be smart to let his head soak for a little. Should help it to clear. After he'd done that he ought to be in better condition to think.

It was a long, murderous hundred yards to the creek. He reached it on unsteady legs, sank down, and belly flat, lowered his face into its cool depths.

Water touched the raw wound in his head, stung sharply. He flinched, drew back, and again sank his face into the stream, this time with more care. An ease began to slip through him after a few moments. He sat up, removed his shirt, splashed himself, scrubbing away the sweaty coating of dust.

It would be fine to strip completely, crawl into the creek, and stay there for an hour or two. He'd feel better after that sort of a treatment for sure—but it was out of the question. He had to start moving, find the outlaws, get to them before they could harm Hetty and Esther. . . . And on foot, wounded, and with no weapon except the slim-bladed knife he always carried inside his left boot, he had one hell of a job ahead of him.

The brief respite had done much to improve the way he felt, and his head, bound now with a bandage made of his bandanna, had cleared. An unsteadiness still bothered his legs, caused his knees to tremble spasmodically now and then, but that he was sure would eventually pass.

Rising, he moved out into the brilliant sunlight to where the sorrel lay. There he scouted about until he located the prints where the horses had all come together into a small bunch. From there it was simple to follow them as they struck out, one in the lead, the remainder in groups of two. He visualized it; it would be Rollie Lister at the head. Behind him would come Abe riding alongside Esther

Grey. They would be followed by Bobby Joe Grant siding Hetty.

They were returning to the valley. That could only mean they had missed him at the settlement after all his precautions, had hurried down the shorter trail that cut along the floor of the valley, and cut him off. He might have made it if he'd hurried—if he hadn't been delayed. But there was no sense hashing that over now.

What would they do with the women? Because they were apparently returning to the settlement, would they release them once they arrived? Esther, perhaps, as she had come and gone pretty much as she pleased. Hetty was a different matter. She'd fought Bobby Joe from the start, and she'd still fight him, and by so doing she would make it impossible for him to let her go.

He'd keep her there in the shack, and the people in the settlement would never know of it until it was too late. Then, when he and the others had taken their fill of her, she would be offered her freedom—or the opportunity of a life as a woman for the outlaws.

Shawn shook off the thought, glanced to the steel-arched bowl of the sky. The sun was directly overhead and bearing down its hardest. They had at least an hour's start on him, possibly more. He looked ahead, up the canyon, and moving hurriedly, crossed to the trail that ran parallel to the stream.

The distance to the town by this route was considerably less, he recalled, and it shouldn't be too tough going. He broke into a slow jog. He'd have water nearly all the way—shade from the trees that grew along the banks of the creek. . . . If only the sun wasn't so damned hot—

In that next instant Shawn felt his knees buckle. A grayness came drifting into his eyes. Strength drained from his legs and he had the sensation of floating, tipping forward. Frantically he threw out his arms to save himself, failed, pitched full-length onto the hot sand.

☆ 13 ☆

Gasping for breath, plastered with sweat, Starbuck lay for long minutes. Finally, he rolled over, picked himself up cautiously. He'd overestimated his strength; he guessed he was worse off from that glancing bullet's blow and the fall than he'd thought.

Moving slowly, mystified by the strange sensation of lightness that gripped and refused to release him, he started for the creek. He couldn't recall having ever experienced the sense of irrelation that possessed him. On the few previous occasions when he'd been shot, it hadn't affected him in this manner.

The fall—he supposed that was it. Being thrown over the dying sorrel's head and landing hard on the solid floor of the arroyo ten feet below. It had been one hell of a moment for him. He was realizing that now.

But he couldn't let it matter. He must get his feet squarely under him and make it back to the settlement, locate the outlaws, and free the two girls. . . . And there was a little matter now of personal property to be recovered—the belt buckle that had been Hiram Starbuck's. He could replace the rest of his gear, but the buckle was something else, and he'd not quit until he recovered it.

He reached the creek bank, dropped to his knees. Brushing off his hat, he scooped a double handful of water, bathed his burning face. Removing the bandage, he dipped it in the stream's cooling depth, wrung it almost dry, and reapplied it.

He felt much better after that, and settling back, rested in the shade of the overhanging trees. But conscience would not permit him to enjoy the recess for long. Within short minutes he got to his feet, and cocking his hat to one side in order to avoid pressure on the stinging, throbbing wound in his head, he once again started up the canyon.

He had learned a lesson. No longer did he try to hurry,

74

to pursue a plan of alternately walking and running, conceived earlier. Now he moved at a steady but not too hurried pace, keeping near the stream with its attendant growth. Occasionally he would halt, find a spot to rest briefly. At such interludes he would again bathe his face, soak and replace the bandage.

The day lengthened with the heat decreasing but little as he pressed on doggedly, climbing out of the canyon, topping the ridge, and finally dropping into the Hebren Valley. He lost the comfort of the adjacent stream there as the road cut away, followed a higher level.

But he did manage to stay within reasonable reach of water and the healing qualities it seemed to offer. Several times he swung away from the twin ruts and crossed to where the creek flowed. It was time lost—but well invested; better to get there late than never at all. And the heat, even when he was near the water, lashed him mercilessly, sucking him dry and robbing him stealthily of strength.

But he would not give in despite the fact that the two women had worked themselves into their present predicament and perhaps should be left to get themselves out as best they could.

After all, the outlaws were their worry—theirs and Oram Grey's and all the other Hebrenites in the valley. Let them face up to what must be done, or if they persisted in living by the pacifist code they professed and wanted to just lie quiet—like a rabbit being chewed up by a coyote—then let them.

Too many times he'd permitted himself to become involved in the troubles of others. He was about due to back off, keep his nose pointed straight ahead, and go about his own business—that of finding Ben and getting matters settled so he could obtain his share of old Hiram's thirty-thousand-dollar bounty.

Then he could start having a life of his own. He could get himself a good piece of land, start a ranch—the Circle S he'd call it. He'd go in for cattle and good horses, specialize maybe in that big tan-and-cream-colored breed he'd seen down in Mexico—*palominos*, they were called. Beautiful, proud animals they were. They made a man's pulse quicken.

Shawn's rambling thoughts died. He pulled to a stop on the crest of a low hill, surprise rippling through him. The edge of the settlement was visible, the squat bleak shacks that stood at the end of the street were just ahead.

He pulled back hastily, hunched behind a clump of sedge. He could see most of the street—the fronts of the buildings. No one was in sight; the place had the same frightened, deserted appearance as before.

He settled his attention on the three shacks. The old Mason house, as Hetty had termed it, was the first in line. The outlaws were using it as their quarters, she'd said. The second, or middle structure, had been converted into a stable for their horses, while the third was empty.

No life was evident around any of the shacks—not even a horse—and that realization sent a spurt of alarm through him. Had the outlaws turned off somewhere between the canyon and the town? Could they have gone on after all, having made a change in plans and left the valley?

He shook his head. He still didn't think such was likely. The idea, according to what Simon Pierce and the others had overheard, was for them to wait for Kilrain and the rest of the outlaw bunch; they'd not pull out until the others arrived.

The men could be inside, the horses around in back or possibly inside their improvised stable. From his position on the hill, he was too far to the front to see the rear of the structures. Taut, worry nagging at him, he dropped back below the crest of the hill, circled wide, and keeping to a small gully, trotted to a point where he figured he'd be provided with a view of the opposite ends of the shacks, and there climbed to the level of the land.

A sigh slipped from his cracked lips. The horses, all five of them, were tied to a sagging hitchrack at the back of the Mason place. The outlaws had returned to the settlement as he had assumed—and that they had not released either Hetty or Esther was evidenced by the presence of their horses with the others.

He mopped at the sweat on his face, glanced to the sky. Not long until sunset. It had taken hours—the entire afternoon—to walk from the canyon to the settlement. He reckoned he was fortunate to make it at all, however.

Now, whatever he was to do must be done at once. Cutting back to the gully's depth, he followed it out for a short distance to where it flattened to meld with the mesa, and again sought out a small knoll that would afford him a view of the houses.

He wasn't too far from them, he discovered with satisfaction—a hundred paces, perhaps a bit more. Scouring the intervening ground with probing eyes, Shawn located a second arroyo, somewhat larger, to his right that angled toward the structures. By keeping down and moving close to the west bank of the wash, he could manage to get in close.

At once he drew back, crawled down onto the still hot floor of the arroyo. Ignoring the throbbing in his head that the bent position summoned, he covered the distance to where he was near the first house as rapidly as possible.

Breathless, head swimming, he drew back against the low embankment, allowed the giddiness and throbbing to fade. . . . He should wait for darkness, he thought again, before climbing out to the level of the yard behind the shacks, but the clamoring urgency within him would hear of no such delay. He'd simply have to risk it in daylight.

Mopping away sweat and breathing back to normal, Starbuck pulled off his hat, raised himself slowly, and peered over the rim of the arroyo. He was midway between the vacant house at the end and the one being used as a stable. The Mason place where the men were holed up was at the far end.

That was good. Gathering his legs under him, taking up his headgear, he came out of the arroyo in a quick leap, and hunched low, dashed across the open ground to the near corner of the empty shack.

Keeping close to the back wall of the vacant house, he crossed behind it, spurted across the narrow yard to the converted stable, and then made his way to its lower side. There he paused to listen, to reassure himself that his presence was still unknown. Convinced, he moved quickly across the last bit of open ground to the rear of the Mason place.

The neglected horses, slack-hipped and dozing at the rack, did not stir as he drew in behind a clump of rabbit brush and squatted on his heels. Sweat was glistening on his face, trickling down his back and chest, and the throb in his head was a steady pounding.

Raising a hand he brushed at his eyes, cleared them of the salty moisture gathered in their pockets, and tried to see through the smudged, dusty window of the house. He could hear the low mutter of voices but it was not possible to locate exactly where inside the shack the speakers had gathered.

He settled back. He'd come this far, taken his chances—and the breaks had been with him. Maybe luck would continue to hold in his favor. Sucking in a deep breath, he sprang from behind the clump and raced to the corner of the old Mason place.

Taut, he listened. There had been no change in the voices, plainer now but still unintelligible. The men, he guessed, were in a room at the front of the house. Still low, he moved forward, halted at the window in the back wall. Again removing his hat, he rose slowly, brought his eyes to a level with the dust-covered sill, and looked through the dirty glass.

Relief flowed through him. It was a small room. In one corner a ragged mattress had been piled. Sitting on it, gagged, hands and ankles bound, was Hetty Pierce.

☆ 14 ☆

Where was Esther Grey?

Cautious, still unable to pinpoint the position of the outlaws, Starbuck drew back. Head below the window's ledge, he moved on across the rear of the weathered old house toward the door that was standing open.

Reaching there, he again dropped to hands and knees, and hat off, peered around the corner. The entrance was into the kitchen. The voices were coming from a room beyond it. Squinting, he could distinguish Abe Norvel and Bobby Joe in what was apparently the parlor. Rollie was there also, heard, but hidden from view by an intervening wall.

He saw Esther then. The men were grouped around a table playing cards. She was sitting behind Norvel. She spoke as Starbuck watched, but her words were inaudible. When she had finished, Norvel glanced to Bobby Joe. The younger man shook his head after which Esther lapsed into silence.

"If you ain't turning her loose, then what are you doing with her?" Norvel's words reached Shawn clearly.

Bobby Joe spread his cards on the table, leaned back. "Aiming to keep her right here," he said, and then jabbed a thumb at Esther. "That there yellow-haired gal of yours'll have company."

"You mean you figure to keep her penned up in that back room like a sheep?" Rollie Lister asked.

"Sure, 'til she gets wised up and wants to stick around of her own notion—like Abe's gal. Only take a couple of nights, then she'll be willing."

Rollie's tone was doubtful. "We best be thinking about the rest of the folks around here. They find out we got her—and Abe's gal—they're just liable to rear up and do something about it."

"Like what?"

"Like using a pitchfork on one of us. Man standing in

the dark and throwing one of them things can be mighty wicked!"

"Not them. Ain't enough spunk amongst the lot of them to put out the fire was their britches burning."

"Ain't so sure," Abe said doubtfully, and turned to look at Esther.

She got to her feet, walked slowly into the kitchen, and sat down on a sagging bench placed against the wall.

Rollie Lister said, "Can tell you one thing for goddamn sure, Kilrain ain't going to like it—not one bit! You know how he feels about having women around."

"He'll be changing his mind once he sees what we got corraled."

"What *you* got," Norvel said quietly. "You can pass that kid around if you like, but Esther's my woman. Making that plain here and now."

Bobby Joe laughed. "Now, I ain't so sure she's all that much yours! She was taking off with that there Starbuck fellow, wasn't she, right along with the kid. You sure she won't go running out on you again?"

Abe made no reply. Bobby Joe slid a glance over his shoulder at Esther, whistled admiringly. "Got to admit she's a real humdinger—but don't you go letting yourself get all roped and tied. Ain't going to be no time for courting and marrying. Whoring around, yes, but nothing more'n that. You recollect back there in the guardhouse at Bliss when we worked all this out with Kilrain, we agreed we'd be like them guerrillas in the war—Quantrell's outfit—remember?"

Abe shifted on his chair. "Sure—sure."

"Said we'd hit and run and hide, taking what we wanted—which included women, and then dumping them when we was through with them. Expect you'll remember that, too."

"Sure, but—"

"Ain't no buts to it. That's the way it'll be and that's how Con will expect it to be. So, if you've gone and got yourself set on that yellow hair, you'd best get it out of your mind right now. . . . Smartest thing you can do for yourself is have her all spread out for Kilrain himself when he gets here."

A chair scraped on the floor. Lister's voice said, "He ought to be showing up," and then the outlaw walked into view, crossing behind Norvel, pointing for the front door. "Six, seven hours late now."

"They'll be here," Bobby Joe said. "Prob'ly was late starting—or they could've run into a mite of trouble."

"Trouble?" Lister repeated, pausing.

"Trouble," Bobby Joe stated. "You forgetting the army's still hunting us? They could've bumped smack into a search detail somewheres. For all we know, Con's dead as old Starbuck or else back in the guardhouse, and all the others with him."

"You're a cheerful son of a bitch," Rollie said laconically, and continued on for the doorway.

Shawn, crouched outside the rear entrance, digested the information he'd overheard. Bobby Joe was correct in just about all of his figuring, Shawn conceded, except where he was concerned. He wasn't dead and he didn't subscribe to the Hebrenite creed—and there was something he'd do about it.

It meant sticking his neck out plenty. The odds were all wrong and he'd be laying his life on the line for people who, in fact, excepting Hetty and Esther, would not thank him for delivering them from their oppressors. Indeed, they blamed him now for the violence that had occurred in their midst. They would condemn him for any more in which he became involved even though it was for their benefit.

He guessed he was a fool to consider doing it; in fact, for all the blessings he'd receive from the Hebrenites, he definitely was. But Shawn wasn't thinking so much about them as he was about Hetty Pierce and maybe Esther.

They were the ones who needed him; the women, plus the fact the law of the land was to be flaunted by this Con Kilrain who had dreams of being another Quantrell at the head of a pack of ruthless renegades. . . . Every man had a duty when he became apprised of such, and Shawn Starbuck had never felt he was an exception to that unwritten rule. . . . And then there was the matter of his own gear—of old Hiram's prized belt buckle.

Pulling back, he made his way to the window of the room where Hetty was being held captive. Rising again, he tapped lightly on the streaked pane. Hetty turned quickly. Her eyes spread with surprise and then filled with tears of relief. Shawn nodded reassuringly, but with no plan in mind, he simply motioned for her to remain quiet and not worry.

Moving back to the door, he once more took up a position there. Esther still sat on the bench, idly fingering the folds of her dress. Lister was at the front entrance. Bobby Joe and Abe Norvel still slouched around the table. Afraid to trust Esther, Shawn stayed well out of sight as he tried to establish the arrangement of the shack in his mind.

The entrance where he crouched led into the kitchen. In that room's opposite wall an archway opened into a short hall off which lay the bedroom where Hetty waited, and the parlor. A fourth room, probably another bedroom, evidently was connected to that area. The front door, only a portion of which was visible to Starbuck, was placed near the center of the parlor's forward wall and opened onto a small landing and yard that faced the street.

Getting into the back room and freeing Hetty while the outlaws were in the parlor was out of the question. He would have to come up with something else besides trying to slip by them—and Esther. She was an unknown quantity and he couldn't risk depending upon her for help.

There was also the problem of a weapon. He must locate and recover his belt and pistol; the rest of his gear could be picked up later—assuming everything worked out and he was still in need of equipment. But a pistol or his rifle was absolutely essential; he could accomplish nothing against the sort of odds he was going up against without a gun in his hand.

He needed to draw the three men, and Esther, out of the house; that was the answer—and the big chore. Once that was done, he could slip in, recover his forty-five and release Hetty, and get her out of the house. Esther, too, if that was what she wanted.

He wondered about the tall, yellow-haired woman. Would she leave if she had the opportunity? She had been running away from the valley, and Abe Norvel, when he encountered her on the trail. Would she again accept the chance to flee? He wished he knew the answer to that. He'd know then if he could trust her. As it now stood, he was afraid to include her in any plans he might make.

"Somebody's a coming!"

Lister's voice broke through to him. He pivoted his attention to the doorway where the outlaw stood.

"Somebody?" Bobby Joe echoed. "Your eyes getting so bad they can't tell who it is?"

"Maybe," Rollie answered, and pushing open the dust-clogged screen, stepped out onto the landing. For a long minute he stared off into the lower valley, shading his eyes from the glare of the setting sun with a hand cupped over his brow.

"Con and Shep—"

Bobby Joe and Norvel got to their feet, started forward. The younger man said, "Just them? Ought to be more."

"Well, there ain't," Rollie drawled, and moved on out into the yard with Bobby Joe and Abe trailing after him.

☆ 15 ☆

Starbuck came to attention. If all three men would move into the street, or even well out into the yard, he'd have the opportunity he sought—not a good one but at least a chance to enter, free Hetty, and grab up a gun.

Esther. . . .

His jaw tightened at thought of her. She was still there in the kitchen, blocked his way. He'd have to risk it—and if she made a move to warn the others, he'd have to stop her. He glanced again to the yard through the open doorway. The men were sauntering into the street. At that moment Esther rose, walked to the archway, stood there back to him, watching. At once Starbuck came to his feet. Entering swiftly, he closed in behind the woman. Throwing one arm about her waist, he drew her tight against him, clamped a hand over her lips.

"It's Starbuck," he said in a whisper. "I'm here to get Hetty. You want to stay—or come?"

He felt her tense body slacken with relief. She managed a nod. He released her. "Out the back—wait."

As Esther turned away, he cast a glance to the street. The outlaws had halted, were all facing to the south. Driven by the need to accomplish hurriedly what he had set out to do and be gone, he stepped into the short hallway, cut sharp to the door at its end. Opening it, he moved in and bending down drew the knife from his boot and slashed the cords that bound Hetty's wrists and ankles.

Pulling down her gag, he said, "The back—hurry."

She stared at him, eyes worried. "You're hurt! We—Esther and I thought you were dead—"

"Talk about it later," he snapped. "Esther's waiting in the back for you."

Immediately he wheeled into the hallway, again threw a look to the street. Bobby Joe, Lister, and Abe Norvel had not changed position, still watched the road that led up the valley.

Shawn glanced about hurriedly. He had only moments, he knew—but he must have his gun. His gear was not in the parlor or the hall. He moved deeper into the room where he could see into the adjoining area. His jaw clicked shut. Piled in the back corner were his saddle and other belongings.

Again shifting his gaze to the outlaws, reassuring himself they had not altered position, he crossed into the front bedroom. His belt and holster were not on the saddle. He swore angrily, then saw his pistol lying next to a holster and belt left by one of the men. Somebody had taken a fancy to the silver buckle, made an exchange.

He didn't quibble. It was a swap he'd rectify later at a more opportune time. Snatching up the strange belt, he wrapped it about his waist, jammed his weapon into the holster, and returned to the parlor.

Pulling up close to the wall of the room, he put his attention on the street. He could hear the slow regular thud of oncoming horses. Bobby Joe was grinning broadly. Abe and Rollie Lister's faces were wooden, devoid of expression.

Shawn spun about. He could see Hetty and Esther standing just outside the kitchen door. Moving silently and fast, he hurried to them.

"Want you both away from here," he said in a hard voice. "Rest of the bunch are here and it's—"

"What the hell took you so long?" Bobby Joe's bantering tones cut in on Starbuck's words. "You been dragging a dead cow all the way or something?"

"Or something," a voice replied. "What's the rush? You got something special good waiting?"

"Depends on what you're a thinking about."

"Well, after a year in that goddamn guardhouse it sure ain't no Sunday school picnic I'm looking for."

"Are they the rest of the outlaw gang?" Hetty asked in a low voice. "Thought there'd be more."

"Seems they're all that's left. One's Con Kilrain, the other one's Shep, from what I heard. . . . You've got to hurry."

Moving by the two women, he pointed to the hitchrack. "Take your horses, lead them. Keep behind the houses. Long as they're standing in the street, you won't be seen."

Esther nodded, stepped to where her pony waited. Hetty paused, considered Shawn with a frown.

"Aren't you coming?"

"Later," he answered. "They've got some property of mine I aim to get back. Owe me a horse, too. Big thing is for you and Esther to get away from here."

Hetty did not stir. "You're not planning to fight all of them—you, by yourself?"

He grinned. "Not if I can help it, lady."

He shifted his attention to Esther Grey. She had freed the reins of her horse, was looking uncertainly toward the houses near the church. Hetty, stepping up to her mount and finally ready to leave, turned to her.

"What's the matter?"

The yellow-haired woman shook her head. "I—I don't know what to do. I can't go back to the house—to Oram—Mr. Grey—my father-in-law."

Starbuck peered through the doorway and the tunnel-like hall. The newcomers had pulled up before their waiting friends, were now dismounting in the stiff, rigid way of men having been in the saddle for too many hours.

The older, dark-faced one with the grim, set mouth would be Con Kilrain, Shawn supposed. Shep was young, like Bobby Joe, had the same loose-jointed, uncaring manner to him. All would be entering the house shortly—and one of the group would lead the horses around to join those at the rack. Anxious, he swung to the women.

"Get moving!" He motioned impatiently to Esther. "Figure out somewhere else what you want to do. Go with Hetty to her place. You've got to get clear of here or I've done a lot of sweating for nothing!"

Hetty bit at her lip. "Not my place—I'm afraid to go home. . . . My folks—"

Shawn swore, took another look at the front of the house. The outlaws, walking leisurely, were coming across the yard toward the door of the shack.

"Go there anyway," he insisted in a low voice. "Tell them I'll be along in a few minutes and explain. That'll maybe keep them off your backs until we can come up with a better idea."

Hetty nodded reluctantly. Esther, giving the reins of her pony a jerk, started across the open ground.

"Go 'til you get to the other side of the next house, then cut alongside to the street. When you don't see them standing out front any longer, it'll be safe to cross over."

Hetty, trailing Esther, paused again. "Can't understand why you won't come, too."

"Told you. They've got my gear. I want it back."

Hetty looked at him narrowly. "You're not planning to slip off—leave me?"

Starbuck brushed at the beads of sweat gathering on his forehead. "Give you my word," he said tensely. "Hurry!"

Esther had reached the far side of the converted house, was leading her horse into the yard that separated it from the end structure. Shawn waited until he saw Hetty also round the corner and then stepped back to the doorway. Keeping low and being careful, he turned his attention to the interior of the shack.

Relief was easing the tightness that had gripped him; he'd gotten the two women safely away—and he had his gun. At least he could face Kilrain and his bunch on a halfway even basis. He had a quick wish that he could catch them all together in one of the rooms; he could manage them that way—the lot of them. Only luck wasn't favoring him that well.

Norvel was carrying something into the front bedroom— probably Kilrain's and Shep's gear. The outlaw chief and Lister were standing in the center of the parlor talking. Shawn's eyes whipped hurriedly about; he saw that Bobby Joe and Shep, evidently close friends, were still in the street engaged in laughing conversation.

His glance touched the sudden glint of silver at Bobby Joe's middle. Anger stirred him. It had been the young outlaw who'd taken his belt with the silver buckle. He'd not be wearing it for long. He brought his attention back to the men in the parlor, straining to pick up their words.

He needed some idea of what their plans were before he formulated a scheme of his own. . . . If they were aiming to ride out of the valley immediately to stage their first bullion wagon holdup, it would be simple to lay a trap for them at the gate when they returned.

But if they intended to wait, to hang around the settlement, complete their take-over, and prepare it for an outlaw stronghold, then he must set his thinking to other lines and act accordingly. That would call for catching Bobby Joe alone, recovering—

"Sure hate to hear that about Medford and Joe." Rollie Lister had turned, was facing the kitchen. His words were clear. "You getting somebody to take their places?"

"Naw," Kilrain said, sinking into one of the chairs. "They's five of us. That's a plenty—and the split'll be better." The man had a deep, drawling voice that showed a hint of Southern upbringing.

Shawn became aware in that next instant that Shep and Bobby Joe were no longer standing in the street. In that same fragment of time he heard the scuff of boot heels, the thud of hooves at the side of the house, and rose quickly.

Abruptly he was face to face with the two outlaws. Both men stiffened with surprise. Bobby Joe yelled, and both reached for their pistols.

Starbuck's hand flashed down, whipped up as he wheeled. His weapon blasted the stillness of the dying day, drove both outlaws back for the shelter of the building's corner. Pivoting fast, he legged it for the nearby arroyo.

☆ 16 ☆

Starbuck went into the arroyo in a low, flat dive. He struck the sandy floor hard, winced as the impact sent pain surging through his body. Breathless, he gathered his legs under him, hearing a wild cursing back at the shack as Bobby Joe and Shep made their explanations to the others.

"Only gun in town—that one." It was Rollie Lister's voice.

"He the one you said was dead?" Kilrain's question was dry, sardonic.

"Sure thought he was."

"Seems he ain't. . . . Get after him!"

Starbuck was already up, racing along the wash wishing it curved toward the settlement rather than to the opposite direction. His chances would be far better among the buildings, however few, than in the open.

"Yonder he goes!"

At Bobby Joe's shout, bullets splatted into the sand around Shawn's feet, thunked into the low wall of the wash. He threw himself to one side, dodging, ducking, looked about desperately for cover.

The back of the general store was fifty strides to his left. Reaching it meant forsaking the comparative protection of the arroyo and exposing himself as he crossed the open ground that lay between—but it was still a better bet.

Ducked low, he raised his pistol, snapped two hasty shots at the shadowy figures moving toward him in the half dark, and lunged out of the wash. Whipping back and forth erratically, he ran with utmost speed for the shelter of the low-roofed building.

Guns crackled spitefully, steadily. Lead plucked at him, droned angrily by his head. He reached the structure, dropped in behind a large wood box attached to its wall.

Sweat was streaming off him. He was heaving for breath and his legs seemed to have lost all their strength—

but he knew there was danger in remaining stationary. The outlaws would split up, come at him from two sides, have him cornered.

Still crouched to avoid silhouetting, he moved on, continuing along the wall of the store until he came to the street. If Kilrain and the others hadn't as yet divided forces, he should cross over. It would be easier to hide, get himself set if he could gain the opposite row of buildings.

He could hear the hard pound of boots coming from the direction of the arroyo. It was difficult to judge whether the men were still in a group or not. . . . It didn't really matter, he decided; he was forced to gamble, anyway. Taking a deep breath he went to a low hunch, and spurting into the street, headed for the feed storage barn directly in front of him.

He reached it just as the outlaws rounded the back of the general store. Five guns blasted simultaneously. Bullets slammed into the weathered boards of the warehouse, clipped through the leaves of nearby brush.

Not hesitating, he raced on, came to the rear of the structure, ducked around its corner, and halted, lungs again crying for wind. He looked ahead. A short distance away was the blacksmith shop. Coals glowed dully in the forge and a thin trickle of smoke, barely visible, twisted up from the rock chimney into the thickening sky. But as it was elsewhere along the street, no one was in sight. The Hebrenite village was like a prairie dog town; at the first indication of peril, all evidence of life simply disappeared.

Beyond the smithy stood the taller bulk of the hotel with its stable aside and somewhat to the rear. From there on he was again faced with open country. Starbuck shook his head, finding no answer as to what his next move should be.

Bobby Joe shouted something into the night. An answer came from farther down the street. The men had separated, were beginning a sweep through the village in a systematic, army-forage-line manner, stalking him as they would an enemy.

He considered the hotel. It offered the most effective concealment but he hesitated to make use of it. Hetty and the Pierces would be inside, along with Esther Grey and possibly others. To enter could bring Kilrain and his bunch down upon them, expose them to injury and death.

Best seek a different place where, protected on at least

two sides, he could have it out with Kilrain and his followers without jeopardizing the lives of the Hebrenites. Casting about, his eyes fell upon a sod shanty hunching half below ground level to the west of the blacksmith shop. It was apparently a storm cellar or storage room of some sort.

From it he would have a good sweeping view of the settlement and of anyone approaching from that direction as well as from the sides. To get at him from the rear a man would have to circle far wide and still would come within his range of vision.

Delaying no longer, Shawn broke clear of the wall along which he crouched, sprinted across the field, and jumped down into the slight pit behind the shanty.

"Here! Over here!"

Squatted low back of the hut, he heard the sudden yell, could not spot the man who had sung out because of the darkness. It sounded like Rollie Lister but he wasn't certain.

Moments later boots hammered in the street, then fell silent. The outlaws were gathering somewhere in front of the feed warehouse, or possibly it was the blacksmith shop. He couldn't tell for sure but there was no doubt they had him located.

He glanced to the western horizon. Complete darkness would soon envelop the valley and that would be of help. If he could hold out until then, he would be able to drop back to the brush a hundred paces to his rear, and under the combined cover of night and the scrubby growth, find a more advantageous point.

Just where that might be he wasn't sure; there weren't many places in the settlement where a man could fort up unless he went into one of the buildings, and that he was reluctant to do. He was an unwelcome and despised stranger among the Hebrenites now; he'd not draw them into the conflict and make matters any worse.

A shadowy figure appeared at the north corner of the blacksmith shop. Starbuck watched the man closely. Motion at the opposing end of the same structure drew his attention to that point. And then farther up, at the rear of the feed storage barn, the outline of a third man took shape.

They had spread out, were planning to move in from several points—five to be exact. He rubbed at his jaw; he'd spotted four of the outlaws—where was the fifth?

Worry began to tag at his mind. Had he allowed one of them to get in behind him?

Keeping his head down, he scoured the irregular alleyway along the buildings with care. Only four half-hidden figures, growing more difficult to see with each passing minute, were visible. He could make out no sound or motion on the open ground behind him either.

Lamplight flared in the window of a house near the church, a single yellow square in a broad sea of darkness. The distant sound of a cow lowing came from up the valley, and inside the feed warehouse he could hear the muffled sobbing of a child. It hadn't occurred to him, but the men who operated the community's supply depots probably had living quarters in the rear of the buildings.

Abruptly he saw the fifth man—a slim, dark shape on the roof of the hotel. He had time only to jerk back, flatten himself against the short wall of the hut. The outlaw fired. Starbuck spat as dust sprayed into his eyes and mouth and nose. A voice yelled from back of the smithy.

"You get him?"

Another bullet thudded into the shanty's slanted roof. Shawn, stretched full length, hugging the mud brick wall, steadied his weapon upon its edge, aimed carefully, and pressed off a shot. The outlaw rose suddenly to full height, a stark figure against the sky, took a stumbling step forward and pitched over the edge to the ground.

Instantly Starbuck changed positions, knowing the flash of his gun pinpointed his location. Bullets smacked into the sod of the hut and then Bobby Joe's voice lifted above the echoes.

"The bastard got Rollie!"

A dim figure emerged from the smoke and shadows to his left, unexpectedly close. Shawn threw himself back, full length, fired. There was a muffled curse and the figure ducked away, faded into the night.

A second shape began to materialize. Shawn drove it back with a quick shot, missed, pressed off another. It was difficult to see, to be accurate in the acrid-smelling gloom. With Rollie it had been different; he made of himself an easy target, but there in the black void behind the buildings it was another story. Motion caught his eye directly ahead. He tightened the trigger. The hammer of the forty-five clicked on a spent cartridge.

Hunched low, he rodded the empties from the weapon's

cylinder, hastily thumbed fresh shells from the loops of the belt he wore, and started to feed them into the pistol's chambers.

Shock and dismay hit him. The shells wouldn't fit. They were of a different caliber. His pistol was a forty-five. The loops of the belt he'd grabbed up in the shack were filled with cartridges for a forty-four.

☆ 17 ☆

Angrily he threw the handful of cartridges aside. He hadn't given the possibility of their being a different caliber a thought—likely because there'd been no time back in the old Mason place to consider it.

He grinned wryly; Bobby Joe would be up against the same problem only he would be in a position to do something about it, either borrow a suitable weapon or get the proper shells from one of his partners. Chances were he had already discovered the difference and had done just that.

The vague figure in front of him that had drawn his attention had paused, was scarcely visible as the man crouched low. A faint clicking sound told Starbuck that he, too, had been forced to reload.

Shawn drew himself to hands and knees. One thing was certain; he must get away from the sod shanty and do so fast. With no means to defend himself, he would be at their mercy—and they would close in quickly, doubly determined to get him after he'd knocked Rollie Lister off the roof.

Rollie. . . . That was the answer. . . . Find the pistol he had been using. If it proved to be of the wrong caliber, then get to Lister's body, take possession of his supply of shells.

Shawn holstered the useless gun, and bent low, crossed to the brush west of the shanty. There, partly concealed by the scattered clumps of rabbit brush and white-flowered plume, he angled for the rear of the hotel. Halfway a rustling in the heat-withered branches of the scrubby growth brought him up short. Abruptly a man was before him, arm upraised. Weak moonlight glinted on the weapon in his hand.

Starbuck hurled himself to one side as the pistol blossomed orange in the night. He felt the scorch of the bullet upon his arm, caught a fleeting glimpse of the outlaw's

94

drawn face—Shep. He veered, drove himself straight into the taut shape.

They came together in a jarring collision. A yell exploded from Shep's blared mouth as Shawn's shoulder speared into his chest, bowled him over backward. An answering shout went up from somewhere near the feed warehouse.

Before Shep could yell again, Starbuck was upon him, pounding at his face, his head, and neck while his eyes searched frantically for the outlaw's weapon somewhere on the ground close-by. Suddenly Shep broke clear, rolled away.

"Over here!" he shouted.

A gun blasted through the night. The bullet struck something well beyond them, caromed off into the black with a high, shrilling noise. Shep cursed wildly.

"Don't shoot—dammit!"

Boots were thudding on the hard-baked soil. Shawn, still looking for Shep's pistol, continued to press the outlaw, driving him back, keeping him off balance with a steady hail of blows. He slowed, aware of the nearness of the others. They were close—too close.

Wheeling, he ducked low to avoid being seen, ran a short distance on a direct line due west to confuse Shep. Again reaching the edge of the cleared area, he darted into the scrub, swung once more toward the hotel. Rollie's pistol was still his one hope—unless it had been damaged in the fall.

Breath was rasping so loudly between his teeth he was sure he would be heard. Sweat blinded him and the ache in his head was a continuing pound of thunder. He threw a hurried glance over his shoulder toward the bulking structures along the street.

He could see no movement in the shadow-blotted flat behind them, but Con Kilrain and the others were there—somewhere—but just where it was impossible to tell. Bobby Joe, Norvel, the outlaw leader, and now Shep were roaming loose in the dark, could at that very moment be closing in on him unseen.

Stumbling onto Shep had been sheer accident, a measure of good luck. If it hadn't occurred the outlaw would surely have gotten in behind him—and chances were he'd not be among the living by then.

The high shape of the hotel was immediately to his left. He paused, glanced to the roof. Rollie's body should be lying near the corner. Continuing, he trotted to that pool of darkness spreading below the structure. Somewhere close-by unseen horses shifted restlessly. He halted, a stab of caution going through him—and then he remembered that Hetty and Esther had led their mounts to the rear of the hotel. Undoubtedly they were the source of the noise.

He moved on more slowly, stumbling through piles of debris. His foot came into contact with a solidness that gave against his toe—Lister. The man had fallen partly across the bottom step of the stairs leading to the landing.

Shawn bent swiftly, rolled the outlaw to his back. Moonlight, now gaining in strength, spread across the man's slack features. It was unnecessary, Starbuck knew, but he felt for Rollie's pulse, assured himself no life remained. It was a subconscious action; if Lister still lived, he would be entitled to aid, regardless.

But the outlaw was dead. Shawn began to probe about in the loose dirt and trash. A glint of metal a few steps away brought him about. He moved to the spot quickly. It was the pistol.

Grabbing it, he checked a cartridge. Another forty-four. His own belt of ammunition was still useless, but there was Rollie's. Returning to the body, he flipped back the tongue of the heavy brass buckle that locked the leather strap around the outlaw's waist, jerked it free. Almost all of the loops were filled he noted as he drew it into place.

Starbuck took a long, satisfying breath. He wasn't naked in a thorn patch any longer; he was again armed, ready to match Kilrain and his bunch bullet for bullet. Grim, he dropped back to the brush, getting as far from the hotel as possible so as not to draw the outlaw's fire in that direction if they spotted him.

He was not forgetting the child he'd heard crying inside the feed storage barn. It would have been one of Jaboe McIntyre's offspring. He hoped it and none of the other members of the man's family had been struck by one of the bullets that had sprayed the structure.

He halted in the pale light now spreading over the land, not certain what his best move would be. He could double back to the sod shanty, resume the stand he'd made there. It wasn't likely the outlaws would expect to find him at that location again.

Or he could swing completely around the hotel, cross the street at its lower end where darkness and distance and the smattering of brush would conceal his movements, and return to the Mason place. The horses were there. He could take his choice, collect his gear and ride out—leave Hebren Valley and its troubles quickly behind.

It wasn't his fight, anyway—at least, it hadn't been at the start. The outlaws had already moved in and taken over the town when he arrived. He'd be smart to get out of it, be on his way, let the Hebrenites cope with their problems as best they knew how—and in the manner they wished. They had experienced such crises in the past and come through them; there was no reason to believe they could not do so again.

But there was a big difference in the crisis confronting the people of Hebren Valley now and the uncertainties that had plagued them in earlier times. They were doomed to remain and endure persecution, not find relief and sanctuary in flight.

And like small children, too, they were lost in such a situation. They needed help of a kind that only he could give—want it or not. Only he was equipped from experience and with a weapon that would enable him to stand in the way of the outlaws. The Hebrenites must accept that truth.

He had no choice. He saw that now. He could not just ride on—hell, he still had to corner Bobby Joe and get back his belt buckle.

Keeping well down, he started for the partly buried sod shanty. Figures in the pale light at the rear of the blacksmith shop caught his attention, halted him. Three men were standing motionless, as if waiting. . . . And then a fourth running toward them from the adjoining feed storage warehouse.

Starbuck straightened as anxiety gripped him. What was Kilrain up to? The answer came suddenly. A spurt of fire brightened the alleyway. An oath ripped from Shawn's throat as understanding came to him. The outlaws had put a torch to the warehouse—and inside were Jaboe McIntyre and his family.

☆ 18 ☆

A woman was screaming into the night. Shawn saw a man dart into the alley behind the burning building, recognized the lean figure of McIntyre. He was carrying a child. Placing the youngster on the ground a safe distance from the flames, he wheeled, rushed back into the thickening clouds of smoke.

Starbuck, forgetting the presence of the outlaws, hurried across the open field to the blazing structure. Reaching there, he started to enter, and suddenly remembering, cast a quick glance to the luridly lit area where Kilrain and the others were standing. The outlaws had turned, were walking away, seemingly having no interest in him and none whatever in the doomed warehouse. Puzzled, he went on.

He had thought it was simply a way to draw him into the open, permit them to have it out with him. Instead— he shook his head as he dashed through the open doorway into the heat-filled interior of McIntyre's quarters, unable to understand. They had something else in mind, that was certain—some sort of plan that would enable them to gain the upper hand in a simpler, safer manner.

All thoughts were swept from his mind in that next instant. McIntyre, with two more children, one under each arm, sweat and soot streaking his face, beard singed, stumbled into him as he emerged from the choking pall.

He saw Starbuck, hauled up in surprise. His eyes narrowed, and then he bucked his chin at an adjoining doorway.

"In there—my wife! Make her come out!"

Shawn pushed by the agitated man, fought his way through the dense haze into the adjacent room. He could see a vague shape moving frantically about, gathering clothing, pieces of furniture, and other articles, piling all haphazardly onto a bed that had begun to smoulder. He crossed to her, seized her by the arm.

"Get out of here!" he yelled above the crackling of the flames. "Whole place is going up!"

She turned a shocked face to him, jerked free. "Our things—from home. . . . Got to save them—"

Starbuck stepped to the bed. Knocking aside the bulky pieces of furniture, he gathered up the corners of the bedspread, pulled it into a bulging bundle. Throwing it over his shoulder, he held it with his right hand, gripped the woman with his left. Whirling her about, he propelled her through the doorway and toward the building's rear exit.

The heat was intense. Flames had cut through the plank wall, dried by countless days of blistering sun, were licking hungrily at the ceiling. McIntyre, a rag tied over his nose and mouth, loomed up again in the smothering fog.

"Go back!" Starbuck shouted, pushing the woman at him. "Too late for anything else."

Jaboe bobbed his head, threw an arm about his wife, forced her into the open.

Shawn followed, trailed them through the bank of pungent smoke to where the Hebrenite had deposited the children, and dropped the bedcover bundle near them. Several of the Family had come from hiding, were standing by, some comforting the McIntyres, others simply watching the building's destruction with expressionless faces.

The flames mounted to their peak quickly, were spearing the night sky with darting yellow tongues. Now and then a sharp crackling and an occasional explosion sounded inside the structure, and showers of sparks would spurt into the duller glow as something combustible burst into flames.

The flames were beginning to lower, to die out, and the charred outlines of the gutted structure with its jagged, smouldering walls showed through the thinning banks of smoke. A few of the onlookers, curiously silent through it all, were fading off, heading back for their quarters. There were hardly any expressions of sympathy for the McIntyres, Shawn noted, just a mute acquiescence to the loss.

"You'll be putting up at the inn."

Starbuck recognized Oram Grey's modulated voice. He wheeled, having been unaware of the man's presence, saw him speaking with Jaboe McIntyre. In him also was the same unruffled acceptance of the calamity.

McIntyre nodded, eyes on the building that had served

as home as well as for the Family's storage depot. Fire yet glowed in the interior where sacks of grain sizzled and steamed hotly as in the crater of a seething volcano.

"Seed's all lost, Oram," he murmured. "Never saved a single, solitary cupful."

The Hebrenite leader shifted his moody eyes to the smoking ruin. "We can grow more—and a new house can be built in which to store it. Only wood and grain has been destroyed—not our will to do."

McIntyre said, "True," and moved over to where his family huddled with their possessions.

Shawn stepped up, took the blanket bundle, again slung it over his shoulder. McIntyre gave him a noncommittal glance, gathered two of the children to him.

"Bring little Aaron, mother," he said to his wife, and started through the smoke-filled darkness for the rear of the hotel.

Wordless, the woman reached for the hand of the third child, and moved to follow her husband. Starbuck, trailing last of all, looked to the side, again wondered about the outlaws.

They were not to be seen anywhere along the alley, but as he drew near the hotel, and the old Mason house at the end of the street where they quartered became visible, he could see light in the window and shadowy figures moving about inside.

They had returned to the shack, had settled down. Again he wondered what Con Kilrain had in mind. That he and the others were forgetting his presence, ignoring the fact that he had killed Rollie Lister, and calling it quits was an impossibility; with them it took blood to square up for blood.

McIntyre led the way up to the hotel's stairs, stepping around the body of the dead outlaw, and entered the building. Simon Pierce was waiting inside the door. Beyond him stood Patience, several articles of night clothing draped over an arm. Farther on Starbuck caught sight of Hetty and Esther. Evidently the younger girl had overcome her reluctance to face her parents. Their relief at seeing him was apparent.

"Room's ready for you," Pierce said, smiling at the soot-and-smoke-marked couple. "You want to wash up, there's water in the tub and pitcher."

"I've got some things here you might need," Patience added.

"Thanking you kindly," McIntyre replied, "but we saved a little—what we're wearing and a few things Mercy was able to grab. . . . Would like some salve. There's a few burns."

Patience nodded, hurried off into another part of the building. Jaboe, releasing his grip on the hands of the children, wheeled, took the bundle from Shawn, and shepherding his family before him, steered them into the room.

Pausing in the doorway, he looked back at Starbuck. His smeared face, showing angry red in spots where live sparks had fallen upon him, was withdrawn, almost hating.

"Obliged to you for helping, but I'm remembering that because of you——"

"Don't give me that!" Shawn cut in, anger and impatience finally getting the best of him. "Was those outlaws who started it. Saw them, only it was too late to do anything about it."

"He's not to be blamed, Jaboe," Pierce said in a calming voice. "He was only the tool, a part of a plan—one beyond our understanding."

"Plan!" Starbuck shouted the word. "What's the matter with you people? That fire was set by Con Kilrain and his bunch. They're taking you—this whole town—over, saddle, cinch, and singletree, and you do nothing about it, just stand around and let them get away with it. They'll have——"

"It's all according to the way it is to be," Pierce murmured.

Shawn wagged his head. "Don't mean to dispute your beliefs, but there's only one reason for that fire—Kilrain. He's got something in mind."

Simon studied him briefly, eyed the bandanna bandage still encircling his head. Then, "That makes no sense. Why would they do it of their own wish? A greater wisdom prompted——"

"You can expect them to be doing a lot of things like this before they're through," Starbuck broke in.

"Perhaps——"

"We are but a part of a single plan—such is what we believe," Oram Grey said.

Shawn pivoted. The leader of the Family had come up the back steps unheard and unnoticed, was standing in the open doorway.

"We do not question, we simply accept."

Starbuck sighed, lifted his arms, let them fall to his sides in resignation. "You've got a strange way of looking at things. You're telling me that Kilrain and his crowd can go right ahead, do anything they like, and you'll let them do it?"

"Our answer to oppression is to remove ourselves from it, not oppose or attempt to fight it. To do so gains nothing. It serves only to create greater contention that must be coped with later. Violence leads only to more violence, and each time it grows. . . . If a man turns his back upon such, it is then brought to an end, and doors to future trouble are closed."

Shawn remained silent for a time. Finally, "Guess I can understand some of your reasoning but I can't say I agree with it. And it's sure your right to live anyway you want—only this time you're up against something different. Your ideas won't work."

Oram Grey stalked into the room, a tall, lean sober-faced figure. His black eyes peered out from beneath their thick brows with a steady piercing intent.

"There can be no reason why it will not. Always it has been the answer."

Grey was making no reference in any way to the meeting that had taken place between them that previous night during which he had requested Shawn's aid in delivering the settlement from the outlaws. Apparently he had undergone a change of view—or still did not wish his followers to know that he broke the principal tenet of their faith. . . . If that was the way he wanted it, Shawn decided, then he would respect that silence.

"They won't let you pull out—move on—if that's what you've got figured as the answer."

Simon Pierce nodded hesitantly. "They stopped him, Oram—this morning. Left him for dead."

It was difficult to think Grey was unaware of the outlaws' determination to keep the valley a locked vault, and Shawn wondered if the Hebrenite leader didn't actually realize it but, for the sake of his people, refused to admit it.

"Why would they object? Everything would be left to them—supplies, houses, our crops. We'd ask only permission to go in peace."

"One mighty big reason," Starbuck said. "They don't want the location of the valley known."

"We'd not tell. This we would promise, on our word—"

"You—there inside the hotel! Come out on the porch. Got some talking to do!"

It was Con Kilrain's harsh voice.

☆ 19 ☆

A small cry broke from Hetty's lips. "It's the outlaws! They've come to—"

Oram Grey lifted a broad hand for silence, smiled comfortingly at her. "Don't be afraid. There's no cause for alarm. They only want to talk."

He moved by Shawn, aiming for the lobby. Starbuck caught at his arm. "Do your talking from the inside. You can't trust—"

"There's no reason to fear," Grey insisted.

"No reason! What does it take to make your realize that you're dealing with killers?"

"Killers? Perhaps, but he said he wanted to talk. . . . He has a plan."

"Hell!" Starbuck exploded in disgust, and then lowered his head apologetically to the women standing nearby. "Only plan Con Kilrain's got is one to take over everything around here—and he'll stop at nothing to do it."

"You—inside! Coming out or am I coming in?"

Simon Pierce stepped up to Oram's side. "I'll stand with you, Elder," he said.

Shawn sighed wearily, released his grip on the man's arm. He brushed at the sweat on his brow. "All right, have it your way. But keep remembering this, you can't trust any of that bunch out there—not one. They're different from any you've ever come up against. They're killers who'll die before they'll let themselves be captured and sent back to that army prison—and they'll do their figuring accordingly. Be smart—don't take any chances."

"How about it, you sodbusters?"

Shawn recognized Bobby Joe's voice, hard-edged and pressing.

At once Oram Grey, with Pierce at his shoulder, entered the lobby and crossed to the entrance. The two men paused there briefly, as if girding themselves for battle, then stepped out onto the gallery.

Starbuck, moving fast but careful to keep out of sight,

slipped in close to the window adjacent to the doorway. Cautiously he drew back the edge of the curtain.

Kilrain and Bobby Joe Grant were in the center of the street. A dozen strides to their left was Abe Norvel. The outlaw called Shep had stationed himself a similar distance to the right. They were not permitting themselves to collect in one group.

"I'm Oram Grey—the Senior Elder—"

"I don't give a hoot and a damn who you are, grandpa," Kilrain said in a jeering tone. "What I've got to say goes for everybody in this dump."

Starbuck, hand resting on the butt of his pistol, felt fingers grip his wrist. He glanced around. Hetty was standing beside him looking up into his face. Her features were strained, eyes filled with concern.

"Shawn—I'm afraid—for pa."

He nodded. "They would've shown more sense if they'd done their talking from in here."

"I know. I heard what you told them. But they don't believe in fear—or in not trusting."

"Man walks into a den of rattlesnakes, trust's not much protection. I'll watch sharp, try to keep something from happening to them."

"That fire," Kilrain was saying, his words pitched to carry the length of the street to those he could not see but knew were listening as well as to the pair standing on the gallery, "we set it."

Oram Grey's reply was calm. "We know that. You were seen."

The outlaw paused, stared at the older men. He turned his head, muttered something to Bobby Joe, who laughed. Moonlight glinted softly off the buckle of the belt he was wearing. *My belt,* Starbuck thought, and felt the stir of anger. It was an insult to the memory of old Hiram.

"Reckon you've been told this already by my boys," Kilrain continued, "but I'll tell you again, sort of make it official. I'm taking over the place, making it my headquarters."

The men on the porch remained silent, simply waited, two bent, graying figures, meek and pitiful.

"You folks do what you're told and we'll get along fine. Give me trouble and you'll wish to God you'd never been born!"

"What do you expect of us?" Oram asked.

"Grub—plenty of it, along with everything else it'll take

105

to keep us going." He hesitated again as Bobby Joe made a remark, laughed, and added, "Includes women and whiskey."

"There's no liquor here—"

"You've got plenty of grain. You can make it. 'Til then, reckon we can bring in our drinking—you just see to the rest."

Oram Grey began to shake his head slowly. He took a step forward. "We can't agree to that," he stated clearly. "We'd be slaves."

"Yeh, guess you would."

"Then we'll leave. We'll take our people and move on. The valley will be yours to do with as you wish."

"Like hell you'll leave! Nobody moves out of here without my say-so! You think I want the law knowing where I'm holed up?"

"We'll not speak of it. You'll have our word."

"Word—that don't mean a goddamn thing to me, grandpa! I want you here—every last one of you. Going to need you to look after us, keep us eating and sleeping and such—"

"So's we can grow fat and rich," Bobby Joe volunteered.

"That's right."

Oram Grey wagged his head stubbornly. "No, we can't do it. We won't. . . . We'll leave—somehow."

The slap of a pistol shot shattered the hush. Splinters flew from the plank flooring at Grey's feet. Both men jumped back, Oram's hat coming off in the process and rolling crazily along on its brim.

"I ain't just jawin' to hear myself," Kilrain said in a dead cold voice. "You damn well better get that in your head right now! There ain't none of you pulling out—and when the rest of your tribe gets back from selling them cattle, they'll pitch right in and help with the rest of you. . . . I'll be taking the cash they got, too. . . . You won't be needing any."

"We'll not stay—be made slaves," Oram Grey insisted quietly.

"Reckon you will, grandpa. This here's the place where you'll live and you'll die—one way or another. And any time one of your bunch gets out of line, you can figure on paying for it plenty. Like that there fire we set tonight. Was just a little sample."

In the pale moonlight Oram's white hair looked to be

pure silver. He drew himself up to his full height. "We won't stay," he said again. "We were born free, and we'll die free—not as slaves—"

The pistol in Con Kilrain's hand flared again, hurled its sound into the night. Oram Grey staggered, a look of pained surprise on his thin face as he clutched at his chest. Slowly he began to sink. Somewhere inside the hotel a woman began to sob.

Starbuck, a wild anger lashing at him, jerked away from the window. Pistol in hand, he lunged for the door. Hetty threw herself upon him, pressed him back.

"No! It'll only mean more killing—you, pa, some of the rest of us!"

Shawn hesitated. She was right, of course. He might cut down Kilrain, possibly even Bobby Joe, but Norvel and Shep, off to opposite sides, would drop him quickly—along with anyone else who happened to be in the general line of fire. . . . Besides, as long as the outlaws were unaware of his whereabouts, he had the upper hand and could do much more good.

"Reckon you all savvy now what I'm saying, and that I ain't just horsing you around."

Con Kilrain's irritating voice was an abrasion rubbing Starbuck raw. Again at the window he watched the outlaw calmly rod the empty cartridges from his weapon.

Simon Pierce, kneeling next to Grey's crumpled shape, stared at Kilrain.

"You've killed him. . . . He's dead."

"Sure he's dead. What I aimed at him being. No big loss no-how. Old man like him ain't good for nothing—same as a one-armed cripple. . . . And he had himself a loose jaw. Would've been handing me back a lot of lip all the time.

"Now, they's no need for any more of this. I've laid the law down to you. Follow it and you'll live peaceable and there'll be no trouble. . . . That's part of what I'm here to tell you. The next thing's—"

"It all right if I get some help, take him inside?" Pierce interrupted, coming to his feet.

"Nope, you stand right where you are, mister. He ain't going nowhere shape he's in. When I'm done talking, then you can lug him off to the boneyard and plant him. Take that other'n laying out back of the place, too.

"Now, that next thing I was talking about—you're

107

hiding a drifter—jasper that shot one of my boys. I want him. Where is he?"

Simon Pierce stood mute.

"Well, no sweat. Know he's around somewheres—and I ain't wasting no more time or men digging him up. Some of your bunch is covering him and I'm giving you orders here and now to roust him out and hand him over. Hear?"

"Could be he's gone," Pierce said. "Know he was planning to ride—"

"He ain't gone. We just seen him a bit ago, and he ain't had a chance to leave town—so don't go lying to me about it. Now, you've got 'til sunup to hand him over. I want him coming right out that there door behind you. First he's to throw that gun he's got into the street. Then he's to follow it. Savvy?"

Simon nodded woodenly.

"Good. . . . If you don't dig him up, then I'm putting a torch to the church. If that don't do it, the store'll be next—and I'll keep right on building bonfires until you show some sense and march him out here. Clear?"

"Clear," Simon Pierce said in a low voice.

"It better be." Kilrain hitched at his gun belt, bobbed his head decisively. "Come sunrise I'll be standing right here. . . . You sure better have him waiting for me."

☆ 20 ☆

Shawn understood now the strange actions of Kilrain and his men after the fire had started; they had made no effort to hunt him down, simply figured to avoid the risk of a shoot-out and the possible death of another of their members by ignoring him. It was easier and safer to force the people of the valley to hand him over.

Silent, he watched the outlaws fade back into the shadows, and then again started for the porch. It was Patience who stopped him this time.

"They might see you and—" She could not say the words. "We'll look after him," she finished and, followed by Jaboe McIntyre and another man of the valley, stepped out onto the starlit gallery. Moments later they reappeared, the two men carrying Oram's body between them, Simon and Patience walking alongside.

"That room off the hall," the woman said in a businesslike voice as they crossed the lobby, "we'll use it."

Other members of the Family, witnessing the murder from their quarters or being advised of it, began to arrive. They came in quietly, filed into the bedroom where Oram Grey was laid. They had their last look at the stilled sunken face, now reflecting the great age of the man, and moved on into the larger area of the hotel's lobby where they stood about in hushed groups.

Patience produced a thick white blanket, and assisted by Hetty and some of the women, began to prepare a shroud. A coffin would not be necessary, the girl told Shawn when he offered to help in the construction of such; the Hebrenites believed the mortal remains of their departed should be permitted to return to dust as speedily as possible.

In the dim lobby, with the remaining Elders and various members of the sect, Starbuck felt apart—a stranger among passive people with ways and customs that were odd to him. He was the outsider, the unbeliever, and from the hastily averted glances he caught time and again when

109

he looked around, he realized they felt he was the cause of their tribulations—at fault for the death of Oram Grey.

He supposed he was to some extent. However, if he hadn't stumbled onto the valley and the Hebrenite village, Con Kilrain and his renegades would still have taken over and forced their will upon the inhabitants. He hadn't been the cause of their coming; he hadn't led them there; his presence had only brought matters to a head sooner.

Perhaps there would have been no killing. That was a question that now could never be answered. But one thing was certain in Shawn's mind, Oram Grey would have defied Con Kilrain regardless; he was a brave man, determined never to allow his people to become slaves.

However, that thin dividing line that separated cause and fault was of no interest to Starbuck. His mind was now filled with thoughts of the crisis that would come with the rising of the sun. He drifted slowly to the window, looked out into the deserted street. Moonlight had strengthened, mingled with the glow of stars, and now lay a soft, pale radiance—gentle and friendly—over all. But death had walked there in that mellowness—and would do so again.

"Shawn—"

He turned to face Esther Grey. He had noted her earlier standing aside from the others, as did he; she was one of the Family, tolerated but shunned and ignored. If it disturbed her, it did not show. In her hands she held a strip of cloth, a bandage. There was a smear of medicine of some sort on it. Removing his hat, he bent forward slightly, allowed her to replace the stained bandanna.

"I'm sorry for the way this is turning out," she murmured when she had finished.

He shrugged. "No need. Cards don't always fall like you'd want them to."

"What will you do?"

He hesitated for a long breath, said, "Only thing I can, play out the hand."

"That's foolishness. . . . You could leave tonight. I'll get you a horse—manage it somehow."

Starbuck gave her a wry smile. "Still got to get back my gear," he said. His face sobered. "You realize what Kilrain and his bunch would do to all of you if I ran out?"

"Perhaps nothing—there's no way of really knowing. If they did take it out on the Family, it would be no more than what they deserved."

He shrugged. What Esther suggested would be fine for him, but it would spell the worst kind of trouble for the Hebrenites; and he couldn't save himself at the expense of Oram Grey's people.

"We'll see," he murmured. "Could be it'll all work out better than we think."

A huddle being engaged in by Pierce, McIntyre, Micah Jones, Vinsent, and another bearded individual broke up suddenly.

Esther frowned, said, "They've made up their minds. I hope they plan to help you."

"Could use a bit, sure enough," Shawn replied and turned to meet Simon.

"We've talked," Pierce said. "We've decided that something must be done before more blood is spilled."

Starbuck waited in silence.

"We've agreed that you should leave here."

McIntyre nodded. "We'll get you a horse and provide supplies, then we'll take you to a place west of here where you can get out of the valley. Only a few of us know the trail—it leads up to a pass. It's hard to find, hard to travel, but if a man'll lead his animal—"

Shawn had folded his arms across his chest, was shaking his head slowly. "Expect you'd best go back and do some more talking. It's plain you don't understand what'll happen around here if you help me get away."

"We don't want no more killings," Micah Jones said. "If it has to be put blunt—we're telling you to leave."

"You think my going will stop their killing?"

"If you're gone, there'll be no reason."

"Fooling yourself," Starbuck cut in impatiently. "What Kilrain sure doesn't want is for me—or anybody—to ride out. You heard him say that."

"He's after you for shooting his man."

"Part of it—but that's not the big thing. He has to be sure nobody gets out of here and tells the law or the army where he's hiding—and spoils a good thing for him."

"But if you gave your word—or we did—"

"None of you seem to realize what Kilrain and the others can do—and will! Shooting down a man in cold blood means nothing to them. You saw that tonight—right out there on the porch."

"We don't aim to put up any resistance, give them cause—"

"You'll be giving them plenty of cause if you don't

111

produce me in the morning. They don't respect your beliefs or your bravery when you stand up to them without a gun. They laugh at you, figure you for a fool—and grab the advantage. . . . Can't you see you're throwing your lives away?"

Ezrah Vinsent stirred indifferently. "No worse than meeting them with a gun and dying from one of their bullets. Dead's dead."

"Won't deny that but at least you've not let them trample you into the dirt like you were a weed or a bug of some sort."

"We've always been peaceable folk, avoiding violence, even at the expense of our land," Pierce said slowly.

"Know that—and you're going to keep on paying that price until there's none of you left—which won't be long. You can't go on believing in that. Might've worked a hundred years ago, maybe even fifty, but it won't work now.

"Thing is, the world can get along without you, but nowadays you can't get along without the world. It's over there, the other side of the hill, whether you want to admit it or not. That's why you're losing your sons and your daughters. They can see it and they're pulling out because they know the old ideas won't work anymore.

"Be a real fine thing if it would. A man's entitled to peace, to live and work and think the way he likes. But there're always the Kilrains and the Bobby Joes and such who'll come in, take what they want by force unless somebody stops them."

Frustrated by the older men's bland indifference, by his failure to get through to them, make them understand, angry at himself for becoming involved and allowing himself to get so worked up, Starbuck wheeled, strode to the window, again looked out into the night.

There was a stillness in the crowded, stuffy room when Starbuck finished. A lamp on one of the tables began to sputter. An elderly woman in a solid black dress turned hastily, snuffed out the flickering flame.

Micah Jones shifted heavily. "It'd be wrong for us to use violence. Keep telling you that, Starbuck—and we plain won't allow it! Oram believed in that, same as did all the Senior Elders before him, and our people, too. We ain't no different in our believing."

Shawn came back around slowly, considered the lowered, intent features of the men before him. He could tell them their leader, facing up to reality, had visited him in the night, sought to have him remove the outlaw threat from their midst. Oram Grey was dead and words could not hurt him.

But they could destroy the memory of the man and all that his followers thought he stood for. To tell them that Oram Grey in desperation had advocated violence in its strongest form would be cruel—although such revelation could be the one factor that would swing them to his way of thinking. . . . But he'd not do it; he'd find a means other than by indicting a fine old gentleman who could not now explain or defend his actions.

"Not asking any of you, personally, to take a hand—just that you understand what I've got to do and not interfere."

Hetty looked up at him quickly, a worried frown on her young face. "You can't fight them alone—not all four of them!"

"There's only one gun. I took it off Lister's body because I've no cartridges for my own. Even if there was someone willing, there'd be no weapon to use."

"But you can't do it by yourself! It would be suicide!" Impulsively Hetty wheeled, faced her father and the others in the room. "You can't let him do it alone! You've got to help, somehow! Does he have to get down on his knees, beg you to let him throw away his life to save yours?"

Starbuck laid a hand on the girl's shoulder, brought her around gently. "Best this be left to me. I've been up this trail before, know what I'm bucking."

"But, by yourself—alone—how—"

Shawn glanced to the rear of the lobby. Through the open door he could see men carrying in Rollie Lister. The women were preparing a shroud for him, too, it appeared. His gaze returned to the immediate room, drifted over the faces of those gathered there. A dozen or so children were present—boys and girls in their early teens, or not quite to that point. They were watching him and their elders closely, eyes betraying the doubt and confusion that gripped their minds.

"Don't know that myself—yet," he said to Hetty, and then swung to Simon Pierce. "Let's get it settled. Need to know where I am. Realize there's enough of you to throw a rope around me, put me on a horse, and take me out of the valley if you're of a mind to. Or you can hand me

113

over to Kilrain. Want the answer now because sunup's going to be here before we know it."

Again a silence fell over the room. Simon adjusted his empty sleeve, then nervously scrubbed at his chin. He touched Micah Jones and the others with a long glance, looked at Shawn.

"You saying you'd stand up to those outlaws by yourself, whether we want it or not?"

"Only thing I can do."

Again Pierce's gaze swept his fellow Elders, this time as if seeking confirmation. "All right, let it be your way. We'll not interfere."

"And you'll not help either!" Hetty cried, whirling on her father. "You'll just sit back, let him go out there and die! I'm ashamed of that—of what you are—of what we all are! And if this is the way I'm supposed to think and the sort of life I've been raised to live—I don't want any part of it. . . . I'll take the world Shawn comes from."

Eyes flashing, cheeks glowing, Hetty stepped in close to Starbuck, turned her face to him. "Maybe I won't have any weapon when you step out there into the street, but I'll be with you. . . . I want you to know there's one person in this valley who realizes what you're doing and's not afraid to die with you."

☆ 21 ☆

A full hour before first light Starbuck eased himself out of the hotel's rear entrance. Sticking to the shadows, he crossed to the barn and thence to the brush below the settlement. He knew it was probably a waste of time but he felt the need to see if Kilrain and his partners were so sure of themselves that they would throw caution to the wind and spend the night in their usual quarters.

He didn't hold out much hope for such; the outlaw—certain of his ground insofar as the Hebrenites were concerned after demonstrating his ruthlessness by shooting down Oram Grey and burning the feed warehouse—was still no fool. There remained one threat to the empire he was hoping to build—a man with a gun who could meet him on even terms, perhaps kill him. He'd run no risk of that coming to pass but maintain a wariness until the threat was removed.

Nevertheless, Shawn was looking into all possibilities. He could be misjudging Con Kilrain's intelligence, and because he needed an edge, he was investigating all angles. He was not fooling anybody, much less himself, into thinking he could go up against four hardened killers and come out unscathed. The only way he could come out of such an encounter alive was by first seeking out an advantage, and then making the most of it.

Hunkered in the rabbit brush and sage, he studied the old Mason place. The horses were gone from the hitchrack, stabled in the adjoining shack, he assumed. A lamp burned in the parlor, threw a weak yellow glow against the walls and through the windows and open doorways.

An invitation, Shawn thought, beckoning to him, asking him to move in close and let one of the outlaws—whichever one had been posted to watch—put a bullet in his head and thus solve the problem even before dawn broke. He grinned. *No dice, Kilrain. . . . I'm not that big a sucker.*

Glancing to the east to be certain there was still ample time, he continued south until he was well below the settlement, and there crossed over, dropping into an arroyo—the same used that preceding day when he had returned from his fruitless attempt to leave the valley with Esther and Hetty.

Kilrain could be using the same wash, employing it as a place, somewhat apart from the houses and buildings, from which to keep an eye on all that went on. With that in mind, Shawn continued up the arroyo but now with greater care.

Approaching the first bend, which lay directly behind the Mason place and its adjacent neighbors, he drew in close to the bank, and straining to see in the poor light, halted.

No one was in the arroyo as far as he could tell. He shifted his attention to the outlaws' quarters. The lamp in the parlor reached through the connecting entries, illuminated the kitchen and the back bedroom where Hetty had been held captive. Clearly, both were empty.

He had guessed right about Con Kilrain. The outlaw was taking no chance on being surprised by his intended victim slipping in and catching him and his friends asleep. Indeed, the lighted but vacant quarters indicated he sought the exact opposite.

They could be holed up most anywhere in the settlement or along its fringes, Shawn realized, beginning a careful backtrack. There was no sense in trying to ferret them out. Best he occupy himself in the time that remained by coming up with a plan to meet Kilrain's demands—and still stay alive.

Back at the rear of the hotel, he started to mount the steps, halted when a figure arose from the half dark at the side of the steps. His hand dropped swiftly to the gun at his side, fell away when he saw that it was Esther.

She came forward to meet him, features serious, worried. "I've been waiting for you."

"Something wrong?"

She shook her head. "Nothing more than usual. I'm going to meet Abe. . . . I don't know where he is, but he'll see me and come to me. . . . I just wanted to say thank you and tell you that I hope things come out all right."

He studied her thoughtfully. "Guess you know one of us has to lose. They may get me—and I'll have to kill Abe if he gets in front of my gun."

"I know," she murmured in a lost voice. "I only wish I could do something—help—"

"Obliged for the thought. Want to say I'm sorry, too, we didn't get through that gate first try. At least you'd be out of it."

"And you—"

He nodded. "Reckon so." But he wasn't at all sure. The fact that he had left the Hebrenites in the clutches of the outlaws would have weighed heavily on his mind, and the probability that he would have turned back once he had the two women safely away was strong. "Well, got to start figuring what I'll do. . . . Good luck if I don't see you again."

"Good luck to you," Esther said, and moved on.

Starbuck climbed the steps, entered quietly, and made his way to the lobby. He could hear voices in the kitchen beyond the dining room, guessed Simon Pierce and the Elders were still up and hashing over their problems. Or perhaps they were just waiting for sunrise. It would be like riding out the minutes before an execution.

Crossing the deserted lobby, he took up one of the straight-backed chairs, placed it at the window. Drawing back the curtain, he sat down. He had waited at the same point earlier, had listened to Con Kilrain deliver his ultimatum, had watched him gun down Oram Grey. It was an excellent position from which to view the area immediately in front of the hotel—but that was of little use to him. He should be in the street, not looking into it when the moment of confrontation came.

He tried to figure how Kilrain would set up his deathtrap. All four of the outlaws would not be in a single group—he was positive of that. Such would place them in a dangerous situation and Con had already proven he was taking no unnecessary risks.

Likely Kilrain would be the lone representative standing in front of the hotel. Bobby Joe Grant, Shep, and Abe Norvel would be covering him from strategic positions elsewhere along the way, just in the event matters didn't work out exactly as anticipated, and their would-be victim came out of the doorway shooting.

He glanced again to the horizon in the east. A pearl glow was making itself visible above the dark hills, extending the first hint of a new day. A wry thought entered his mind; he guessed he was pinning on Oram Grey's paper star after all.

His shoulders lifted, fell resignedly. Reaching down he drew his pistol—Rollie Lister's actually—absently checked the loads. He had a cartridge in each of the six openings of the cylinder, a practice to which he did not ordinarily subscribe, but again he felt it wise under the circumstances. That extra bullet could be the one to save his life.

His own weapon, useless without bullets, was thrust into his waistband. He would feel more comfortable with it on his hip and in his hand when the time came to make use of a weapon, but there was no way to make that possible. He might as well leave it there in the lobby, relieve himself of that much excess weight . . . Unless . . . Starbuck frowned, considered the heavy forty-five through half-closed eyes. . . . Maybe—

A sound behind him brought him around. It was Hetty. She had been in the kitchen with the others. He gave her a short smile.

"I didn't hear you come back in," she said, her voice faintly accusing, as she drew up a chair next to his. "Did you find out anything?"

He shrugged. "Like I figured, they weren't fools enough to stay in the Mason shack. Did have it all set up for me—lamps lit and all."

"Are you going to try and find them?"

"Nope. . . . Good rule at a time like this is to let the man looking for you do the hunting." He paused, jerked his thumb toward the kitchen. "Been quite a meeting. Lasted the whole night."

Hetty sighed. "Just talking—and waiting. They won't do anything to help you. Sad part of it is they wouldn't know how if they wanted to." She turned her eyes to the window. The vague pearl band was now a bright flare reaching up into the sky. "Shawn—it won't be long until the sun's up."

"Not long," he agreed, making no issue of it before her.

She sighed deeply. "You weren't depending on them were you?"

"No."

Her voice was wooden, hopeless in its quality. "Have you thought me of a way—a plan that'll—"

"Keep me from getting killed? Not yet. Not much I can do until I see how Kilrain aims to handle it. He'll scatter his bunch, can depend on that. Just where's the important thing to me. Once I know that, I can go from there. Did get an idea about that part."

118

The fan of pearl was showing streaks of color. All along the street the shadows were thinning and definition was returning to the objects turned mysterious and unfamiliar by the night.

Hetty was staring at him. "An idea—can I help with it?"

"Could be, but I'll not run the risk of you getting yourself hurt. Important you stay inside the hotel out of danger."

"I will, but it really doesn't matter. Nothing does, it seems. I guess I've sort of grown up during the night."

"We all have, probably. . . . Something like this can do it—can make you realize how little some things count and how much other things do."

Chair legs scraped against the kitchen floor. A door opened somewhere allowing a light wind to breeze through the hotel, sweep clean the mustiness stagnating in the lobby. Somewhere nearby an overzealous rooster crowed shakily.

Starbuck rose, glanced once again to the east. He was frowning, torn between the need to put the plan that had come into his mind into effect, and the wisdom of forgetting it.

Still undecided, because it involved Hetty, he said, "Want to get outside, be there when the time comes."

Hetty got to her feet, relief easing some of the tautness in her face. "Then you're not going to just walk out the door—let him shoot—"

"Not about to. He'll not take me that easy."

"But if you don't—"

"Think I've got a way around it. Just came to me. I'll need your help but it's no deal unless I've got your promise to stay inside—not leave this lobby."

The girl nodded eagerly. "I'll promise, Shawn. What do you want me to do?"

"Kilrain's orders were for me to throw my gun out into the street," he said, taking the useless forty-five and handing it to her. "Then I'm to step out onto the porch. What I want you to do is stand inside the door. When he hollers for me to do it, count ten and toss out the gun. . . . You've got to be sure he doesn't see that you're the one doing it."

"I understand. You want him to think it's you inside."

"That's the idea."

"But when you don't show yourself—"

"Those few moments I'll gain after you throw out my

gun are all I'll need. Bobby Joe and the others will have their sights lined up on the door. When they see the gun hit the street, they'll figure there's no danger of me trying to shoot my way out, and come out from where Kilrain's got them hiding. . . . And I'll be out there watching and waiting for that."

Hetty clasped the heavy weapon in her two hands, faced him, eyes dark and deeply worried. "It sounds all right—but I'm still afraid for you."

"Don't be. A little edge like that's all a man needs. Fact is, I've been in worse tights—and luck's been running with me. Expect it'll keep right on."

She nodded vigorously as if to convince herself. "I know it will, and I'll pray for you, Shawn, pray that you'll not get hurt and that you'll come back to me. Then we can go away—together—leave all this behind and—"

He reached out, laid a finger upon her lips, stilled the words. "No," he said in a low, firm voice. "Not together, Hetty. It's not for me—the kind of life you're looking for and deserve. I've a brother to find, one I've been hunting for a long time. I can't quit until the job's done. . . . After that—maybe—"

She was utterly silent, features dark, her eyes filled with the dullness of rejection. And then abruptly she turned, dropped the pistol onto the chair. Reaching up, she put her arms about his neck, and drawing him down, kissed him hurriedly.

"I'll still pray," she murmured, and taking up the pistol again, moved toward the door.

☆ 22 ☆

Shawn let himself out the rear of the hotel with caution. Light was now spreading over the land and there was the possibility that Con Kilrain had posted one of his men to cover that exit.

Taking full advantage of the shadows, the bin where cut wood was stacked, and the walls of an extending closet, he ignored the steps and dropped to the ground from the landing. Wheeling at once, he cut south, followed a course much the same as he had taken earlier when he had gone to have his look at the outlaws' quarters.

He'd make his play from there. What was more logical than to hide himself in the one place where he knew absolutely none of the gang would be? It made good sense to him, and moving with hurried care, he skirted the settlement, reached the arroyo, and traveling its sandy track, came to where he was opposite the Mason shack and its adjacent decaying companions.

As before there was no way he could tell if any of the men were inside, and he could not risk finding out. He'd simply have to lie low until proceedings began and he had some inkling of where the outlaws were—then do what appeared to be the most effective thing.

Hunched in the wash, shoulders against the wall, he watched the flare in the east change slowly into long fingers of salmon and rose, thence to a sheet of purest gold, and finally, as the rim of the sun peeped over the ragged hills, to a white hot blue.

In that same instant he heard Con Kilrain's voice break the hush that lay over the settlement. Kilrain was making good use of the dramatic, knowing his precise punctuality would serve to impress the Hebrenites more firmly as to the inflexibility of his will.

"All right, drifter—time's come!"

The sound of the outlaw chief's voice startled a dog, set the animal to barking furiously.

121

"Don't go getting no cute ideas now. You ain't got a chance in hell—'cause there's four guns covering you."

Shawn delayed no further. The outlaws, wherever they were, would have their attention focused on the hotel's doorway. Rising, he vaulted over the edge of the arroyo, raced to the back of the Mason place. Darting through the rear entrance, he crossed to the front, drew to a halt.

Crouched close to the door frame, he threw his glance up the street. Kilrain stood in approximately the same spot as he had that previous night. His thumbs were hooked in his belt, his legs were spraddled, and his crumpled broad-brimmed hat was pushed to the back of his head. The arrogance of the man was infuriating.

"You hear, drifter? Throw out your iron—now!"

Mentally Starbuck ticked off the count. Promptly at the beat of ten he saw the faint glitter of steel as his pistol arced from the hotel entrance, fell to the street in a spurt of dust.

"Fine. . . . Fine. You're playing it smart."

Shawn saw Bobby Joe then. The young outlaw had been standing at the far corner of the general store. At the surrendering of the pistol, he stepped into full view at the edge of the building's board landing. Motion across from him, at the forward end of the blacksmith shop, betrayed Shep's position.

Two of them—plus Kilrain, accounted for . . . Where was Abe Norvel?

Disturbed, realizing that with each passing second a part of the advantage he had managed to gain was being wiped out, Starbuck again searched the street for a sign of the missing outlaw. He should be to Kilrain's left; such would permit him to cover the lobby door from a different angle as well as guard his chief's flank. . . . He could be in one of the other shacks—the one at the end of the row. It would be nearest Kilrain.

He must know—positively. Norvel's bullet coming from an unexpected quarter could cost him his life. Grim, he turned, cut back through the rooms of the Mason place intending to cross over to the shack being used as a stable. If Abe wasn't hiding in there, it was almost a certainty he'd be in the third house.

Pressed by the urgency of fleeting time, he rushed through the doorway into the open—and froze. Directly in front of him was Norvel leading a horse. Beside the outlaw was Esther Grey, also walking her mount.

Starbuck's hand flashed down for the pistol on his hip. Norvel, knees bending slightly, went for his weapon.

"No—Shawn!" Esther cried, rushing in between them. "We're leaving—"

Starbuck, not removing his eyes from the man, base of his thumb hooked over the hammer of his pistol while the remainder of his big hand wrapped about the weapon preparatory to drawing and firing, rocked back gently. Kilrain's voice reached him from the street but he gave it no attention. . . . One thing at a time. . . .

"It's true!" Esther continued, her features taut with fear. "Abe's quit Kilrain—giving it up. . . . We're going away."

Norvel, holding also to his pistol, nodded slowly. "What we're doing," he murmured. "Can believe it or not."

"I'll be more apt to believe it when you take your hand off that gun," Starbuck said in a low voice.

In the tense hush Norvel shifted his eyes to Esther. It was as if he needed reassuring. She nodded at once. Slowly then he let his arm fall away.

"Kilrain know about this?" Starbuck asked.

"No—we'd never get out of here alive if he did," Abe replied.

"Then best be on your way," Shawn said, and moved on, seeing the smile of relief and gratitude on the woman's lips. "Good luck."

"Same to you—friend," Norvel responded in a low voice.

". . . ain't waiting no longer—"

Kilrain's tone was angry. Shawn, turning into the narrow yard that separated the converted stable from the end shack, threw a glance over his shoulder. Esther and Abe Norvel had reached the lower section of the arroyo where they could no longer be seen from the settlement, were mounting. . . . He owed much to the yellow-haired woman; in persuading Norvel to break with the outlaws she had done him a great favor. . . . He was pleased to think that this time she'd make it out of the valley.

"Come out of there—hands over your head! Hear?"

Starbuck reached the front of the house, halted. Con Kilrain was in the open before him, easy to see, to cut down with a bullet. On beyond, Bobby Joe and Shep still held to their positions. Norvel, he supposed, had been stationed about where he now stood—except that he would be inside the shack.

123

"Goddammit—you'd better come out or I'm—"

"I'm here, Kilrain—right here!"

Cool, nerves tuned to razor sharpness, Shawn stepped into the street. He sent his first bullet into Shep, believing him to present the greatest threat because he was directly opposite and in position for a quick shot. He saw the outlaw buckle, start to fall, and jerked to one side—aware of a sudden loud commotion along the buildings.

It was a shattering racket of pounding and hammering that began to bounce back and forth between the building facades, echo discordantly, and quickly added to by the barking of a score of frightened dogs.

A distraction, pure and simple, calculated by Simon Pierce and the others to be no more, no less. Shawn knew instantly what was happening; the Hebrenites were helping after all, providing him with that breath of time he so badly needed to duck away, avoid the return bullets from the weapons of Bobby Joe Grant and Kilrain that he must expect. . . . And too, it could be they were demonstrating to the young ones of the sect that the outlaws provoked no fear in them.

Low, running hard, he dashed back along the area behind the shacks. He rounded the corner, crossed behind the last structure, and started for the street.

Con Kilrain was before him. He had anticipated Starbuck, was crouched, weapon leveled. Pure hatred distorted his dark face.

Shawn fired instinctively, spun half about and went flat as shock and pain met him straight on. Stunned, and again from some inner direction, he rolled over, came to his knees, triggered a second shot at the outlaw leader.

Through blurring vision he saw Kilrain sinking slowly, head sagged forward, arms limp. The outlaw hung motionless for a fraction of time, as the second bullet ripped into him, and then toppled stiffly.

Bobby Joe. . . . There was still Bobby Joe. . . . By the general store. . . .

The thought hammered dully in Starbuck's clouded brain. He dragged himself upright with effort. His whole right side was numb, seemed not to be a part of him. Gathering strength, he started for the street, continuing the course he had been taking when he encountered Con Kilrain.

He was going the wrong direction. . . . Bobby Joe was

not that way—not toward the hotel. He was farther up—the store. . . .

Reasoning stumbled about in his flagging mind, finally registered. Reversing himself, he cut back for the rear of the sagging shack. He gained the corner, began an unsteady turn, half falling in the effort. As if from a great distance behind him, he heard the crash of a pistol. Roaring pain seared again through his body, driving him down.

He fired twice at the vague, weaving shadow he saw running toward him—Bobby Joe. He knew that it was him because of the sun shining on the silver buckle he was wearing. *My buckle!*

The dim shadow halted abruptly, staggered to one side, fell. Starbuck, at the stage where pain was so massive as to be an anesthetic, stared woodenly at the prone figure. Muttering incoherently, he dragged himself to where the outlaw lay face up, sightless eyes staring into the brassy arch of the sky. Somewhere he could hear a voice calling, crying his name. . . . Hetty's voice he thought, but he couldn't be sure.

Fumbling, working at it doggedly, he released the tongue of the buckle, freed the belt encircling Bobby Joe's waist. With great effort he pulled it clear. He looked up wearily at the blur of faces that suddenly were all around him.

"I'm taking this," he mumbled thickly. "Happens to—be—mine," and then accepted gratefully the smothering fog of blackness that welled up from nowhere to block out all pain and thought and engulf him in unconsciousness.

☆ 23 ☆

It was Simon Pierce who touched off the blaze. Standing bareheaded in the blistering Texas sun, the empty sleeve of his homespun shirt neatly folded and pinned, he dropped the burning fagot into a pile of dry twigs and stepped back.

No cheers went up from the members of the Family scattered about him in a loose half circle. All watched silently, seeing in his act the foretelling of death for a faith and belief that had seen them and their forebears through many trying days.

As the flames surged upward, ravaging the juiceless branches and leaves camouflaging the barrier that had turned aside all would-be newcomers to the valley, Starbuck glanced about. The ceremony was partly for his benefit, he realized; but also it was meant to impress the younger Hebrenites with the fact that the future for them was to be different.

Grasping the headstall of the horse beside him—a black that had once borne the weight of Con Kilrain—he steadied the nervous animal as the fire crackled fiercely. He'd turn the animal in to the first lawman he could find, buy himself another. Chances were the black had been stolen by the outlaw and Shawn had no wish to be strung up for a horsethief.

Three weeks—twenty-two days to be exact—had slipped by since the showdown in the village, time during which it had been touch and go for him while he fretted under the constant ministrations of the Hebrenite women who were determined that not only would he recover but also that he would heal unblemished from the outlaw bullets that had smashed into him.

And he had. What had been told to him concerning the medical and surgical skill of the women was true; he was as fit as the day he stumbled onto the secret valley.

But it was secret no more. He had brought change, and he was seeing the proof of it now in the leaping flames

126

consuming the gate that had sealed off the canyon and the broad valley beyond it for so many years.

"We ain't aiming to keep folks out no more," Micah Jones said, turning to him. "We're going to welcome them, invite them to make a home here."

"Not that we're giving up the things we've been taught," Pierce, who was now the Senior Elder of the sect, added. "We figure our way's still the best—that violence is wrong and turning from it is what folks should do. We'll offer our ways to those who come. If they see fit to accept them, well and good. If not, it's their right and we'll try to understand."

"What about your young people?" Shawn asked, glancing to where Hetty stood with several others in the shade of a small cottonwood. She was smiling and talking animatedly.

"They can stay, or they can go—when they're of proper age. It's to be their choice. But with new folks moving into the valley, we don't think they'll be wanting to leave."

Shawn agreed. The cattle drivers, along with the teamsters, had returned some days back. Enroute they had encountered a wagon train headed west. A rider had been dispatched to intercept the emigrants, tell them of the valley and invite them to settle on its fertile slopes. The offer had been accepted, and now everyone anxiously awaited the train's arrival.

Starbuck looped the reins over the black's neck, toed the stirrup, and swung into the saddle. Those same teamsters had answered his question regarding Hagerman's Hash Knife Ranch and the Carazones Peaks country; of Hagerman they could tell him nothing, but the Carazones Peaks—southeast and a long hundred miles away.

Settling himself, he glanced around at the faces of his friends, smiled at Hetty who paused, touched him with a soft look, and resumed her conversing. Simon Pierce stepped up, solemnly offered his hand.

"I'm speaking for all the Family—come back. There'll always be a place here for you."

Starbuck nodded. "Just might take you up on that someday," he replied, and again letting his gaze slip over the small crowd, he rode the black through the now open mouth of the canyon.

Someday . . . maybe . . . after he'd found Ben. It could be soon. . . . Ben just might be at Hagerman's ranch. . . .

Big Bestsellers from SIGNET

- [ ] **BLOCKBUSTER by Stephen Barlay.** (#E8111—$2.25)
- [ ] **BALLET! by Tom Murphy.** (#E8112—$2.25)
- [ ] **SERENA by Jeanne Duval.** (#E8163—$2.25)
- [ ] **SHADOW OF A BROKEN MAN by George Chesbro.** (#J8114—$1.95)
- [ ] **WOMAN OF FURY by Constance Gluyas.** (#E8075—$2.25)
- [ ] **ROGUE'S MISTRESS by Constance Gluyas.** (#J7533—$1.95)
- [ ] **SAVAGE EDEN by Constance Gluyas.** (#J7681—$1.95)
- [ ] **CRAZY LOVE: An Autobiographical Account of Marriage and Madness by Phyllis Naylor.** (#J8077—$1.95)
- [ ] **THE SWARM by Arthur Herzog.** (#E8079—$2.25)
- [ ] **THE SERIAL by Cyra McFadden.** (#J8080—$1.95)
- [ ] **TWINS by Bari Wood and Jack Geasland.** (#E8015—$2.50)
- [ ] **MARATHON: The Pursuit of the Presidency 1972-1976 by Jules Witcover.** (#E8034—$2.95)
- [ ] **THE RULING PASSION by Shaun Herron.** (#E8042—$2.25)
- [ ] **THE WHITE KHAN by Catherine Dillon.** (#J8043—$1.95)
- [ ] **KID ANDREW CODY AND JULIE SPARROW by Tony Curtis.** (#E8010—$2.25)

THE NEW AMERICAN LIBRARY, INC.,
P.O. Box 999, Bergenfield, New Jersey 07621

Please send me the books I have checked above. I am enclosing $_____(check or money order—no currency or C.O.D.'s). Prices and numbers are subject to change without notice. Please include the list price plus the following amounts for postage and handling: 35¢ for Signets, Signet Classics, and Mentors; 50¢ for Plumes, Meridians, and Abrams.

Name_____

Address_____

City_____State_____Zip Code_____
Allow at least 4 weeks for delivery